***

Carl's Side

Lila Drowos

***

Table of Contents

Prologue

Chaos was spreading throughout the ship. The ship moved side to side eerily as it started to sink slowly. The boat had no holes, and it hadn't hit anything. Yet water seeped into the boat as hundreds of terrified passengers ran around in a panic.

Near the center of the ship, in an empty lounge where there were no panicking people, a woman with long, wavy, light-brown hair and honey-colored eyes held the hand of a terrified little boy. A man with chocolate-colored hair and a matching beard walked in slowly, keeping his dark eyes on the boy, who had the woman's eyes and the man's hair.

The whole ship was shaking hard and sinking fast. The lights flickered on and off. The nervous boy looked up at his mother with a question in his wide, innocent eyes- what do I do? The woman had no answer. She just wrapped an arm around him. He whimpered like a wounded puppy.

Cracks were now *spreading* across the walls. Suddenly, a blast of pure white light erupted throughout the ship. The woman cried out as she fell to the deck, clutching her head. The boy shrieked as loud as he could, hoping any other passenger would hear him. Either none did, or they were busy trying to save themselves or their own families, which was, of course, understandable but not helpful at all.

Suddenly, the man flew backward and slammed into the wall. He was knocked unconscious, his limp form sliding down the wall, until it slumped to the floor. Blood trickled from the corner of his lip, and he groaned. The boy stood defensively next to his mom. He was clearly terrified, but he did not seem physically harmed like his parents. His eyes darted to the door as if he would bolt out of the room, maybe to the lifeboats, but instead he frowned, staying with his family. He wouldn't have gotten very far anyways.

The ship was thrashed against the angry waves outside. The woman screamed as her head started pounding and her vision swam. She tried to block out the world. She still didn't understand what had happened. One second the ship was floating on the water, completely fine, and all of the passengers were having a good time, but then *BAM*!!

Then, she heard a voice—a cold, dark voice, laughing cruelly. She looked around and noticed a horrifying pair of red eyes watching from the shadows. She blinked rapidly, trying to clear her vision as the eyes flashed in front of her.

"Soon, you'll be mine. One way or another. Your whole family. The whole world! You'll be mine!" The evil voice laughed. The woman screamed and tears slid down her face as the red eyes swam across her vision, clearly amused by her struggle.

"No, please—" She whispered, trying to stay strong for her sons, her family. "Please..."

There was another laugh as her vision slowly faded into darkness. She struggled to see what was going on. Her head was pounding, and her thoughts were swirling in unhelpful circles. The red eyes were now wavering like everything else she saw, but they seemed to smirk before they blinked back into the shadows. It seemed like she wasn't in the boat anymore— all of the water was gone. That was a good thing, though, or at least she thought so. At least she didn't drown.

Suddenly, she heard footsteps and then more voices that sounded very far away. She tried to listen but only caught a few words— "Ship sank... No survivors... So sorry... Unknown cause... Nobody left." The voice sounded official and... sad. Maybe a news reporter? "I am sorry, everyone."

No... The woman thought desperately, trying to get up and move.

We're right here! Please, someone help us! She wanted to call out, but her mouth would barely move. It formed a round circle, but no sound came out-- only her slow, hard breathing. Her whole body hurt, and she couldn't understand anything beyond the pain, the voices, and the mysterious red eyes... She wanted to keep struggling—needed to keep struggling for her family, but it was hard to move. *Please... please help us...*

She had to save her son, her husband, and the other passengers who definitely didn't deserve this. And the other one...

her other son… hopefully safe at home with his babysitter. He needed her! She struggled to get up, blindly stumbling around. Her head was pounding harder. She seemed to keep being pulled down by a force hidden in the darkness. Was she tied up somehow? She cried out as she struggled. Everything hurt.

Finally, she gave up hope and let her body fall back into the darkness with a soft thud. She cried and cried, although it made her dizzy. It hurt to cry, but she couldn't stop. She wanted to stop, to be brave for her family, but she just couldn't. She cried for the innocent strangers from the boat, the passengers that would never find their families again— friends she could have met but never had the chance. She cried for her family, her wonderful little boys who looked up to and needed her, her husband whom she loved so much. Her beautiful family.

Everything felt heavy and sad, and she realized that fighting was useless. She knew she could never beat the pain and the darkness—not as she was, anyway. The woman didn't even remember her own name. She didn't know where she was. She didn't know where her family was. Her body was stuck in place. She reached out her hand, and it landed on cool, damp stone.

Where am I? she wondered. *Where is my family?* The stone felt small, and the surface she touched was smooth and cool. Where was she? A cave? A cellar? It was dark and cold and bare, and it gave the woman a bad feeling. *I'll fight for my family!* she promised herself, although she didn't know how. It felt as if some sort of dark magic had happened, but the woman dismissed the thought—mostly to remind herself that magic simply didn't exist, but also because it hurt too much to try to understand it. Was magic even meant to be understood? No, probably not. But that didn't matter, because magic wasn't real either way, the woman reminded herself.

She shivered. It was like a dream—no, a nightmare—but even more painful. Not realistic, but *very* real. And it hurt. She begged silently for help until she couldn't focus anymore. What was happening to her?

She heard a whisper from far away, calling out to her. "*Mum…?*"

Was that her son? It sounded more like her younger son's voice. How had he gotten there? She simply *had* to fight for him. He needed her. She heard that evil laugh again, from the strange red eyes. What part did they play in all of this? Why had the thing with those eyes captured them and sunk their ship, if it even had? Where were her sons, her husband? The only sound was her panting, echoing into the air around her.

"Help…please help..." she managed to croak once more, struggling into a sitting position as her whole world went dark. The red eyes came back, haunting her vision, smug once more, there to claim their prize. She had just given up on herself, knowing nobody would ever hear her through the darkness, the pain… and the silence.

***

Chapter One

Life on the Run

I ran in silence, carrying a hulking backpack. It was so heavy it was starting to hurt my back. At that point, there was nothing else for me to do but run. Under the cover of night, I looked like all of the other shadows. Nobody could see my light brown hair or dark eyes. It was so dark as I ran past office buildings, homes, and parked cars and trucks. I passed the garbage dump, the museum, and the mall—all the way out to the edge of the sleeping town. The giant tent loomed ahead of me. Panting, I pushed up a giant tent-flap and stepped inside.

As I exhaled, the backpack on my shoulders seemed just a little lighter. The warmth of the tent made me feel safe. At the back of the tent, I saw a tiny marble counter. On its cluttered surface sat tons of bottles filled with mixes and experiments that my friend claimed were potions and spells—fortune-telling magic that could supposedly read the future. I didn't fully believe in it all, but I trusted her. I reached for one of the bottles.

"Carl?" a voice called out. The voice of a girl. I jumped, startled, pulling back my hand. The voice was deep and mysterious, almost glittery and magical but also sort of spooky as it echoed around the tent. My eyes darted around, but I did not see the speaker.

"Where are you, Ivy?" I asked. No answer. After looking at another of her 'potions', I straightened up. I began to fiddle with my shirt, waiting. I called her name again, my voice shaking slightly.

Ivy was one of my best friends, but I was worried about how this conversation would go. I knew what she would think of me for running— *ungrateful coward*. So, I would be careful.

"I'm right here," she replied coolly. I almost tripped, but caught myself. Ivy crept into sight from behind the counter. "So...Carl," she said calmly, watching me with sharp eyes.

Silently, I studied her pretty, auburn hair and lovely green eyes. I was pretty tall for my age, so she was a little shorter than me. That was something I'd usually tease her about. I stood up straighter again. "Hello, Ivy," I said, with a smile that she didn't return. She was frowning. I never visited in the middle of the night. I barely visited at all because of my uncle. "Why have you come? You know better." she said. I couldn't tell if she was being sarcastic or not.

I scoffed and took a deep breath. "Why shouldn't I have come?" I asked calmly. "I can do whatever I want."

Ivy clearly wasn't buying it. I had never been a good actor. She knew something was wrong; knew I'd done something bad. She knew I wasn't supposed to be there. I knew it too. Did I care at the moment? Not exactly. I was a runaway. A fugitive? No, a runaway.

"You know your uncle Jean doesn't like me." She reminded me. This time, it was clear that she was being sarcastic. She was probably remembering how rude he always was to her. How rude *everyone* was to her. Many people laughed at her or teased her for her 'magic'. She was alone, like me. I took another deep breath. This was the wrong subject, but she wouldn't let me change it. I really needed her help, as she probably already guessed.

"I...I can do whatever I want." I repeated quietly, looking down. I refused to meet her eyes. I could tell she was getting impatient.

"No, you can't," she blurted.

I felt a violent surge of annoyance. "Why not?" I asked loudly, not removing my eyes from the floor. Who was she to tell me what I could and couldn't do?

Her eyes narrowed and searched for mine. "Because! You're just a kid—" she started.

I narrowed my own and looked up. "We're the same age!" I shrieked indignantly, interrupting her. I guess I *was* still a kid, but that was unfair. "And YOU live alone!" My mouth slammed closed immediately. I shouldn't have said that.

Ivy's face heated up as her eyes darkened. I could feel myself heating up too.

"Ivy, I..." I started quietly, but there was no point. She was angrier than ever. I shouldn't have mentioned her family.

"Carl. Why aren't you with your uncle?" Her voice was low and shaking. A challenge.

I didn't answer. I couldn't. She looked directly into my eyes, and it felt like she was staring into my soul. Was that something that magic could do? I squirmed nervously.

"What happened Carl?" she asked in a soft, passive-aggressive tone.

"I would rather live on the streets than live with him," I muttered. She looked at me curiously, even more upset by my words. My uncle was all I had. She had no family at all, and was clearly thinking about how ungrateful I was. I knew she would be.

"You don't know what it's truly like to be alone," she said quietly.

But I did. And that hurt. A lot.

"I do. I might as well, anyway. I'm basically alone." I said miserably, looking away again. "He's awful, Ivy!"

"Not awful enough for this." She grumbled.

Of course. She would have paid anything just to have Jean, no matter how awful he had been to her, and here I was, running from him. She'd never forgive me, but it wasn't her choice.

"I wanted answers, so I came here, to you," I said, my voice suddenly hoarse.

Ivy said nothing. She just looked at me. I held her gaze.

I waited as she glared at me. "Ivy, please!"

Ivy looked away and started fiddling with her potions. When she looked back up at me, there was a fire in her eyes. For just a moment, I felt like the 'bad guy'.

"Goodbye, Carl." She started shoving me out the door.

"Please, Ivy! I need answers! I need help!" Tears sprang into my dark eyes, but I quickly swept them away with my hand.

Ivy froze and considered. It lasted a split second before her face darkened again.

"Fortune-tellers are not reliable enough," she told me sarcastically. "Certain people wouldn't appreciate me still 'helping' people."

Okay, so some people didn't like her magic. Okay, so my uncle was one of them. Well, maybe that wasn't okay at all. But I believed in her. Didn't that count for something?

She shoved me away. "Ivy!" I hollered. She ignored me. "IVY!!" I grabbed her hand in a last attempt to stop her as she began to turn away. She stopped mid-turn.

"I said no!" Her voice got louder. "You want to trade lives? I'd run back to your uncle in a second, and you could be a stupid fortune-teller if you want."

I knew she must have been upset because she never called her magic stupid. Ever.

"I believe in you."

"You're the only one."

"You know that's not true, Ivy. Please," I begged.

"Go home, Carl." Her voice broke. "Please. Your uncle is probably worried."

"Worried? Him? Never." I dismissed the idea with sarcasm and a hint of annoyance, but my voice was somehow sad. I didn't mention that I didn't have a home anymore. What I had with Jean was certainly not a home. I sighed as Ivy glared at me. I shouldn't have said anything at all. I shouldn't have even come.

"Ha-ha." Ivy's fake laugh was just as sarcastic. "Ha." She made a face at me and I groaned.

"Please, Ivy?" I begged. "I need your help!" I wasn't sure what I was asking for. Anything, I guess. I didn't really know what I wanted.

"Hm," was all she said as she studied me carefully. My heart skipped several beats.

"What does 'hm' mean?" I asked slowly, knowing she could change her mind any time. My future might as well have been up to her.

She studied me and nodded. "I guess it means that I'll find you the answers you want," she decided. I sighed in relief. "But not today."

***

Years ago, my parents and older brother went on a ship. The ship sank. No one knows what happened to the passengers. Most people think they're dead, but I refuse to believe it. They're alive, I just know it. People just laughed... or worse, smiled sadly at me and commented on what great people they were, which always angered me even more.

Nobody believed me. No one cared. I was alone.

"They're alive." I would say to anyone who would listen, which was only a few people anyway. They must have swum away from the sinking boat; they were amazing swimmers. Still, nobody believed me. There were stories, of course, but none as optimistic as mine.

"Sorry. It's impossible." A few people were sympathetic. When I was little, I stayed with my babysitter, and she was always kind and understanding. Her name was Beatrice. She had bleached blonde hair, and she was sweet, smart, and caring. She was like a second mother to me when I was little. She would pretend to listen and agree, but I knew she didn't. And that was that. At least I was safe.

The safety and comfort wouldn't last long, though. A few days later, I found Beatrice, my babysitter, searching through mountains of paper. I thought she might have been looking for my parents. I felt very hopeful for a moment. People were trying to help! Were the police involved? A detective, like in those spy movies? Any minute she'd say that my family had been found and I would be going home. Maybe it had all been a trick in the first place. Smiling, I crept closer to peek at the papers and asked her what she was doing.

"I'm finding out who you should go and live with, sweetie." She'd replied kindly. "You can't stay here forever." She was smiling sweetly like usual, although she didn't really look happy at all.

My eyes widened. *But where will I go?* I thought. I had started shaking. This had to be a joke. I felt like control of my life was slipping away from me, just like that. I had realized I wouldn't be living with Beatrice permanently, of course, but I didn't want to live anywhere else until my parents were back. I knew they would come back. Eventually. I thought my parents would be found soon. Or that they were playing hide and seek. I thought it was all a mean trick and they would pop out at any moment and take me home. But they hadn't yet.

"B-but…" Tears sprung to my eyes, and without another word, I ran up to my room, locked the door, then sobbed all day. I didn't come out, and Beatrice didn't come looking for me. I was very little and very confused. I had to find a way to make her let me stay.

I didn't want to, but I went to live with my uncle, Jean. My uncle was cruel, and it was no wonder I hadn't known him well. My parents definitely wouldn't like the lazy, harsh man. He could barely take care of himself, or at least wasn't used to it now, because he had me. Even though I was little and confused, he started to make me do difficult house chores. All day. Every. Day. He even made me homeschool myself every night. Thankfully, he had lots of old books lying around. I would wake up at five-thirty in the morning each day and fall asleep at close to eleven at night, sometimes later.

At around five in the morning every day, Jean would barge into my room. Without even checking if I was awake or listening at all, he would start talking.

"Today you have it easy. You have a lot less than you usually do," he would say, pretty much daily. "Make the beds, do the laundry, make me breakfast, trim the garden…" Then, Jean would list a whole bunch of chores. With no other choice, I would listen to them all. "And…make me dinner," he would finish.

His list became longer every day, but I thankfully had a great memory. I later gained the strength to accomplish the work.

I was too young and too shy to argue with my evil uncle. The only thing that kept me going was my family. Eventually, I just gave up and prepared myself to act as his slave once again. *Someday, I'll stand up to him,* I promised myself. *Someday.*

Early in the morning, Jean would fall back asleep on the couch as a black-and-white movie droned on an old TV. Sometimes, the news would be on. I would sneak glances at it to see if there was any news about my parents. Usually, it was just clips of the president making speeches and stuff. He was a large man with red hair and kind eyes. He always wore expensive suits. He made lots of jokes on TV, none of which were very funny, and he always seemed to forget simple stuff. Sometimes, he would just stare into space with a blank expression, as if he was trying to recall something important. There was just something off about him.

I would set off to make the beds and do the laundry.

By the end of the day, I would be sweating from running around the old house. I would try to make Jean a late dinner of whatever he wanted, too timid to resist. I taught myself to bake and cook at a very young age just so Jean would keep taking care of me, if you could even call it that. There was no choice. If I refused, I would be kicked out. I *needed* my uncle to accept me. I would set his table, set the food out, and run into my empty room. This became routine for me. *Calm down*, I would remind myself. *At least you have a home.* But I knew I really didn't. I just had to keep waiting, hoping, until my family came home.

Each night, I would look around my room, painted a fading white, completely empty except for a small cot in the back corner and a dusty shelf. I had put piles of books along the walls but that was it. The paint was peeling off of the walls and I almost didn't fit on the small cot. I blinked away tears. I was too strong to cry. I would walk over to the small cot, and sit there, trying to read an adventure story through my blurry eyes. If anything other than my family was keeping me going, it would be the characters in the stories I read. They understood me. It was the most incredible feeling as all of those amazing adventures soaked into my brain from old, worn paper. There was this one legend about trolls that could freeze time— the old powers. I would love to have those powers. I would pause the world around me and take a break from my uncle's extensive list of chores. That was one of my favorites… until my uncle burned it. I wish I was as brave as those characters. I would call the police on my cruel uncle, or run away and find my parents. They were out there somewhere.

The stories reminded me of the time before my parents disappeared. That was a different life, and I didn't have many memories of it. I lived with my mum, my dad, my older brother, and my grandfather, who had unfortunately passed away just a few years before I went to live with Jean. He would always tell me this story of a time he went on an adventure through the woods and came across a vampire who he beat through *"a bit of skill but mostly luck"* (his words, not mine). I always found his stories to be a bit ridiculous, but I never minded. The feeling of my grandfather tucking me in with far-fetched vampire tales was very comforting. Stories gave me that feeling all over again.

Sometime late at night, Jean would walk in and throw a pair of dirty pajamas on top of my bed. He handed me a cracker. That was my reward for doing everything for him. One cracker. At least it was better than nothing, I guess. He would jerk his head toward the cracker. "Eat it. And get into your pajamas. *Now*," he would snarl. I would eat the cracker, and put on the pajamas. "Clean up the rest of the house," the lazy man would instruct.

"But the house is clean!" I always protested. "I spent the whole day doing chores!"

"Is that a complaint?" He glared down at me. "If I let you stay here, you need to clean EVERYTHING!" By *"everything,"* he usually meant his leftover dinner and any trash he dropped carelessly on the floor, which, knowing him, was usually a lot. I don't even know why I tried. He would never give in.

"Everything?" I would squeak nervously. Even asking questions could be considered rude when talking to my uncle. He constantly reminded me how disrespectful I was. I was lucky not to be on the streets, he would tell me.

"EVERYTHING!!" The man would bellow, and so I would set off to finish my job.

Jean would be in bed by the time I was done, and it would be very late. I climbed into my bed and stared up at the moon. Where were my parents, I wondered? If they were playing a trick on me, it wasn't funny anymore. But if they were testing me, I would fight for them. I just had to believe that they were okay. I knew I wasn't in the right place. Jean's house wasn't where they wanted me to be. My family was strong. They would come for me, eventually. They would fight, and I would as well. Well, at least that's what I always said. I was never brave enough.

But that was over now. I would live alone on the streets. I would survive, somehow. I would not go back to Jean's house. *Never.* I promised myself. I could never go back now, anyway. Even if he wanted me. Living on the streets was better than living with him. Sighing, I sat down on a log. I took off my backpack, placed it on the log and began to rummage through it. I pulled out each item and started a little pile of my stuff next to me.

"Let's see… I have snacks, a blanket, money, water bottles…" Everything I needed. I pulled out my favorite book and smiled as I added it to the pile. I looked at my pile, feeling better knowing I had at least some personal items to keep. I felt around in the bag, checking to make sure that I had everything I needed. I felt something else, then pulled out a soft teddy bear and another memory took over my mind.

"Here," my mum had said, handing a teddy bear to me, three years old at the time. My eyes widened, and I hugged him, pulling on his arm and smiling. "This is Sir William. He will keep you safe." I stopped playing with the bear and let go of him. 'Sir William' dropped to the floor. He seemed to hit the tiles in slow motion with a soft thudding sound, like in horror movies. I was so confused. Why did the bear need to protect me? I looked at my mother, who was picking up Sir William. Wouldn't she protect me?

I gave voice to my question. "Won't you protect me?"

She smiled sadly and handed me Sir William. "I'm going on a boat, sweetie. I'll be back in a week," she told me. I frowned. A boat? Without me?

"But will daddy stay?" I asked softly. She shook her head.

"Beatrice, your babysitter, will stay with you," she said. I started crying.

"Please no. I want you and Daddy." I sniffled. I loved Beatrice, but I wanted my mum and dad. She didn't answer. "Is Louis staying?" I had questioned. Louis was my older brother and best friend. My mum shook her head. I sniffled. I couldn't believe they were just leaving me! How come Louis got to go on the boat and not me?

"It's okay. It's just a week." Mum smiled, although it was more sad than happy. I knew she was just trying to make me feel better. It wasn't working.

"Why can't I come too?" I asked, though the question sounded more whiny than I would like to admit now.

My mum wrapped me in a hug. "You're too young," she answered sadly. "I'll see you soon, I promise. Sir William will keep you safe."

I could picture the moment in my mind clearly. It was a sad movie that I was forced to watch, again and again. I didn't want to remember.

I clutched Sir William, one of my only friends as a child, tightly, and a tear rolled down my cheek. I laughed softly at how life had changed since then. It wasn't a happy sound. I swiped away more tears as I put everything back in my bag. At least I had some things. My things.

I wrapped a blanket around myself and sat on the log. It was cold. I decided to rest there for the night, which was probably a bad choice, but I was too tired to think about it much. It was *so* late. Well, more like early. The sun would be rising soon. My back would not be forgiving in the morning, though. I dropped my backpack and curled up like a cat, wrapping my blanket around me, then fell asleep.

The morning came faster than I thought possible. I sat up and yawned. I had slept, but I was still exhausted. My back and neck ached from the restless night on the rough log. My dreams were awful—invaded by sinking boats, evil uncles, and, strangely, evil red eyes. These dreams had been haunting me for a while, but never this bad. I stretched, opened my bag, and I ripped open a granola bar. I savored every bite as my breakfast. I gulped down some water and snatched the money from my bag, putting it in my pocket just in case. I swung my backpack over my shoulder and decided to go to Ivy's tent. I couldn't just sit around. I knew it wasn't right to use her magic for my own purposes, but I needed to know the truth. I needed to find my parents, or at least figure out what happened to them. I needed closure. I couldn't go to the police, and I definitely couldn't go back to Jean or Beatrice. I would visit Ivy as many times as I needed to. I took a deep breath and rushed in that direction.

Colorful leaves crunched under my feet as I flew toward the tent and threw open the flap, stopping for nothing. I was in a rush. "Ivy!" I called. "Hello?" No answer. For just a moment, I felt bad. It was too early in the morning and I didn't want to wake her. The silence was sharp and still.

"'Ello?" Ivy's voice yawned from deep inside the tent.

"Good morning." I said, rubbing my tired eyes.

She appeared through the tent flap. Even in the early morning, she was wearing a worn, gorgeous purple dress that made me feel very conscious of the blue T-shirt and black sweatpants I had been wearing all day yesterday— and all night as well.

"Carl!" She was clearly surprised by my appearance so early in the morning. "What are you-" She paused and studied me carefully for the first time, certainly noticing my tired eyes and the chipped pieces of bark in my messy hair. "Oh my—what on—you look so exhausted!"

"Just tired," I groaned, shaking myself awake enough to give her a sleepy smile.

"Oh, yeah," Ivy said, sucking in a breath. She gave me a small smile, welcoming me inside of her tent, again. She knew. I had so much going on that I had been up half of the night caught up in my thoughts. She didn't even ask anymore, which I was grateful for. I was lucky to have a friend like her. "Need anything?"

I took a step closer and looked around her tent and took a deep breath. She looked at me expectantly. It couldn't hurt to ask once more, anyway. "Do you happen to have anything for me?" I asked, super-hopefully. "Any fortunes?" I knew immediately by her face that she didn't.

"I'm sorry," she said quietly. "I can't always see everything right away. The visions appear in my crystal ball when they need to."

"I know." She had told me that before, and I respected that. I understood. *I guess her ball doesn't seem to think my problems are as much of a priority as I do…*

"What kind of answers are you looking for anyway?" she asked curiously.

"I don't know," I replied, half-honestly. "I'm looking for a place to go. I want to know what I'm supposed to do. I… I need closure, honestly. I just… need to find my parents, Ivy. I need…" my voice broke. "I need to know that they're okay."

I knew Ivy understood. She was always good at understanding people, especially me.

"Well, hopefully we'll get you some answers soon," Ivy said with a little wink, putting her hand on my shoulder. She knew I was desperate for an answer. Any answer, as long as it made me understand… understand anything. Understand what I was meant to do and maybe figure out how to do it. And I was worried. *What happens next?* I wanted to ask. But that was a question for another time. Her powers didn't go that far.

Ivy was just trying to help, so I returned her smile anyway. "Hopefully."

***

It had been a week since I had run away. I was sitting on my log, the one I'd slept on my first night as a runaway. Since then, I'd learned from my mistakes and instead slept on a patch of grass in the shade of a leafy tree. I'd also been visiting Ivy each day, looking forward to our daily chats about… anything. It was just nice to have a friend. It was much easier, and I was getting more used to my new, temporary life. I was sitting under my claimed tree when I suddenly heard loud footsteps. They got louder and louder. Then, the sounds turned into voices. Familiar voices.

"Sir, please. Calm down. As far as we know, he's not in any danger. It will be okay," a voice was saying, trying to comfort someone. Who?

I was so surprised when they walked past me that I almost choked on absolutely nothing. It was Jean, followed by a group of police officers! What on Earth was he doing there?!

I ducked behind the tree to watch them, making sure to stay hidden. Something weird was happening. I studied the small group of officers, including a burly male, a female officer with a large clipboard, and a boy who was younger than the rest, but still in uniform—maybe a deputy or a junior officer in training. I watched them march behind my uncle, peppering him with questions and comforting him. Jean's eyes were tired and his hair was messy. He looked *awful*. I had wondered how he was doing without me acting as his servant. I guess this was my answer. Maybe he called for me every morning and started his list only to realize that I wasn't there. Maybe it was kind of mean, but I had to smile at that thought, just a bit. He deserved it, after all.

"Where is he, my only nephew?" Jean cried with much-too-heavy despair. I gaped at him. Well that explained it. I shook my head and listened. He was sobbing— no, *pretending* to sob. He'd always been a good actor. Of course, it was all a lie.

It almost felt like he cared, but the bitter truth was that he didn't. I so desperately wanted to believe him— I wanted him to care. I wanted a home. I wanted answers. But he just wanted the policemen to find me so he could have a worker again. He was just as lazy as ever.

"Sir, please calm down. We will find him." The burly police officer promised.

"What happened to him?" The female officer asked, writing another note on her shiny blue clipboard. "When and where did you discover that he was missing?"

"Uh, he... my dear boy was kidnapped in the middle of the night." My uncle lied in a wail of fake despair. What a twisted version of the truth. How horrible could he get? "I loved him so much! He was the only thing left of... of...." He burst into fake tears, and my heart thumped against my chest. Yet again, I found myself almost wanting to believe him. I scolded myself internally. No, his lies were good, but they were still lies, and I didn't like lies. Still, my heart was slowly sinking.

They continued their search until they concluded that I wasn't there. I tried to catch my breath. My heart was racing. I knew they wouldn't stop until they found me. Jean needed me for his chores, after all. When they finally left, I sighed in relief and my heartbeat slowed. The policemen and my uncle were gone.

I wasn't going back, not now or ever. I simply wouldn't. Jean couldn't control me anymore. Now I needed the truth more than ever. I needed to find my parents before Jean found me. I winced at the thought. I had to do something! If I went to the police, they would tell me— no, force me — to go home. Even if they said that, I couldn't. Home? The thought almost made me laugh, more of a scoff than a sound of joy. Jean's house was never a home to me, and it never would be. I didn't even have a home anymore. But I would find one— I know I would!

I decided to go see Ivy again, even if I'd seen her just the other day. I needed her help more than ever, or even just someone to talk to about what had just happened. Ivy could help me, I knew it. She just needed time. I needed time too. My life had changed so much, and I wasn't sure what to do with it anymore. But I'd find out. If I found out the truth about my parents, I'll know where I belong, I was sure of it. I had promised myself never to go back to Jean. I couldn't and wouldn't do that, anyway. *You don't own me anymore, Jean,* I swore in my head, stepping forward and checking to make sure the officers were truly gone. I wasn't going back. At least not until I found something, anything to help me. Until I found a home. My home. Maybe even any home, as long as it was a real home.

***

Chapter Two

A Cruise with a Vampire

"What?!" Ivy shouted suddenly, her voice echoing as it bounced across the previously silent and sharp night air. Her voice was shaky and loud. I stepped back from the tent walls. Was something wrong? "This changes everything!" She was talking to herself— that wasn't a good sign. It meant she was using her magic. Maybe *now* wasn't the best time to visit. I made myself step forward and peek into her tent.

"Ivy? I called. "Are you okay?"

"Uh... I've been better!" I heard the soft *clink* of glasses touching each other. "Magic is hard—it almost never works the way you want it to. Magic has a mind of its own. It can sometimes make you dizzy... too much could even change the user. Big magic, like a crystal ball."

I knew that, of course, because she'd told me. What had she done? Had she used her crystal ball? Did she... have my answers? I was quiet for a moment.

"Ivy?" I waited patiently in the entrance for her to continue. I heard her make a startled noise like she had forgotten I was there. "What did you see?" I prompted her.

"Carl, I saw your p—" She paused like she was hiding a secret. I could almost hear her grin. "—Your answers! I think this may help!"

My heart soared, and I smiled. Finally. So, this *was* something good!

"Come in, come in!" Ivy said excitedly. I stepped further inside and saw her standing over her glass ball, which was resting on a wooden stand. Again, she almost never used her crystal ball, which meant that something big was going on. The ball was glowing, but a part of it was covered by a shadow, which Ivy was studying. Ivy said she could speak to the shadows and understand them. I studied the ball. It seemed pretty normal to me, but Ivy always said that sometimes you find magic when you least expect it. Her eyes lit up as she watched the shadows rotate around the ball, forming different shapes and figures. It was special, almost magical.

"Your parents…" She paused dramatically. I held my breath. "…Are alive! And they're hiding on an island, it seems," she said happily.

I almost choked on my gasp. This was what I needed! My parents! Then I realized what Ivy had said. Hiding? Hiding from whom? Or what?

I opened my mouth to ask, but she wobbled a little, nearly falling. I caught her and helped her onto a chair. She looked at me curiously as she sat.

I watched the crystal ball closer. "What do I do next?" I asked.

But I already knew what I would do. I was going to find my parents. It was dangerous, but I would do it for them. I'd do anything for them.

"Is this really what you want, Carl?" Ivy asked with a frown. I nodded. My mind was already made up. She sighed. "You need to get on a boat. I can't see where they are specifically, but there has to be some undiscovered island somewhere— they're probably there."

"I'm leaving." I told her, trying to be confident. "I'll go tonight, when it gets dark."

Where on Earth would I go? I wished she had seen something more specific. How was I supposed to find some random island? It was definitely risky, but I had to try.

"Carl—" Ivy started.

"When I come back, I'll have my parents with me." I promised confidently. This was the only answer that I needed—the only way—and Ivy knew that, but I could tell she was worried for me. I was too. She was the most amazing friend ever. She had already helped me way more than I deserved. I started leaving through the flap of the tent, but Ivy reached for my hand and stopped me. She looked troubled.

"What's wrong, Ivy?"

"Carl, the rest of your future is unclear if you chose this path. It's all up to you."

What was that supposed to mean?

"I know, Ivy," I said, even though I didn't really know. "It's okay."

It was just some shadows. Magical shadows.

She gave me a smile. Her gentle hand brushed against mine. She smiled softly and planted a kiss on my cheek. "Good luck, Carl," she whispered in my ear.

Because I definitely needed that too.

***

My backpack slid down one of my shoulders as I ran. Honestly, I had no clue where I was going. I remembered what Ivy said. I needed to get on a boat. Most islands had boats going to them at some point. There was a large port at the edge of our small town where most people got on boats, and I decided to try to head there. I swung my backpack over my arms again and ran into the darkness before me. Once again, I was leaving under the cover of night, afraid of being discovered by my uncle, the police, or worse, someone dangerous, like a criminal.

I shivered, mostly because I was nervous, but also from the cold air pressing against my body. I ran for hours, not sure how to get to the port. I was lost with no sense of direction.

I fidgeted with the black shirt Ivy had lent me. I was wearing *her* black T-shirt and *her* jeans, which felt a bit awkward, but I was grateful. She'd given me some old pairs of clothes for my journey. Even though she was shorter than me, I was skinnier so mostly everything fit. She'd also given me a gray sweater, which was wrapped tightly around my waist.

Ahead, I noticed a kind-looking old man on a street corner. I finally stopped and approached him to ask directions. I knew I shouldn't talk to a stranger, but the sun would come up soon, and I was lost.

I wasn't sure to where exactly I should ask for directions, so I asked how I could get to the nearest port. Any boat seemed like a better idea than running around, lost. I had to find the island that my parents were on.

"Looking to get on a boat?" the man asked, smiling at me.

I mean, obviously I was. I was tempted not to answer, but he seemed nice enough. When I nodded, he pointed me in the right direction.

I thanked him.

I walked to the port, smelling wood, paint, and the salty sea air. It seemed like a friendly place, even so early in the morning. The strong scents were almost overwhelming, but in a comforting way. The rising sun painted the sky orange, pink, yellow, and purple.

I looked up at the boats and a strangled noise caught in my throat. I recognized this place, these boats, this scent. This was the port that my parents' boat had left from years ago. I choked as I watched a cruise boat sail away.

As the sun got so bright that it was blinding me and blue light filled the sky, I stepped forward toward the lines of boats. Then I saw the rows of wooden signs labeled with prices for each boat. I slid my hand into the pocket of Ivy's jeans to check how much money I had. Eight dollars. I wasn't sure if that was enough to get on any boat, so I hid it in my pocket again.

But then I saw a man standing in front of a large cruise boat. It looked so familiar, yet I couldn't remember where I'd seen it. The man seemed to be watching me. He was saying something as passengers got on the boat, but I couldn't hear him. I walked closer, trying to tune out my other senses and focus on what he was saying.

"Mysterious boat tour, only five dollars!" Only five dollars? My hand automatically slid down into my pocket and closed around my money. Was it worth spending most of it on a boat tour? I got even closer to the man, still listening to him.

"New boat tours! Come get a five-dollar boat tour! Explore mysterious and unknown islands you've never seen! Discover islands never seen by men!" He gave an exaggerated laugh and grinned at me. "Would you like a ride, young man? You seem lost, maybe not physically, but mentally. Maybe exploring the sea will help you find your way?" He offered way too loudly.

Find my way? Wow. I shuddered. It was almost like he had read my mind, which was extremely creepy. He seemed to be staring into my soul. I found the way he spoke to me suspicious. There was so much about him that seemed off. He smiled at me again, showing big, shiny teeth. He was waiting for my answer. Could a boat ride really hurt?

"Your parents are alive! And they're hiding on an island, it seems." Ivy had said. I thought about that for a minute, studying the strange man and his boat. *"Discover islands never seen by men!"* he'd said. I considered this along with Ivy's other words: *"There has*

to be some undiscovered island somewhere— they're probably there."

If my parents were on an island that was *known to a man,* they would have been found by now, right? The man was still watching me. This interesting boat ride opened up new possibilities for me and my family. I had no other choice.

"Here." I gave in, handing the man five dollars. That was over half of my money. The man grinned, and for the first time, I noticed his creepy red eyes. His shining teeth were way too sharp. His smile didn't seem friendly anymore... it seemed like a smile of amusement, as if he was a predator luring prey into a trap. It made me worry, but I ignored it, for my family. I also realized the man had a black umbrella with white skulls and bats on it. Why the man had an umbrella, I wasn't sure. It was a sunny day with just enough wind and not a cloud in the sky. *Ignore it,* I reminded myself. *He's just some strange old sailor.* I joined the few people on the boat and sat down without making a noise. The whole boat was awkwardly quiet. Suddenly, a noisy horn sounded, shattering the silence.

"All aboard!" the strange man called. Slowly, the boat started to pull away from the docks and the man walked toward the small group of passengers. None of them moved an inch.

"So..." The man turned to me, out of all of the passengers. It seemed like he just wanted to talk to me more. *Why me?* "You are?" he prompted.

I looked up, straight into the shiny red eyes. Into the lion's den. *This is why you don't talk to strangers...* "Carl," I muttered.

The man's eyes lit up as if my name was important to him. He wrapped his arm around me like we were old friends. I shifted uncomfortably. Did I know him from somewhere? "Well, well, well... Finally. My name is Drake," he added with a grin. What a strange name. The grin felt more like a smirk. He was really making me nervous; watching me like a hawk.

"Yeah," I said nervously. "I'll just..." I shuddered, backing up slowly. *He's so creepy. I need to get out of here!* I turned toward the end of the boat, but it was already quickly moving through the water, further and further away from land until the port was just a distant speck. Drake followed me quietly, not lowering his umbrella. I turned away slowly and was met with his creepy snarl. I immediately stepped away, but he advanced toward me and grabbed my arm. I yelped, cowering by the edge of the boat. The murky water extended out as far as I could see. Drake gave a cold smile and started to chuckle before pulling me back to my seat.

"Careful," he said, his voice dark and amused. "Wouldn't want you falling off of the boat." There was something different in his smooth voice. It was almost threatening now, and it was clear that the other passengers had noticed, for they were observing the exchange nervously. I sat down without another word. Something was definitely wrong.

We had been gliding around the sea all day. The water was smooth beneath us, giving me an eerie feeling, as if it was watching me, worried—as if Drake's presence had somehow tamed it, and my presence was somehow going to upset the strange balance. Finally, night started approaching, and it didn't seem like we were any closer to any island. I hadn't seen any, only the eerily calm sea for miles and miles. I wanted to ask how long it would be until we were there, yet I stayed quiet. I didn't want to speak to Drake anymore. But he was my only chance to find my family, and it was only getting later. I took a deep breath.

"When will we be there?" I asked. Drake definitely heard me, but you wouldn't be able to tell by his blank expression. "Drake?" I pressed. "Could we maybe stop, or go faster? We really need to find the island we're going to."

He whirled around. "Why?" he questioned with a smirk, but didn't stop or speed up at all. "What's the rush? Do you have someone you need to go home to?"

This set off alarm bells in my brain. I turned away and stayed quiet. In fact, I didn't have anywhere to go. And it seemed like Drake knew that as well. It was silent for several minutes. Now the sun was setting, and it was getting dark.

I turned to Drake again. He was focused on the water ahead, as if looking up from it would set off a bomb. Maybe he was worried about getting asked too many questions. But when the boat came to a stop, he finally looked up with an even smirk.

"We're here," he declared.

I looked around. We were floating in the middle of the sea, not near any islands, not near anything. Just more water.

Drake laughed. "Oops!"

I screamed as the boat started sinking. Drake's evil laugh echoed through the air. All of the other passengers looked at each other, eyes raging with fear. Drake grinned at me. Not all of us, just me specifically. His grin was evil, not happy, as he looked me directly in the eye. Then he disappeared.

I yelped. I looked around for Drake, but all I could see was darkness and… a bat in his place. The bat had Drake's creepy red eyes. It *was* Drake, I realized! I was almost too shocked to move, but as the bat, who was actually Drake, prepared to dive at me, I immediately ran to the back of the boat and hid in a cramped nook. I couldn't figure out what was going on. But as I played everything over in my mind, it suddenly seemed clear.

DRAKE IS A VAMPIRE! It seemed obvious now but still didn't make any sense. I mean, sure, he had very sharp teeth, a creepy grin, red eyes, he didn't like the light—which was the cause for the umbrella, I supposed—and he turned into a bat, which shouldn't have been possible either! *Vampires aren't real*, I scolded myself. This was probably a dream—no, a nightmare. I shook my head. Then I pinched myself hard. I yelped but then quickly covered my mouth. I heard approaching footsteps on the deck of the boat.

Drake!

I dashed out of my hiding place and through a door where I was met with darkness. I fumbled for a light switch. As my eyes adjusted, I realized that I was looking around the tiny, dusty, old storage room at the back of the boat.

Looking through the storage room at the back of the boat, I hoped I could find a flashlight or something helpful to fight off a vampire. There were piles of crates neatly stacked against the wall, but there was something suspicious about the way they looked, like they'd been there for years. I opened one crate. And another. Nothing helpful. Just some old junk. A suitcase, a camera, a collection of seashells, a little sculpture that looked like an anchor and some stuff that belonged to the old captain of the boat, who I assumed Drake had stolen it from. I opened the last crate and found a pile of papers. I pulled one out. It was a ticket for a cruise. When I took out the second paper, my face paled and I started shaking. No, it couldn't be. That… that was impossible!

There was a picture of all of the passengers who were previously on the boat, and my family's faces were among the group! My mum, laughing; my dad, smiling; and my older brother, Louis, just a little boy then, looking up at the camera, smiling, curious. I felt dizzy. That shouldn't have been possible. It happened so long ago. Yet, I realized they were standing in front of the very boat I was on.

I suddenly didn't trust the wooden boards beneath my feet, I hated the paint on the walls. The stuff in the crates could have belonged to my parents. I could have denied it, saying it could have been a coincidence, but that changed when I recognized a fourth face: Drake, smirking maliciously at my parents. They wouldn't have noticed at the time, but I did. I never should have trusted Drake!

The boat around me started spinning, and I couldn't catch my breath. I noticed cracks in the walls that seemed well covered, nearly invisible until you looked for them—like magic. I could hear Drake's laugh in my head as my knees buckled beneath me. There was a connection between me, my parents, Drake, and this boat. Something was wrong, but it wasn't the kind of normal wrong, like as if you had done a bad deed in the past. This was way, way worse—like a history of bad deeds done by people you thought you knew. And, it turns out, you didn't. I felt everything I thought I knew about my parents— about my *life*— being turned over. I was so shocked that I didn't notice the door creak open. I was shaking so hard that I didn't see the smirk on his face. I noticed the glowing red eyes too late.

Drake grabbed my hand, dragging me out onto the deck of the boat. I tried to escape, but his grip was like steel. I pulled against him, trying to forget about my parents for a moment. Did I even know them at all? It may even have been his fault that they were gone. *Hiding*, Ivy had said. At first, I didn't know who— or what— they were hiding from. But now I did—Drake. Drake, who I somehow met that very same day. Was it all a coincidence, or part of some bigger thing? I gritted my teeth, trying to ignore his look of amusement.

"Well, well, well, it's the goody two-shoes. You're just like your parents. Just like your grandfather." His face darkened at the mention of my grandfather. My grandfather was a part of this too? He had been so special to me, but... he had died years ago. Did I know anyone in my family at all?

I stared into Drake's red eyes. He looked... almost sad. Maybe there was a different side to him. I felt a glimmer of hope, but quickly squashed it. So far, he had only shown pure evil. All he had done so far was hurt my family.

"What did you do to my parents? What did you do to this boat?!" I yelled, struggling against Drake. He acted like he didn't even hear me. "I KNOW YOU HEARD ME! WHAT DID YOU DO?!" Fighting was useless, but I tried anyway, even though Drake was much bigger and stronger than me. The truth was that he knew me, and I didn't know him. He knew my weaknesses, and I didn't know his. Even if I was truly stronger— which I wasn't— he would still defeat me. *One step ahead.* His grip got tighter around my wrist, and his sharp, long nails dug into my skin. His red eyes sparkled.

I tried not to let Drake see the tears glimmering in my eyes. His voice echoed in my head whenever he spoke, his smirk flashed before my vision whenever I closed my eyes. Whenever I tried to drown him out, he somehow kept creeping in. Compared to him, I knew I was weak. *And... he knows. He knows that I know. That's his advantage.*

"You're as good as dead," he spat. His voice got louder, prouder, more aggressive. "You will suffer, and your family will pay! Fighting me is useless. Running from me is useless! *You* are useless! You think that you can beat me? I'm more powerful than you could ever imagine! The universe follows my commands, and I know all of your strengths. You don't even know them yourself. But more importantly, I know your weaknesses! Don't you see? I'm always one step ahead of you, Carl. I will always get there first! I *will* win. And I *will* enjoy destroying EVERY LAST INCH OF YOUR FAMILY!" Drake's voice was almost a yell now.

I shuddered. *Pay for what?* I wondered. What did Drake want from me, and more importantly, my family? Then I thought of a more important question.

"Why?" I whispered. I wasn't even trying to hide my fear. Drake knew everything about me, but I knew nothing about him. I didn't know why he was doing this. Only he did.

Then I decided that his mysterious origin story wasn't my biggest issue now. Another part of me argued that it would definitely be a problem in the future. But that part of me just wanted to know something about myself that I'd never known. It made me sad, almost mad, at my family. There was so much that they'd never told me any of this. I forced myself to shake it off. It was clear that there was conflict—a whole *history* of conflict— but different. There had to be something bigger going on, something that would make Drake this cruel. Maybe vampires were truly good inside. Maybe he used to be good too. I had tried so hard to find a better side in him, somewhere deep down. But I would never know. What could my family have done that made him change for the worse? Something bad had happened, and my family was part of it. I was too… whether I liked it or not. But I refused to be a pawn in Drake's evil games.

The boat started shaking as if it would fall apart any minute. The cracks in the painted wood of the boat, well-hidden and almost invisible before were now obvious and only growing bigger. All of the other passengers had disappeared into the cold night air, like my parents. I shivered. Innocent people, gone like *that*. Drake probably showed them no mercy. The cold air bit into my face, making my vision blur and my face sting. Suddenly, Drake was lifting me with his cold, steel grip. It was then that I really started to panic, and Drake loved it—I could tell.

I'd really messed up. I felt like Drake knew that too. He always knew. Something deep down in me ached. There was more. There were hints throughout my childhood— all of those nightmares and memories of red eyes, those times I thought I could hear my parents screaming for help late at night, the times I felt like someone was watching me… none of it made sense. There was so much more that I was just too blind to see. Drake watched me carefully, like he knew what I was thinking. I choked on what may have been a mix between a sad sound and a scared sound.

Then everything faded, briefly, and shifted. I was in a different place, one where I was happy with my family, one where I was home. A reality where Drake didn't exist, and Jean couldn't hurt me, and I was safe. There were no boats, no red eyes, no mysteries. But the sound of water startled me awake, and I was back.

Drake was dangling me high above the water. I could hear the rushing waves beneath me. The water seemed deep and cold, and the waves were harsh, rising as high as towers and crashing even harder. Huge and heavy, waiting to cover me, submerge me, drown me, hurt me. I cried out, but nobody could hear me. No one was even nearby, and even if someone was, they probably wouldn't be able to hear me over the roar of the rushing water. I had the sense that no one would be able to help me.

I watched the water, waiting below me, getting closer every time Drake moved his arm. He was taunting me. I was stuck in his grasp. If he let go, I would fall. I would have thought that if there was some grand plan of revenge against my family at work, he would want to kill me himself. Dropping me to my doom seemed too quick for this type of enemy. But maybe that was better. No, probably not. It didn't give me enough time to escape. Maybe he knew that. His voice echoed in my head. *I know your strengths. I know your weaknesses. To every attack there is a counterattack, and I can predict all of yours. You are weak. You are useless. You will never defeat me. I'm always one step ahead. Always.*

He was right.

There was more, I realized. I suddenly remembered *and* understood all of the signs my parents had tried to give me; signs that I didn't understand before— the cause of all of the warnings and safety trips, the real reason they didn't let me go on the boat, all of their discussions at night. Even as a three-year-old, I remembered listening, confused, to all of those talks about red eyes and 'vampires'. I even realized their true motive behind making me stay with my uncle if anything ever happened. Drake couldn't find me. Jean wasn't involved, and even though they hated them, I would be safe—I had overheard that too, though my small, three-year old brain didn't comprehend it at the time. My parents had tried to shield me from it, but that didn't last long. They didn't last long.

No, I reminded myself. *You shouldn't think like that.*

Drake was watching me, sensing my thoughts; my confusion, my sadness, and my anger—buried deeper than my other feelings— but mostly my fear. The fear that Drake could read me like an open book made me cry out again. Drake smirked and hissed in my ear, "They'll enjoy watching you die."

Then, he let go.

***

Chapter Three

Diaries of a Pirate Prisoner

I seemed to be falling in slow motion. *They'll enjoy watching you die?* I thought, confused. *Who?* He was killing me now, I thought, by dropping me into the wild waves below, and nobody else was nearby to see. He didn't care enough to spare me the time to escape. I was flailing wildly as I fell through the air, as futile as the struggle was. The wild water was already rising up to meet me.

There is no escaping me. The waves said. *You are coming into my territory now.*

Something weird was going on. Something was wrong. The waves got closer, but I barely noticed them now. I was caught up in trying to understand my own life and what had just happened. It seemed everyone knew me better than I did myself. Drake smirked from above, getting farther and farther away until he was only a speck. He loved confusing me. He enjoyed his triumph over me, he loved knowing, he loved being one step ahead.

No more games.

I closed my eyes, preparing for impact. Then I hit the water.

Everything in my body stung. I felt water seeping into my clothes and my hair. I opened my eyes, moving my arms around helplessly, upsetting the water. I cursed in my head. I tried to make noise, but only bubbles came out, fizzing to the surface as I swallowed water. I couldn't swim. I'd never needed to, and I'd never been taught—obviously. Jean couldn't spare a moment of his *"precious"* life to teach me. My vision blurred into a mess of icy teal water, colorful creatures and silver foam. I fought the water but my energy couldn't last for long. I made one last attempt to reach the surface and cry out as the world went black.

***

"Wake up! Wake up!" said an unfamiliar female voice, sounding aggressive but somehow kind... soft hands, shaking me gently... *What...?* I groaned. I was alive? I opened my eyes and coughed up water. My vision was blurry and my body was aching, but I was alive! I blinked twice. I was on a ship deck, but not the same one I had just been thrown from. I had somehow escaped Drake. *Wait...* I felt around for my belongings. My backpack was gone! My food, my water, my money, Ivy's clothes— gone. My bag had gotten lost in the water, probably, which meant I had lost everything except for the clothes on my back and the sweater around my waist. But I was alive.

Wait. Drake.

"Va-vampire..." I spluttered. "I have to... he's coming... he'll get me..."

She stopped me. "Catch your breath, kid."

In front of me, stood a pirate. Seriously. A real pirate. A tall, dark-skinned, female pirate with black hair that was tightly woven into braids. Hm. She seemed to be around my age; maybe a few years older. She was very pretty. Her voice had a sarcastic yet caring tone to it. I leaned against her for support. Somehow, it just felt *right*. I didn't mean that in a weird way at all.

My face heated up, and I shoved that thought away, trying to make sense of it all. I was in danger, and so was she as long as I was on her boat, because of Drake. He would know that I was alive. He would come. Well, I wouldn't give in to him. So instead of thinking about Drake, I turned my attention back to the girl, back to where I was now. Still, she wasn't like a real pirate, the kind that you read about in historical stories. No, she was more like a pirate from a fantasy. Her boat resembled that too, but a bit friendlier. Like her.

"Who are you?" I asked loudly. Her eyes widened with fear as if we would be heard, like I shouldn't have been there. It's not like I was there on purpose.

"Be quiet, please!" she begged. She looked over her shoulder almost nervously. I didn't argue, but I was confused. Were there more pirates somewhere nearby? I waited silently for more information. Where was I? Who was she? Whoever she was, she seemed concerned for me, and it was nice to have someone try to defend me for once. She seemed nice. She looked back at me, and her face softened. Our eyes met. "It'll be okay," she promised.

I took a deep breath and exhaled. We were *really* close. My face turned red. But she was just helping me, and she seemed fine with it, so I ignored the fluttering feeling in my heart. I barely knew this girl!

The boat we were on was much larger than Drake's, and had more things piled everywhere. It was definitely how I would have imagined a pirate's boat, and it felt good to be here with this pirate. I didn't know her well, but maybe I'd get to know her better. Maybe she could help me. Maybe we could be friends. And maybe there were other pirates, but was that good or bad? The girl *did* seem worried that somebody would overhear us. I wasn't sure what to do, so I sat there quietly, watching her. After all those days, I had finally found someone who cared. Unless you're counting Ivy, I'd never really had any friends.

"I'm Stephanie," she said finally, her voice light and soft. "You can call me Steph, if you want." She reached out her hand and helped me stand up. I smiled.

"I'm Carl." I told her, my voice hoarse.

"You'll be okay," she promised slowly. "...Carl." She smiled, making me blush.

Suddenly, there were footsteps banging up the stairs from below the deck. Stephanie paled as her positive attitude faded entirely, replaced by pure terror. She glanced over her shoulder to the stairs. Someone was coming.

A rough voice echoed from down below as the clear owner of the footsteps grumbled to himself. He was clearly angry. Stephanie—the kind pirate who had acted so brave and sarcastic just moments ago— was suddenly all nervous and fidgety. The man's shadow—not very tall but not the shortest either—was getting closer.

Then he paused his intimidating march and bellowed, "STEPHANIE!"

Stephanie froze, and her hand snapped into salute. "Yes, Mason? I mean, sir! I mean... Captain? What do you need... Captain?" Stephanie nervously glanced back and forth between me and the stairs. Mason, the captain, was coming. He hadn't seen me yet, but I knew that he would. Steph would have to come up with a lie as to why I was there, and soon.

I expected Mason to be big, burly, and mean. But when he stomped out onto the deck, he was the complete opposite— a short, fat, fair-skinned man with beady black eyes and untidy blonde hair. He was wearing heavy black pants, a black shirt with a white skull and crossbones on it, and a dark-blue jacket. He did look very grumpy. He stopped as soon as he saw me, as I expected he would.

"Uh… Who is this?" he asked Stephanie, looking as if he had smelled something disgusting. He glanced at me. His face said very clearly, *"Get off my boat."*

"Uh, a prisoner?" Stephanie suggested timidly, glancing at me apologetically. I stared at her like she had grown another head. Prisoner?! Really? I suppressed a groan. She couldn't have come up with a better excuse? I didn't want to be a prisoner! No one did, really, but *why,* Stephanie?!

"Can we make him walk the plank?"

Stephanie's face fell. I shot her a look. That was worse. That was *way* worse. I knew Stephanie would protest, but this man clearly had way more power than her on the boat. He was the captain, after all. Did that mean that I was getting thrown off of a boat *AGAIN*?! Worst day *EVER*! Yes, Stephanie definitely didn't seem to like the idea. But it was clear that if Mason wanted it, she had no say in the matter. There was nothing she could do anything about it.

"But—Captain—" she stammered.

Mason didn't seem to care about what she had to say. He just grabbed a rope, tossed it carelessly into her hands, and walked away. His message was very clear. *Tie. Him. Up.* Stephanie stared at the rope and then at me.

She saw the look on my face and blushed. "I'm sorry! I'm so sorry!" she exclaimed quietly. "I promise I'll help you."

Help me? "By taking me captive?" I hissed.

She blushed harder. I shouldn't have been mad. She obviously didn't *want* to suggest taking me captive, and she certainly had no other choice. Well, in her mind, at least. I could think of a few other better ideas. She inched toward me. I watched the rope warily. I tried to look away, but I couldn't. I tried to ignore the feeling of betrayal. I didn't know why I was even thinking that way. I barely knew her. But she could see the hurt in my face. "Carl," she whispered. "Look at me."

"Why?" I asked testily. I couldn't help but blush, though. Was it that obvious?

"I'll get you out of here! I promise!"

I tried to look away again, but she stared directly into my eyes.

I managed to croak out a weak, "Promise?" I felt like a little kid.

She nodded. Then she tied the rope around my sweaty hands. Loosely, sure, so it didn't hurt me, but tight enough that I couldn't escape. I still felt betrayed. Then she left.

***

It was getting later, and I was still alone, struggling against that stupid rope. Where were Stephanie and Mason? Suddenly, I heard footsteps and voices.

"WHERE HAVE YOU BEEN?!" Mason yelled. He was talking to Stephanie. Wait, what? So, they hadn't been together celebrating—or at least pretending to celebrate my capture?

"W-watching the prisoner," Stephanie stammered in response. I hadn't really been paying attention to them but that caught my attention. I knew she was lying because I had been alone. *What has she been up to?* I wondered.

I barely heard them starting to argue, Stephanie's arguments getting slightly weaker every time. Stephanie was saying something along the lines of, "But if he walks the plank-" That got my attention again. They were still talking about me. And she was still fighting to protect me. That made me feel a bit better. A little.

Mason's voice answered flatly, "He *will* walk the plank!"

They walked out onto the deck where I was trapped.

Stephanie argued timidly, "But... Please, I... but—"

"WHY DO YOU CARE?! A REAL PIRATE WOULDN'T CARE! YOU SHOULDN'T!" Mason roared. Stephanie's voice faltered. She had no response. That hurt her, I could tell. I started to panic a little, shaking the ropes. This argument was getting me nowhere.

Stephanie saw, so she gave me a small smile and mouthed, *"Sorry, but it's okay, I have another plan!"*

I glared at her with a look that I hoped clearly said, *"You better."*

She got close to me and untied the rope, freeing me, just so I could walk to my wet doom, *AGAIN!* I was having a really bad day, and not the normal kind! Too many people wanted to kill me. I sighed. It was true. My day had been full of vampires and boats. *And cute pirates...* Wait, WHAT?! Uh, I didn't say that. I didn't even think that. Stephanie *was* pretty, but... Just forget it. I sighed to myself. Really, Carl? I was about to die, and *this* was what I was thinking about?

"Please, Captain... " I tried, knowing he probably wouldn't see reason. He didn't seem to care. He was a pirate, so why would he? Because that's all I was to him. I was a stranger, a prisoner on his boat, a useless boy being tossed off the plank for entertainment.

"You. Will. Walk. The. PLANK!" he roared in response. Maybe he was having a bad day as well. Yeah, I was pretty much doomed. From his tone, I could tell as well as Stephanie that there was no point in arguing. This wasn't working. I had to do something, but I couldn't think of anything.

What if Stephanie's plan didn't work? What if I walked off the plank and drowned for *real* this time? What if I was saved from the water only to be hurt again? What if Stephanie was trying to trick me? My head was full of "what ifs" and no actual plans. Stephanie looked a little nervous too, but she flashed me what was probably meant to be a reassuring smile.

"Stephanie, get him ready." Mason ordered. Stephanie grabbed my tied hands and started dragging me toward the plank. I pulled against Stephanie hard enough to make her stop. She looked directly into my eyes. Her face softened when she saw how scared I really was. She was trying to help, I knew, but I was doomed, I realized with a frown. If this kept happening, I was as good as dead already. *Don't think like that!* I scolded myself again. I'd had to remind myself that many times, but it wasn't working. Drake was after me, Mason was after me, and I was after myself, somehow.

Yay.

"What are you doing?" I asked through gritted teeth.

"Jump," she whispered, swiftly untying my hands. My eyes widened. If that was her plan, I definitely was doomed.

"What?!" I yelled. Stephanie shushed me and looked over her shoulder at Mason, who was glaring in our direction. Well, glaring at me... sort of. It was more like smirking. He did seem really excited that I was to walk the plank.

"What's going on over there?" He asked, eyes narrowing at me and Stephanie. It wasn't normal for prisoners to talk to his pirates while they were walking the plank, I guessed. He was looking at us with suspicion in his eyes. This worried me. Could he hear what we were saying? Would he even be able to over the rushing wind and the wild water? Did he know what Stephanie was planning? Would he punish her? Or was I just taking too long for him? I didn't know. There were a lot of things I didn't know.

"Nothing, sir!" Stephanie called back, way too loudly. I narrowed my eyes. Stephanie had to be kidding, right? She had a different plan, of course. She would laugh, then explain how I could survive, and I'd be safe.

Right?

"Stephanie, what's your plan?" I whisper-hissed.

"I already told you my plan, Carl. *Jump!*"

"I can't just jump off a plank! That's dangerous. And crazy! And—" I could think of a thousand things wrong with her plan. But she really just wanted to help. At least she was *trying*. But that wouldn't be enough to save me. I was getting closer and closer to the plank, the water was getting wilder and wilder, and I was scared.

"Trust me," she whispered.

For some reason, that silenced me. My face grew hot. The scary thing was that I did trust her, at least kind of. Mason was watching intently. He wouldn't be satisfied until I was off the plank.

"Stephanie… I…"

She pushed me softly toward the plank—not even a push, more like a nudge— a reminder to move my frozen legs. *She has a plan,* I tried to tell myself. This time I didn't fight it. I was slowly getting closer to the edge—to the water. Trying to distract myself from the fact that I was walking to my certain death, I tried to examine the creaky plank. It was made of dark wood. The craftsmanship was excellent. I walked as slowly as I could, wobbling on the plank.

"Go faster!" Mason yelled, making me lose my focus and trip. Was my speed *really* his biggest issue right? I screamed as I fell toward the water—again.

I heard Mason laugh back up on the ship.

I heard Stephanie groan loudly.

I panicked.

"HELP ME!" I yelled over the rushing water.

"STEPHANIE!" I didn't care if Mason heard. He probably wouldn't. Stephanie probably wouldn't either. This made me angry with myself. For some reason I noticed the tears that were streaming down my face as I fell. The world around me blurred into just swirls of color as I fell.

Above me, Stephanie leaned over the side of the boat, looking slightly worried, but also determined. Yet again, I seemed to be falling in slow motion.

I trusted her enough, I guess. I don't know why, but there was something about her...I looked into her eyes and she gave me a reassuring but sad smile and a small nod. The sound in my ears died for a moment. "Stephanie... Please, help me!" I whispered into the air.

"It's okay!" she called softly, sounding unsure. Her voice had carried to me somehow. Even so, I could just barely hear her. How was this okay?! I was falling off a boat! Suddenly, I could hear her voice in my head. *"Please trust me, Carl. I just want to protect you."* For some reason, I completely believed her. Her eyes met mine. She noticed the tears, the fear. She reached out, as if to grab me, and I reached out, allowing myself to imagine our hands touching.

For a moment, I felt like I was touching solid ground, touching safety. But I was too far away. I was still falling. Suddenly, I saw Stephanie's mouth move, forming the shape of words that I couldn't hear over the roar of the wind. Somehow I knew she was saying something important.

"What?" I yelled, suddenly panicking "Stephanie! I can't hear you! STEPHANIE!" She shook her head, smiling sadly, and I realized that I would never know what she had been trying to say, that nobody would, probably, except her. "STEPHANIE!"

Then, I noticed a small, empty boat under me. It seemed like some type of speedboat. *This must have been what Stephanie was doing!* I realized happily. She cared about me, enough to risk all of this? I shuddered, thinking about all of the things Mason would do if he figured out. Her eyes sparkled with sadness. I reached up to her. She tried to repeat herself, but I still couldn't hear her, and we both knew I never would. I saw her smile sadly at me as she backed away from the edge of the boat. I heard only the echo of her voice, talking to Mason, though I couldn't hear exactly what they were saying. It wasn't important anymore. I sighed to myself.

"Thanks," I whispered to Stephanie, to no one, to the world. I don't know if she heard—if anyone did—and I doubted it. The word remained in the air like a cloud, hanging over me as if it had never been spoken at all. I closed my eyes and tried to imagine what she could have been saying. I tried to imagine my family, safe; me, safe; and Drake, defeated. And, for some reason, Stephanie was there too. Ivy was as well. All of my friends and my family. That was my dream, the reason for my trip.

Home. It was an adventure.

I will find you, I promised to my parents and to my brother. I would travel the ocean until I did. *I will defeat you*, I vowed to Drake. *You may be one step ahead, but I will learn. I'll learn your strengths, your weaknesses. No one will be able to hurt me anymore. I'll get stronger, better, quicker, smarter. I will find a home, and search until I do.*

I wasn't going to be a pawn in Drake's games anymore. I landed on the cushioned seats with a thud. Although it should have hurt to fall from such a height, it somehow didn't. I leaned back. Where would I go now? I shook my head. I didn't know where I would go. I'd never been on a boat like this. I'd never done the sorts of things needed to survive such an adventure.

For some reason, I saw Stephanie's face in front of me, reminding me that I was safe. I so wanted that to be true. *Trust me.* Stephanie's voice echoed through my head, reminding me of the reason I started walking off that plank in the first place. *I want to help you.*

For some reason, I heard Ivy's voice in my head as well. *You can do this, Carl.*

I thanked the voices in my head. I missed my friends already— especially Ivy. I smiled sadly as the boat started moving on its own, making loud noises as it shook, getting ready to take me away, to take me to adventure.

The speedboat got faster and faster until it sped off into the blue sky as it faded into soft oranges and yellows and pinks. It was like becoming a new person—a brand-new Carl.

I watched the huge pirate ship shrink into a speck of dark colors in the distance, the sun slowly coming down above it, and waved goodbye. This wasn't ideal. This wasn't how I imagined the journey to save my parents going, but I was alive and that was enough. Yeah. I was alive. I was really alive, surprisingly. Take that, Drake. Take that, Mason. Take that, universe. You want to try to kill me, but I won't let you. Yeah. I was alive. I was going to live. And I was going to use my life well.

***

Chapter Four

The Troll Under the Bridge

I bolted upright. I was in a boat. *What?* Then I remembered. I was in a small boat that somehow piloted itself forward. I had just barely escaped Drake and the pirates. I was on an adventure. Unfortunately, it wasn't just a dream.

The boat quickly glided across the gorgeous blue waves, which were so much calmer now. I stretched out my arms and looked around. The small boat was moving forward at a steady pace, but there was no way to control it. I assumed Stephanie could somehow control it from far away. Was that even possible? I wasn't sure. I knew next to nothing about boats, especially small pirate boats in a magical world that seemed to be pure fantasy. *Maybe she's trying to get me to somewhere where I'll find answers. Where would that be?* I wondered to myself, trying to think like Stephanie.

Then I saw the small, yellow, lined post-it-note hidden at the bottom of the boat. I tugged it out of its hiding place. A note from Stephanie!

Carl, get to the bridge! Stephanie had scribbled quickly in large, messy letters. I looked around, not seeing a bridge, tilting my head in confusion. Clear light blue water was sparkling all around me, but no land, and no bridge. It was clear that she hadn't had much time to write it, as it was untidy, and it wasn't specific at all. What bridge? I wondered.

Carl, get to the bridge! I read it again. Only then did I look at the bottom of the note, and I saw the smaller letters that I hadn't seen before. *I'm sorry Carl. This was the best I could do. Watch out for the toll troll! Get help in the fairy kingdom. They won't trust you, but they will do what is right.*

I read it again, and then two more times. *I'm sorry Carl. This was the best I could do. Watch out for the toll troll! Get help in the*

fairy kingdom. They won't trust you, but they will do what it's right.
That didn't make any sense! A *troll*? *Fairies*? Why wouldn't *who* trust me?

My life was becoming ridiculous enough to be a fairy tale— one that seemed to come from some kid's worst nightmare. How did characters ever find a happy ending when one thing leads to the next and their life was a mess? I didn't know.

I had learned the hard way that there were two sides of the world— the human side and the magical side; never meant to meet. Drake was messing with the two worlds, and my family was somehow part of it. He had brought us here for one reason— revenge. I needed to fix this.

Suddenly, the boat swerved sharply to the right, nearly knocking me into the water. I saw a blurry shadow of a shape— something in the distance. Squinting my eyes, I realized it was a very small island and a bridge. *The* bridge, possibly. The bridge extended over the water from the island and into a heavy mist over another, larger land mass. It was a wide, stone footbridge— wider than usual— and looked rather sturdy.

The boat got closer and closer to the bridge, and I sighed in relief when I didn't see anything that looked remotely like a troll. Everything seemed normal about this bridge. Maybe Stephanie was playing a joke on me. I really hoped that it was some type of metaphor. And somewhere across the bridge, I'd apparently find answers. Maybe some… helpful fairies? If that wasn't a joke too...

I really hoped it wasn't *all* a joke, even if it meant I had to face a troll— a toll troll, whatever that meant. A toll troll couldn't be that bad, right? But really, just because vampires existed—*one* vampire existed—didn't mean that every single fairy tale creature was coming to take over the world. *Get yourself together, Carl.* The boat went right up to the island and stopped. The bridge stretched out in front of me, waiting for me to walk across.

It didn't seem like there was anything blocking me— specifically a troll— but there also didn't seem to be much on the other side except mist and trees. Why would Stephanie send me to this normal bridge? It seemed like a cruel prank, way too cruel for her, and she didn't seem like the joker type. Would she really do that? Well, how would I know? In fact, I barely knew her. I just thought… Well, I guess I *hoped* she was my friend, but that didn't matter now. The bridge almost seemed too normal. Things were never as normal as they seemed, not in my life, anyway.

I tried to ignore these thoughts— they didn't matter. I kept thinking about Stephanie! But a small part of me knew why. Maybe it was because I thought we were friends. We had a special connection. I silenced that part of me and got to my feet, looking over the bridge that seemed to stretch on and on.

I got out of the boat slowly, looking nervously to both sides. I took a deep breath and began to tiptoe across the bridge. Suddenly, there was a loud rumbling. I screamed as the whole bridge shook, feeling ready to collapse and bring me down with it. Small chunks and bits of wood and stone fell from the sides of the bridge. Dust floated around me, but somehow the bridge managed not to fall beneath me.

I nearly collapsed onto the shaking bridge with relief, but it didn't seem like this was over yet. There was always more danger to come, unfortunately.

A loud roar echoed through the dusty blue air, startling the dark birds in the sky that were hovering above me, watching me with their wide gray eyes, waiting to see what I would do. I wheezed, shaking, as I took a nervous step backward.

A large troll jumped onto the bridge, right in front of me. It glared at me, growling as its eyes met mine. The thing looked exactly like you might imagine a troll in a fairy tale or a cartoon— exactly like you'd see in a corny adventure movie. It had a big, round, lumpy nose, and a fuzzy bit of brown hair on top of its head. Its large body was covered with green skin that was bumpy and plastered with spots. Its head was topped with large, pointy ears like an animal's, and it had large eyes that were a light shade of gray, watching me. It almost looked funny, but I was too scared to laugh, frozen under its angry glare.

I was an invader in the monster's territory. Its glare was like steel, as scary as the worst thing you could imagine. This troll was ready to attack if I even *tried* to move, to chase me if I ever *dared* to run. The troll was ready to hunt— even kill if it had to. I suddenly understood what a 'toll troll' was— it was basically a weapon, trained to hurt humans like me. We were merely obstacles— punching bags to defend their world from.

"Um... hello," I squeaked nervously, shaking and covered with sweat. "M-may I pass, please?" I didn't know what else to say, what else to do. My mind was left blank. My fear had betrayed me. The troll laughed at me like I was a joke. To it, I was. Then it held out its big hand. I eyed it, not sure what to do. Did it want money? Food? I didn't have any. I didn't have anything, really. It was clear that the troll wanted *something*, though. I racked my brain— what did trolls like in stories? What would I give it?

It seemed to sense my confusion, because it nodded its head toward my sweaty hand, which I'd realized had somehow slid into my empty pocket. Maybe I was wrong about the whole *'just a weapon trained to kill humans'* thing.

"You have to give me money," the troll explained, observing me carefully. It was waiting for its prize. "It's for the kingdom." Its voice was surprisingly light and calm, but still dangerous— not quite a challenge. A warning.

The kingdom? I wondered. Maybe the Fairy Kingdom where Stephanie had wanted me to go. The troll's eyes were warning me of what would happen if I didn't give it what it wanted. But I didn't have any more money to give. How would I get it? I couldn't just make cash appear out of thin air. I looked down at the bumpy green hand that was waiting in front of me.

"Please, Mr. Troll—" I started, stopping when its hand pulled back sharply, angry. I took a step back. I needed to get out of this somehow, and I'd thought that being polite to this troll seemed like an okay start. But I was wrong. My polite pleading seemed to make it even more angry. I didn't know why. I'd already realized that it was a bad idea, though— I needed to do more if I wanted to survive.

My eyes darted back toward my boat, debating my chances of escape. None.

"*Mr.* Troll?!" the troll repeated in an indignant yell as its eyes narrowed with obvious hatred. I had said something wrong. Very wrong. "Do I look like a *'Mr.'*? I'm a girl!"

Oh. That was why, then. I hadn't meant to be rude or inconsiderate, I just hadn't considered *that*. But now she was mad at me, her sharp teeth bared. I whimpered. I had offended a *troll*! Zero points for Carl. Yet again, I was headed toward certain doom.

"Sorry! I'm so sorry. Please," I begged. The troll scoffed, but an emotion I couldn't recognize tugged at her expression, quickly disappearing into its normal scowl. I must have been mistaken. "Listen, Ms. Please, just listen. I am sorry, but I don't have any money."

There was that odd strained expression again, before her face hardened a second time. I was absolutely sure now. Something wasn't right about her.

"Look, kid, your money, or you're lunch," she said, suddenly saying the words as if she was reading them from a script.

I would be doomed unless I came up with something. I looked around, trying to think of something to do—to distract her, to stop her, to save myself—or else I was doomed to become a troll snack. How would I taste to a troll? What a weird thought. Now wasn't the time to be considering that. Now was the time for a bright idea.

What else did trolls like to eat in fairy tales? I frowned, forcing my blank mind to try harder, to try to form a plan, any plan. Goats, maybe?

I inhaled. "Speaking of lunch… uh… Look!" I pointed to where the green island stretched into the distance back on my side of the bridge. "There are some big, healthy goats over there!" I had never been the best liar, but it seemed believable enough. "Then you won't have to eat me." I pointed out reasonably.

The troll's face lit up. The troll licked her lips as she considered. Did trolls like goats? Would she even be able to eat the goats? What was I saying, there weren't any! She seemed tempted, but I could tell she was thinking about the rules. She would probably get in trouble for letting a human into her kingdom. But that was her problem, I reminded myself while forcing myself not to feel bad for this creature. She wanted to eat me, after all, and she would without regret, it seemed.

Meanwhile, she was nodding. She'd made her choice. She'd go for the goats—the goats that weren't actually there.

"Mmm, I love goats," she gave in, turning to look at the green fields, where she could find some delicious, imaginary goats. I could see the hunger sparkling in her eyes. It seemed she would *much* rather eat the goats than eat me.

As she turned, I dashed past her as fast as I could, sprinting across the bridge. I saw her eyes flash as I crossed behind her. She looked toward the fields, though, and let me pass.

I thought that because of the troll's size, she'd be slow. I thought I'd be far away before she could come after me. I was very wrong.

The troll quickly noticed that I had tricked her. Realizing that there were no goats, she sprinted after me and grabbed the back of my still damp shirt— the black one Ivy had lent me. The creature was way faster than I would have ever thought by looking at her. Like a cheetah, she could easily beat a human in a race, even me, and I considered myself to be pretty fast.

"You're brave, I'll give you that. No one has ever dared to challenge me. How interesting. You're clever, but not clever enough," the troll said with a halfhearted smirk as she watched me struggle in her steel grip. For a moment, she reminded me of Drake. "Your money or you're lunch!" she repeated loudly. I squirmed in her grasp. Because of her size, she was able to dangle me high above the ground—a rather scary experience. I didn't have money left— my three remaining dollars had washed away when I got thrown off Drake's boat—and I definitely didn't want to be the troll's lunch. Fidgeting, I tried to escape, but she was too strong. The troll just laughed.

I sighed, looking down in defeat. Suddenly, a light bulb clicked in my brain— I had a plan. Finally, I met her eyes.

"Can I at least go and get you something to eat? Please? I'll find you a goat or something. I really don't want to be lunch," I pleaded.

A flicker of doubt crossed her face. I was the boy who cried wolf— or goat. Yet suddenly, I saw a flicker of something else in her eyes. That unfamiliar emotion again. This troll seemed different, suddenly, and I saw her in a new light. I felt like no other troll would even consider letting me do that. I would have been dead already. But this troll… she was different, I guess. Plus, she seemed to like eating goats more than eating people, so it seemed like a fair offer. She didn't trust me, I knew, yet she was considering breaking rules just for me—just so I had the possibility of buying myself some more time. Or so she had the possibility of eating a juicy goat. Either way. I shook my head. Where would I even find a goat?

"All right, I guess, but hurry." She decided, eyeing me suspiciously. "The others can't know." By 'others,' I assumed that she meant other trolls. I smiled gratefully, and she slowly lowered me to the ground. As soon as I hit the wooden bridge, I tucked my legs into my chest and rolled through her legs. Her eyes widened, but I was too fast. I'd caught her off guard, and she didn't have time to react. I shoved her onto the ground and sprinted as fast as my legs could carry me toward the kingdom—toward the other side of the bridge. The troll roared. Because of her size, it was difficult for her to get back up. I was almost there!

Then an invisible border stopped me. I fell back, landing on my side. I groaned.

I picked myself up as a small camera appeared, a small light blinking red, flashing in my face. At first, it seemed like it was floating in mid-air, but upon closer look I saw that it had extended from a rock and was balanced on shimmery waves in the air— the invisible border. It seemed like far too advanced technology for fairies and trolls, but I didn't question it. The machine started to vibrate slowly. "Hello. Name, age, and species, please." A robotic voice that was clearly female requested. It was somehow cold yet also friendly at the same time.

I banged against the invisible border as hard as I could. "Uh… I'm Carl! Eleven years old. And… uh, I'm human." I yelled, hoping I'd be let in. What a weird question. I banged against the invisible border again, pressing my face up against it. "I need to get to the fairy kingdom, now!" I yelled, taking a second to look behind me. The troll had gotten up!

"You are not welcome here," the robotic voice said, suddenly with an edge. "Get out." Was there something wrong? I had only answered the truth, hadn't I? The camera started sinking back along the invisible barrier— back to where it came from.

'WAIT!" I shouted, banging harder against the invisible wall, which I imagined would have looked really dumb without context. The robot-camera paused and came back out, focused on my face. "Please, I need help!" I begged desperately. "Please, please, *please!* You have to help me!"

"I don't have to do anything. Out!" The robotic border snapped, this time more harshly.

I realized that it wouldn't care if I was dying or being chased. It didn't care about me— it was just a robot! An incredibly smart robot, apparently… To it, I was just an intruder. It would never let me in!

Apparently, I didn't *'get out'* fast enough because the red light started flashing. "Intruder! Intruder! Human! Human!" The red light blinded me as the little camera started to retreat back into the shadows of where it had come from.

I growled and continued banging against the invisible wall, hoping it would stop and come back. "No! Please, you don't understand—" But the camera was gone.

I slid down against the invisible wall that was blocking me until I was sitting on the ground, defeated. The troll was getting closer. But then I had an idea.

I jumped to my feet. I wasn't sure if my plan would work. It was one of those things that only worked in cartoons. But if anyone could do it, it was me.

I waited until the troll was in front of me, and then... I jumped.

I jumped off of the bridge. I spread my arms out wide and screamed as I fell toward the rushing water, catching a branch that was hanging from a tree and clinging to it. It bowed dangerously, and I yelped, but somehow, it held.

The troll gaped at me as I dangled from the tree, just as shocked as I was that the crazy feat had worked. The troll roared— she was too heavy to slow down and she was going too fast to stop now! She slammed into the force field. She fell back with a loud *SLAM*. She groaned as the robot crept back out, flashing its red light at her.

"We are currently on lockdown due to human. Facial scan initiating. State your name, age, and species, please." After a few seconds, the tiny robot beeped. "No humans detected. Ending lockdown." A few more seconds past before it crept back into its hiding spot.

The troll, still on the ground, stared at me, still surprised— but not as surprised as me. I had always been very flexible, I guess, but even *I* hadn't known that I could do *that*. I swung off of the branch and tried unsuccessfully to backflip onto the bridge. Instead, I crashed down towards it and just barely managed to land on my feet. I stepped away from where the troll was sprawled on the ground, growling. I suddenly noticed a boat with a long rope sprawled across the inside, waiting for use.

I grinned.

"Hey, troll?" I called.

She looked up. "What do you want?" She muttered. "And my name is *Jolly*."

I tried unsuccessfully to cover up my snicker. "Jolly... the *troll*?"

"Yes… It isn't funny." She muttered, pushing herself off of the floor. She glared at me with the most terrifying glare I'd ever seen. I wasn't even trying to make fun of her name. It was just funny to me, considering how scary she was. I made a mental note not to laugh at— or mess with— terrifying creatures ever again.

Well… maybe one more time.

"Come and get me!" I called tauntingly. I jumped over the side of the bridge again. This time, I let myself fall down to the boat below instead of stopping myself with a branch. It hurt *badly*, but I didn't stop. I grabbed the rope, then climbed quickly back onto the bridge. Thankfully, it wasn't very high above the water.

Jolly chased after me, but I jumped back and smacked my whole body into her face. *SLAM!* I used the rope to tie her up. She pulled against it. It must have been a *good* rope, because it didn't break from her strength or size. Maybe it was a special *troll-proof* rope or whatever.

"Hey! Let me go!" she screamed, twisting against the rope helplessly. She hadn't expected that. Despite the situation, I smiled a bit. I had outsmarted yet another danger.

Then Jolly started to cry—something that *I* hadn't expected. That wiped the small smile off of my face. I raised an eyebrow. She was wiping her eyes, embarrassed, but that couldn't disguise the fact that she was still sobbing. I didn't expect this large, strong troll— who I'd figured could and would kill me in seconds— would be here *crying*. She'd just given up completely. I just watched her, almost feeling bad. I tried to remember that she'd tried to attack me seconds ago, but I couldn't convince myself. She just seemed so… *sad*. So lonely.

"Um… Jolly?" I called softly.

She looked up at me miserably. I shifted uncomfortably. "Um, sorry… it's just… you tied me up… and… I know you probably hate me… but please, let me go!" she managed between sobs. I hadn't expected the outburst, and she hadn't either. She wiped her eyes again and covered them with her big hands.

"I'm...sorry, Jolly." I said, not sure how to react. "You...you were going to eat me." I gave an awkward shrug.

She looked at me, and then looked down, defeated. "I–I don't even like eating humans!"

What? I found that hard to believe, but she seemed so sad— like she really *was* sorry. I pursed my lips, giving her a suspicious look. At that, she began sobbing even harder. I knew she wasn't acting this time. She clearly didn't like her life as a... what had Stephanie called it? Oh yeah, a toll troll.

"It's true! They taste horrible. They need to be deep-fried, and they need salt to even come *close* to tasting good."

I covered my laugh so as to not seem rude. In fact, maybe Jolly *could* help me.

Jolly continued, "I would prefer just eating goats and living in a nice, quiet cave where people can't bother me, but *noo*. As a toll troll, I rarely ever get privacy or time to myself! Although, many other trolls do like capturing and eating humans. Especially other toll trolls." She buried her head in her tied-up hands.

Other toll trolls? I hadn't realized that there could be more. I guess it was a job, not just one specific troll, and certain trolls got sent to do the job. It didn't seem like a choice, however, because Jolly was so unhappy doing it. Or maybe it was a permanent choice, and Jolly didn't know how bad it would be?

"I'm just...so lonely," Jolly added quietly, looking back up at me. Her voice was very shaky now, some tears left to dry on her face. I hadn't expected a troll to be this emotional. She'd seemed so... dangerous. I wasn't quite sure how to respond to that. I *did* feel bad, though.

"Sorry." I said quietly. Then, I had an idea—a really good idea this time, one that would benefit both Jolly and me! "Jolly," I said slowly, "What if you told me how to get inside of the Fairy Kingdom?" Why hadn't I thought of it before? Who else would know the kingdom better than one of its guards— Jolly! She was clearly baffled by the suggestion, but she was listening anyway. So, I continued, "If you help me get in, you help me get help, and you help me get out, I will let you come on the rest of my adventure— if you want. I will be your friend. Your"—I grinned— "best friend!"

Jolly's eyes lit up, all traces of tears or awkwardness gone almost immediately. "You've got yourself a deal!"

***

The afternoon sky was filled with blue, the clouds perfectly puffy and white. The sound of rushing water met my ears, but I didn't fear it this time. In fact, it was peaceful, almost calming, and the sweet scents of sugar and something baking from the fairy kingdom mingled with the soft sounds, giving the whole place a feeling of calm, of joy, of home— something I hadn't felt in a while. Jolly— my new best friend, a friendly troll, and I were sitting on the far side of the bridge, our legs dangling over the edge, looking over the Fairy Kingdom. It turned out that Jolly and I had lots in common, and she was truly very kind.

We were eating sandwiches. We had taken bread and some type of meat from Jolly's cave. She picked a leafy vegetable from a tiny community garden along the fairy kingdom border. I couldn't tell what kind of meat was in the sandwich, but it was amazing. Surprisingly, the unfamiliar vegetable was too. It was better than anything I'd ever tasted.

The moment was so sweet—the calming scents and sounds, the beautiful scenery, the delicious sandwiches, and the laughter. It felt like the best moment of my life—the happiest I'd been in a long time and probably the most joyful I'd be for a while. I savored it, even the smallest details.

Jolly watched with amusement as I ate a whole sandwich in just a few seconds. She offered me another. "Good, right?" She laughed—a clear, soft sound that didn't match her strong, dangerous look at all. I could tell how unhappy she had been just by how happy she sounded now. She just needed a friend to bring out the best in her.

"Wha..ish ..tis.. shuff?" I asked, my mouth already full.

Jolly laughed again, grabbing a sandwich for herself and taking a large bite of it. "The meat is from a magical bird called a Golden Gaile," she answered after swallowing. "They're very rare and hard to catch. The fairies have a sanctuary where they breed them, and thankfully you can get their meat without killing them." She saw my questioning look, and added, "Don't ask— it's really weird. It's not exactly real meat. It's still good, though, and we eat it all of the time. Fairies are actually vegetarian— in a way. They don't harm animals."

She took another bite. "The plant is called a gashroot; they only grow here in the fairy kingdom. We grow lots and eat them in sandwiches and salads. See, fairy culture is very interesting—" she paused. "You're hungry." She laughed again as I reached for a third sandwich, still listening intently.

"Sorry." I grinned sheepishly, finishing my sandwich within just a few seconds. I licked my lips, silently debating whether I should take another one. I decided not to. "This is the best food I've ever tasted," I declared.

Jolly smiled. "Thank you."

The truth was, I hadn't eaten in days. I hadn't even showered or changed my clothes.

I was waiting for her to start talking about fairy culture again when I suddenly thought of a more interesting question. "Hey, Jolly? Why don't humans know about you guys? I was told all of my life that trolls and fairies and vampires and witches and wizards and magic are fake—the stuff of fairy tales. That's clearly not true. Are those lies? Or do people just not know the truth?" I had actually been wondering about that for a while. It was really weird. The only traces of magic on our part of the world existed in fairy tales.

Jolly's face darkened. "Long ago, you did." She stood up suddenly and held out her hand. "Come," she said. "I'll show you."

She led me across the bridge to the charred remains of a city. I stared at it. "Humans lived near us, in the Human Territories. They made us tools and resources and showed us technology, and we gave them land and food and magic. Then they started a war. Only your leaders know about it, and they do their best to cover up their mistake. Maybe they don't even remember."

I remembered seeing the president on Jean's TV. He was always staring into space as if he had forgotten something important. I knew there was something off about him!

Jolly's voice broke as she continued. "The humans stole from us, then tried to bomb our city and run, but we got to them first. We met on the outskirts of the kingdoms." She swallowed. "Many were killed—theirs as much as ours. I was just a girl. We won, they left, and they never returned.

"But wouldn't the humans have noticed this whole other world?" I pushed. Why hadn't we if it had been here all along? Why hadn't *I* until Drake wanted me to?

"Simply because humans are stubborn and blind. Things are never as normal as they seem. If humans really looked, they'd see elves and vampires and fairies living among them. Humans only see what they want to see."

"But why don't they want to see this world?"

"Carl, think about it! They started a *war*!"

I tried to imagine it: blood and smoke everywhere; a mob of angry people with weapons and torches, attacking hundreds of fairies, trolls, and other magical beings. I swallowed. The people did their best to forget the magic because they knew they were at fault.

"Fairy tales *are* lies, because not everyone lives happily ever after," Jolly said softly.

I suddenly felt like I'd intruded on something very deep and personal, but the hard part was that it was as much a part of their history as it was of mine. Trying to change the topic, I cleared my throat and said, "What other species are there? I've seen trolls, of course, and also vampires, and I know that fairies exist."

"Well," Jolly said, brightening a little as she started counting on her large fingers. "There are also elves, who live underground. Oh, and wizards and witches, who live in the Magical Territory. They're ruled by the strongest wizard of that time, who is given the title of master.

"That is *so* cool, Jolly!" I exclaimed. "The other humans need to hear this."

Her face darkened just as quickly as it had before. "The other humans can't hear about this, Carl. What if they attack us again?"

I suddenly felt the urge to defend humans. "They won't. They'll see reason." Surely if humans saw all of the wonderful creatures in this world, they'd change for the better, right?

"No, Carl, I'm afraid they won't. Humans will do anything to get what they want, and they fear anything that is different. That is why they cannot see our world. They simply do not *want* to, and they are not *wanted* here either."

"Okay." I agreed glumly. Her point was reasonable enough. She smiled gratefully. Feeling awkward, I decided to change the topic *again.* "I can't wait to meet the queen of the fairies."

She wrapped her arm around me. "And I think it's about time that you do." She smiled, leading me across the bridge. She paused at the invisible barrier and knocked on it carefully.

"Hello." The camera crept out, flashing red, and Jolly gripped my hand. "State your name, age, and species, please."

***

Chapter Five

Human in the Fairy Kingdom

Before I even knew what was going on, I was walking through the fairy kingdom, my hand in Jolly's. She'd quickly explained how to get through the invisible barrier, and half-dragged me past it. The kingdom looked *very* different on the inside. Everything was so... small! The kingdom was picture perfect, every detail exact. Flowers grew along the stone pathways winding throughout the city. Perfectly white clouds blew by. *Huge* mushrooms were scattered across the green grass. As I bent down and looked closely, I saw that the mushrooms had doors and windows carved into them! They were the fairies' houses! I peeked in one window and saw a blonde fairy. She was about the size of a small mammal with sky-blue eyes, a red dress, and wings. Whoa.

She saw me and panicked. I mean really panicked. Her eyes slowly got bigger, and she started screaming. "HELP! IT'S A GIANT! WAIT... NO! A HUMAN! HELP!" She shrieked.

My hands went to my ears to block out her high-pitched screams. "Wait! Quiet down, *please*! I promise I won't hurt you!"

She flew out of her mushroom, still screaming. "HUMAN! THERE'S A HU—"

"Shh!" I stood up worriedly, careful not to step on her or her home.

"IT'S GONNA GET ME!"

"Be quiet, *please*! I promise, I'm a nice human!" I whispered. It bothered me slightly when she called me an "it," but I ignored it.

"W-who are you?! What do you want?"

"I'm Carl," I told her, talking as if she was a small child. "I'm just a normal human."

She didn't seem totally convinced, but she had stopped screaming, and that was a start. I put out my hand for her to land on. She nervously flew up to rest on it. Then she looked up at me with terror in her eyes. "Please don't hurt me," she whispered.

I looked straight into her pretty blue eyes. "Why would I hurt you?"

"Because… you're a human."

Oh. Right. The war. The fights. Jolly's story. I swallowed and bent down, still letting her rest on my hand.

"A nice human, though. Not all humans are bad." I smiled. "What's your name?"

"I'm...Clover."

"That's a pretty name."

"Thanks."

I suddenly thought of something. "Can I call you Clo?"

She laughed and nodded. "And you are… Carl, right?"

I nodded.

"You're pretty nice… for a human. I've never had a human friend." She seemed excited by the idea.

Then she saw Jolly. I prepared my free hand to block an ear from her screams. There was a large, scary toll troll in her kingdom, after all. Surprisingly, Clover just smiled and waved. "Hello, Jolly! How are you?"

I blinked. I wasn't quite sure how the two knew each other, but I wasn't about to ask.

Even more to my surprise, Jolly smiled back. "Hello Clover! I'm doing well. Although… *someone* got past me and convinced me to come with him." Jolly gave me a look. I felt nervous for a moment, but then the troll burst out laughing.

I decided to play into the joke. "Well, that just shows how smart I am." I winked.

Clover, the small fairy, laughed.

"Another troll should be here shortly for the next shift," Jolly said.

I turned to Clover. "Why do the toll trolls guard the fairies but not themselves?" I asked. The idea had been confusing me for a while.

"Fairies and trolls are in an alliance. Our queen and their king are friends. That's why we have trolls guarding our bridge." Clover explained, and Jolly nodded in agreement.

"Of course we guard ourselves. But we get food or tools in exchange for keeping out their enemies too. Toll trolls also get money from the humans which we split," Jolly added.

Ah, so fairies and trolls used human money then. Interesting. But they probably ate the humans anyway... or at least turned them away, even after they'd been paid. It seemed like an unfair situation for the humans, I thought, before remembering that we were the ones who attacked them first. "You're at war with the humans because...because..." I couldn't even finish the sentence. I remembered how horrible Jolly's story was and felt bad for asking.

Clover must have read my mind. "Yes. Their leaders chose to 'forget' us, and even though we erased the memories of the people, your leaders tried to continue the wars for a while. They are hopeless." The tiny fairy sighed.

Jolly continued explaining for her. "Humans have no leader, and they run wild around the world, destroying everything in their wake. Now they don't even *believe* in any of our species. No offense." When someone says 'no offense,' you should probably prepare to be offended. I *was* kind of offended, actually. I realize that was completely selfish. I was better than my leaders... I had to be. I remembered with a stab of guilt that I hadn't even believed in fairies before I had gotten to their kingdom. That was all of the lies and brainwashing designed by the government, led by the forgetful, red-headed president. Our leaders today tried to escape every mistake as well, from unfair treatment to violence. It was so easy for them to cover it up. I swallowed hard, keeping my eyes down. I had to change the subject.

"Well, we should be going," I told Clover quickly.

Jolly sensed my discomfort and nodded. "He's right."

Jolly and I started to walk away when Clover chimed in. "Uh, guys, the fairy palace is this way! Come on!"

I turned around. "Huh? Clo... you're coming? Even though I'm a..." I swallowed. "A human?" She would be deemed a traitor if she was seen with me— and Jolly too would get in trouble. But Clover flashed a glittering smile. Of course she did. She was almost always smiling, it seemed, and it almost made me want to smile too.

"Yeah! Uh...That is, if you want me to," she replied casually, trying to act less excited than she was. It didn't work. She was practically bouncing in the air.

"Of course," I answered truthfully, happy to have some more company. I mean… The more the merrier, right? "I was just surprised that you would come and help a human."

"Not all humans are bad." Clover winked at me. I smiled a bit.

"B-but, Clover, you'd be deemed a traitor!" Jolly protested, crossing her arms.

"No more than you." Clover smiled sadly. "I don't have a life here. I don't mind. Now let's get going."

I smiled. I had friends, and they were going to help me. It wasn't like family, but it was similar. These friends were my family, at least for now. It was the next best thing. And it was amazing—I could tell—for all three of us.

Clover led us in the complete opposite direction of where we had just been going—over a tiny, fairy-sized stone path. I had to chuckle to myself. It was so small! Jolly and I hurriedly followed her, trying to keep up with the tiny fairy, whose wings seemed to be going as fast as a hummingbird. She led us through the kingdom, stopping every once in a while to show us something. Occasionally, she got so excited that I had to jokingly remind her that she wasn't our tour guide. Lots of fairies were flying around doing their work, ignoring us completely. There were even some male fairies.

Suddenly, my mouth dropped open. We were looking at a huge stone castle with beautiful murals painted on the walls, glass windows, and a large star engraved on the top. It was absolutely *gigantic*— so the trolls could get in, I guessed. More large trolls guarded it, sharp weapons and spears in their hands.

"It's beautiful," I whispered with wonder. Clo nodded, satisfied, then simply started flying toward the guards. My eyes widened with alarm. What was she doing? I carefully grabbed the back of her long, red dress and tugged her back. She yelped. "What are you doing?!" I whisper-hissed.

"Well, Carl, I'm… I'm going to the palace! Isn't that where you wanted to go?" Her tiny hands landed on her hips.

"You can't just *barge* into a palace," I insisted. I was kind of scared of what might happen if I just stomped in to the castle, followed by a fairy and a troll, and that was only if we could even get past the guards. Not only that, but the palace was so lovely and peaceful that I almost didn't want to disturb the silence.

"Well, I'm sure if we explained that we're..." Clover started to respond, then hesitated. "Wait, *what* are we doing here?"

It was then that I realized I'd never told them about my parents or Drake or *anything*. I was worried that if they knew I was dragging them on a crazy adventure just for *my* parents and *my* problems, they'd think I was selfish and wouldn't want to help me. Nothing we were going to do would help them. Even worse, it could be dangerous, especially for Jolly! It was her job to stop me from getting in the kingdom in the first place. Yes, she'd wanted an adventure. I just wasn't sure that she would want *this* one. But it would be selfish not to tell them, wouldn't it? I should care more about my friends' safety than being alone.

"If I tell you, you might not want to come. You might not want to be my friend. You might...You'll think I am selfish," I admitted, blinking hard. *Don't cry,* I thought, sticking my hands into my pockets.

"Never, Carl. We're with you to the end," Clo promised.

"Yeah. You're my... best friend," Jolly agreed softly, almost sheepishly.

"Really?" They both nodded with so much conviction that I had to smile. I did want to tell them. Really. If they were going to help me, didn't they have to know why?

No. A small part of me said. That was the part that was scared, the part that would do anything for acceptance. That was the selfish part that didn't want to do anything that could hurt me, or worse, them. But that part was wrong, wasn't it? *No.* That same part insisted. *You know I'm right. You know that they'll see it too. The bad part of you. They'll leave you. Is it wrong to want to keep your only friends? Answer me honestly.* I shivered. I didn't want to answer. I was being selfish, and they deserved to know.

"I'm looking for my parents." I blurted. "When I was little, they went on a boat and... they disappeared. I think it has something to do with this world. I... I know. It's selfish. It's my problem, and my family, and I shouldn't have dragged you into it..." I rambled.

Surprisingly, Clover didn't turn around and fly away. Instead, she flew up to my hand and hugged my pinky. Shocked, I smiled at her. "Why would you even think that, Carl? We're your friends and we want to help you!" She said. I could tell that she was holding back tears.

Jolly wrapped her arms around me too. "I didn't know you felt that way. I'm so sorry about your parents," she said. "But Clover's right, Carl. We're your friends. You have to trust us."

I suddenly realized that I was used to seeing the worst in people, or worse, having people see the worst in me. I would do anything for their acceptance— but having friends meant that I already was accepted, didn't it? And with Jolly's strong arms wrapped around me, I realized I didn't have to worry about being accepted anymore. I had true friends, something I'd always wanted. My vision blurred slightly, but I blinked my tears away.

Clover smiled thoughtfully for a second, and then put her hand on her chin, as if she were thinking. She made a "hmm" noise and tapped her head. She still wanted to help me. She cared. I smiled gratefully and watched her think for a minute, before she sighed, and shook her head.

"No, you're right, Carl. They wouldn't let us in." She tapped her small head again, her fingers running through her hair. She laughed, but this time it was more of a nervous laugh. "I mean, they'd let me and Jolly in, but they'd eat you." she added.

Thanks. I got that, I wanted to say, but I didn't. She was just helping. Or trying.

Clover sighed, and then shared a look with Jolly. Apparently, they could read each other's minds now. But when she turned around, Clover's face told me that this was no laughing matter. And when Jolly nodded, looking grim, my face darkened. Something was wrong. The girls stared down at the cobblestone path beneath our feet. I stared down too. That was not good.

"So let's do it," Jolly said suddenly. I thought she was talking to Clo, so I didn't answer. When no one else said anything, I looked up at Jolly, who was staring at me. Oh!

"All right then," I said automatically. Then I studied their grim faces. And I mean *grim* faces. Those were, "*This is a bad idea but it's the only way. It's for your own good. You want help, don't you?*" faces. Wait, no. I tried not to think about it too hard, but those were totally, "*Sorry Carl, but if you get killed or tossed in a dungeon along the way, it's not our fault*" faces as well. That thought stayed in my head. I gulped. That was definitely bad news. "Wait, do what?" I asked quickly. Both of them quickly looked down, now refusing to meet my eyes.

Uh oh. What had I just agreed to?

"Uh… Carl…" Clover was fidgeting with her dress. She looked up, and I looked straight into her eyes, giving her what I hoped was a serious "*tell me*" look.

"Do what?" I repeated. They both sighed, and Jolly shared another look with Clover. The small fairy nodded, clearly reluctant. This time, I knew what it meant: "*Should we tell him?*"

As much as I appreciated that they were trying not to worry me, I needed to know whatever their plan was. They were doing it for me. If I got captured or hurt while the plan was going on, it was my fault. I wouldn't blame them, although they would blame themselves. I had to know. I had to do this. So Jolly nodded too.

Then, Jolly said something that I didn't like. "You have to trust us, Carl. We have a plan."

And then Clover sighed and said something that I *really* didn't like. "Let's sneak into the Fairy Palace."

***

Chapter Six

Sneaking into the Palace

"We can't!" I argued for what had to have been the millionth time.

Jolly and Clover groaned, annoyed by my complaining. They didn't like the plan either, of course. I realized I was being totally selfish. Childish, too. It was their home, not mine, and they were doing it all for me. That was why I absolutely could not let them.

"We have to." Clo retorted miserably. She was as unhappy as me with the plan, if not more. "You were sent here for a reason, Carl!"

"The queen won't listen to a human, especially if that human sneaks into her castle! What do you think is going to happen? I'll just say, 'Hey, Your Highness, I'm Carl. I just snuck into your palace and I need help. Have you seen my parents? I've heard they're hiding out on an island.' And you think she'll listen to that?! You think she'll say, *'Oh sure, Carl, of course I know them. In fact, the island is right over there. I'd be happy to take you there myself'?!* That's NOT going to happen guys!" I yelled sarcastically.

Clover took a step backward. I hadn't meant to yell at her. I'd hardly yelled at anyone before. My face turned red. I had just yelled at the friends who were doing everything in their power to help me. I sunk to the ground and buried my head in my hands.

I took a deep breath and looked up. "I'm sorry," I said softly.

Clo just sighed, but Jolly shook her head and paced back and forth. "She might be able to help," the troll insisted sternly. She tilted her head at me, as if to say, *"Can I go on?"*

I glanced at the gorgeous castle, then sighed and nodded. I knew as well as my friends that there was no other way.

Jolly inhaled and started explaining her plan. She would distract the guards as I slipped through the bushes of the garden to get into the castle with Clover on my shoulder. She would direct me to the queen and tell her our situation, since the queen knew her family well and might listen to her. Clover added that the queen was open-minded and tried to help others. I wasn't sure if I believed her because the queen allowed trolls to eat people without getting to know their stories first. But the humans did start the war. Maybe she was kinder than I'd thought. Plus, I'd never even met her. Maybe she *would* help me after all.

Then, we would get out of the palace right before the guards appeared, shouting, *"Stop!"* or *"Halt!"* or *"Villains!"* or *"Get them!"* or whatever guards shouted. That part, I'll admit, I made up in my head. Had I been reading too many adventure novels? Eh, probably. Then, we would get my parents and go home. *Boom.* I sighed. This was never going to work. I just knew it. Did they really think I'd get my happily ever after? *We can do this. We can do this. We can do this.* I repeated in my head over and over again. Honestly, I could think of a million things that could go wrong with the plan, but I didn't argue anymore. It's not like I could come up with anything better. "Fine." I sighed. "Let's go."

The plan went wrong almost immediately, like I knew it would. I was trying very hard to ignore the feeling, but I really knew this was going to be a mess as soon as Clover whispered, "Go!" to Jolly from my right shoulder.

Jolly walked over to the two guards on duty, a tall one with a deep voice, and a short, fatter one with a raspy voice. "Who are you?" The taller guard asked as soon he noticed her.

"Uh, I'm here for the next shift," she answered.

The taller one shrugged dismissively. "You're an hour and a half early," he stated.

The shorter troll elbowed his partner who winced. "Let the troll speak." His eyes sparkled with greed. "You can take my post!" He handed her a spear, wiped sweat from his brow, and stretched. I wondered what it would be like to stand outside of a castle in the heat all day. Probably not very pleasant. While they were turned to the side, distracted, I sprinted for the door.

The huge door slid open with a loud creak, and I slid through quickly, banging my shoulder on the way. *Uh oh. Way to be subtle, Carl.*

Startled, the guard dropped his spear, which clattered to the ground. "Hey! You there! Stop!" I looked over my shoulder just in time to see the guards chasing after me, leaving a shocked Jolly standing in the doorway by herself. I turned away again and ran as quickly as I could, while Clover sat on my shoulder, giving me directions. She jerked her head toward the stairs, and I started the run up, panting already. The next floor was very high up, and the winding stairs were *way* too tall. Finally, I made it to the top, completely out of breath. I looked around in a panic as footsteps pounded on the stairs. The polished wooden floors were covered by an expensive golden rug and shining suits of armor on wooden stands lined the halls. The hall was also decorated by tons of windows that gave an astonishing view of the fields of the kingdom. I was still shocked at the size of everything. Every window had blue lace curtains. I ran to one, but they were locked and too high to jump from anyway. The guards were coming fast, and there was no way to get out of the hall. It was a dead end! I had to hide. My eyes darted around, looking for a hiding place. Suddenly, I saw the perfect spot.

"Listen." I whispered to Clover, choosing my words carefully. "You leave. Fly out through the tiny crack in that window." I pointed. "Forget me and never come back."

Her face darkened. "No! I won't leave you!" She hissed.

My heart pounded against my chest. She was a good friend, and I didn't want her to leave, but that was selfish. She would certainly fit in my hiding spot, but it wouldn't last long. If she stayed, we'd both be trapped and the guards would catch us. Not only would I be eaten or captured, but she'd be in trouble as well. The least I could do for her was help her escape now.

"Please, just go! It's too dangerous to try and help me!" I pleaded, remembering my encounters with Drake and Mason. Bad things always seemed to happen to me. The footsteps continued on the stairs, now accompanied by heavy panting. It was now or never.

"No!" Clover insisted. "I won't leave you!" I closed my eyes and suppressed my groan. She was kind—too kind—and I appreciated it, really, but I just couldn't let her get punished for my problems.

"Fine!" I said through gritted teeth, then realized how aggressive my tone was. I took a deep breath. "Fine. You're very sweet, Clo. But please, just fly through the crack in the window and meet me after," I begged. "*Please.* I promise I'll be safe."

Clover looked like she was about to argue, but she could see the tears in my dark eyes, the tears that I knew were there. I was ready to get on my knees and beg. I didn't want this either.

She hovered near the window for a second.

"Don't be a stranger," I said softly, trying to smile.

Clover then flew back to me. "Be safe, Carl," she whispered. "I promise."

She squeezed my hand with her tiny fingers and then squeezed through the little crack in the glass window, disappearing behind the blue curtains.

I took one of the suits of armor off of its fancy stand. It seemed to weigh a million pounds. I just barely managed to slip the armor on. It was gigantic on me. I walked over towards its stand. The heavy metal *clunked* with each step. I managed to get onto the stand, but I was definitely going to be sore after this. The chest plate weighed me down, but I stood tall and proud, as if there was nothing inside. From the outside, it was a normal suit of armor, polished and untouched, just as it was before. If I stood on my toes, I could almost see through the helmets eye slits.

"Where are you, little human?" a voice asked from down the hall. The voice was gentle, like a person talking to their pet, but somehow threatening at the same time. "Come here. We won't hurt you." The voice was the unmistakable, squeaky rasp of the smaller, greedy troll. From my position, I could just barely see the foreheads of the guards creeping down the hall. As they got closer, I saw more and more of them.

"Shut up, Gerald. He's not *that* stupid. He's not just going to tell you where he's hiding. He can't know that we're onto him or he'll have an advantage over us!" The taller one scolded the shorter one.

"Oh, COME ON, Terry," Gerald retorted. "I knew *that*. He already knows that we are looking for him. I just wanted to make it clear that we won't hurt him." He laughed, although it was a dark and unhappy sound.

The two didn't seem to be the smartest, even though they were dangerous and knew how to use weapons. Maybe I could trick them. I coughed softly.

"Gerald, Terry, this is your queen. Report to me immediately!" I forced my voice to have a soft, light, pretty tone.

My throat burned with the effort. Thankfully, I had always been good at voice impressions.

I saw the shorter head, Gerald's, look up, suddenly alert. He started walking back towards the stairs, only to have his arm grabbed by Terry. "Come on, Terry. The queen wants to see us. We have to go now." He tried to shake Terry away.

"Wait!" Terry stopped his partner. "What if it's a trick?"

I started sweating. Gerald seemed to be completely convinced by my voice, but Terry was not so confident. I held my breath. But I guess I'm a better actor than I'd thought, because Gerald shook his head, now annoyed by his partner. "Oh, you're always so doubtful. Do you want to get in trouble with Queen Gilly?" Gerald asked his partner dismissively.

"No," Terry mumbled. Gerald crossed his arms, satisfied. Terry simply shook his head and sighed as they walked away. I was too scared and grateful to move. I just waited there. All I could think was: *Oh, so that's her name. Queen Gilly.*

Not even a few moments later, I heard an alarm blaring. "CODE RED! THERE IS A HUMAN IN THE FAIRY PALACE. PLEASE DO NOT PANIC! I REPEAT, CODE RED! HUMAN IN THE FAIRY PALACE. DO NOT PANIC! Thank you!"

I gulped. That was the *real* fairy queen. Gerald and Terry must have told her that I was here! I gulped. She was probably sending guards for me this very second. They wouldn't stop until they found me, just like Jean. A part of me wondered where he was. I shook those thoughts away. This was too serious.

Suddenly, red light blinded me, and the sound of banging metal numbed my ears. I was confused, but then I realized the helmets of the suits of armor were glowing a terrifying shade of red that rivaled Drake's eyes. Not only that, but they were moving! They had come to life… with me inside one of them! I stayed very still and held my breath, careful to make no noise.

"Locate the human boy," they said in unison. They all shared the same cold, emotionless voice. It gave me chills. If they found me, I would be in very big trouble— even more so now. Would they even listen to me when I asked for help? Or would they just see me as the human who snuck into their palace and hid in a suit of armor? Would they see how desperate I was? Or did they think that I was as emotionless and cruel as the magical suits of armor? The suits of armor that were marching away with me trapped inside. Thankfully, they hadn't noticed me. *Yet.* They continued marching down the hall.

The suit that I was hiding in was at the back of the group, so I tried to sneak out of it, thinking none of the others would notice, but that didn't go as planned. My suit of armor just stopped marching.

"There is something inside of me," it said stiffly. The other walking suits of armor turned to mine. If they were real people with real eyes, they'd be glaring at me. I cringed at how weird this whole situation was.

"Locate the human. Locate the human," the suits of armor chanted. I resisted the urge to cover my ears. Their voices were like nails on a chalkboard.

The helmet above my head fell away and red light blinded me as one of the other suits of armor decapitated mine with its sword. Thankfully, I was small enough inside the suit that I could easily duck below the neck. The rest of the suit collapsed on the floor, trapping me under a heavy iron chest plate.

Trolls with spears, knives, and swords ran from the corners of the hall, surrounding me. One of the trolls lifted the heavy armor off of me, and I sat up, gasping for air. The suits of armor returned to their stands, including mine, which picked up its head and left as if nothing had happened. One of the trolls poked at me, gaping stupidly. One of the others nudged him

"Please—" I started.

"Come," one of the guards ordered, cutting me off. "The queen wants to see you."

Before I could think of anything else to say, the trolls grabbed me and started dragging me down another hall. They dragged me all the way to a room with a golden, fairy-sized jeweled throne. I was almost startled to see such a small throne in such a huge throne room.

I heard the flutter of wings. "So, who are you and what are you doing in my kingdom?"

***

Chapter Seven

Magical Trolls and an Audience with the Queen

The queen flew around her throne gracefully and sat on it as if it was fragile. I gaped at the queen. She was beautiful. She had golden, light honey-colored hair and perfect, delicate wings. She was wearing a long, summer yellow, lace dress complete with a white ribbon around her waist, with a matching yellow rose in her hair. She seemed so fragile, yet so regal.

I'd never met a queen before. It was kind of awkward for me. I had no clue how I was supposed to act. *Should I bow?*

"Whoa." I whispered. The queen glared directly into my soul with beautiful eyes. I shuddered. There went my chances of the queen listening to me, even if there hadn't been much chance to begin with.

The guards around me sank into a bow, and I copied them immediately. The queen was looking at me. Her face had shifted from a glare to half-anger and half amusement, maybe even interest or curiosity. That was good, I thought.

"Well?" she prompted, staring straight through me with her perfect teal eyes. Teal was my favorite color, and I thought her eyes were gorgeous. But looking closer, they weren't perfect. There was something wrong with them, and I just couldn't put my finger on what.

I cleared my throat. "Your majesty, I'm Carl," I said. "And—"

"Funny name, isn't it? Very...human," she mused. I frowned. What a weird thing to say. I obviously *was* a human. I didn't think that my name was funny at all. The queen just smirked at me. "Now, what would a human like you be doing in my palace? You must be a clever boy." That was also weird. I didn't say anything for a minute, so she continued. "It is technically illegal for you to be here. You probably know that. You seem too smart not to. Should I put you in my dungeon? Or would you escape?" she asked.

Why was she asking *me* if she could put me in a dungeon? What kind of strange game was she playing? Did she want me to beg? Simple. I wouldn't beg. I would compliment her instead. I smiled to myself. The game was on.

"You must be Queen Gilly. It is a pleasure to meet you. I've heard wonderful things about you—that you're an incredible, open-minded queen who listens to others' perspectives."

The queen knew what I was trying to do and seemed amused by it. "Hm, caught ourselves a smart one, haven't we?"

"No one caught anyone," I smirked. "I came here all on my own."

"Okay. I'll give you five minutes of my time," she offered.

That was just enough. So, I took up that time, explaining my story in detail, leaving out Clover, Jolly, and a few other small details to protect them. And me.

"Well, well, well," the queen said, giving me a long slow clap. My body stiffened. Her game was still going. "Somehow, I find that it's still illegal for you to be here!" she exclaimed in mock surprise. Of course, I knew that, but why "listen" to me if she wasn't actually going to *listen* to me? And why was she acting this way? What was the point? Was I just entertainment for her? Was she going to help me or just have me killed? The pieces just didn't fit together. And she didn't match Clover's description of her at all! "I think I should put you in a dungeon."

Wait, *what*?! "No! I—" I started, but I had nothing else to add to that.

"Well?" she prompted with a smirk that was way too evil. Something still wasn't right, so I stayed quiet until I could figure it out. "No comment? Huh, that's a shame, you seem like you have a lot to say, clever boy." The queen laughed. "Okay. Dungeon it is," she decided.

Out of the corner of my eye, I saw Clover watching through the window and motioned for her to duck. She disappeared again beneath the blue lace curtains.

"Ma'am…" My mouth was dry. I was terrified. My mind was blank, and I had no strategy to get out of this. But she did. She was still going. "Your highness, please…"

She ignored me. "But…The fairy dungeon is too small," she pointed out mockingly.

What is she doing? I wondered. The guards stared at her, raising their bushy, brown eyebrows.

The queen continued. "And the human dungeon is not secure enough," she added with mock thoughtfulness. Then I realized. I realized that *this* was the whole point of the queen's strange games. They just needed a reason. They wanted to punish a human, so no matter what I did, they were going to punish *me*.

"Can anyone tell me what that means?" Queen Gilly asked, as if she were a teacher asking a question to a bunch of schoolchildren, not a queen talking to an army.

"Troll dungeon! Troll dungeon!" a troll called out excitedly, sounding like a five-year-old. He had a long, brown, messy, piece of hair sticking out of his head, too stubborn to be neat, and his dark green body was covered in strange black tattoos. His face was marked with a large scar.

"So we'll put him in the troll dungeon?" The queen asked with a smirk.

I saw Clo peek through the window again, trying to eavesdrop on our conversation. She looked pale. I could barely breathe. Suddenly, the queen turned to the window. My mouth was dry, and I could barely breathe, but I needed to help Clover! So, I willed myself to shout, "Duck!" and then covered my mouth. Clover hid right as the queen was facing the window. The queen glared at me. She was done with the games. But so was I.

"OPEN THE WINDOW!" I screamed. The window slowly moved open, and I heard a soft grunt, followed by the fluttering of wings.

"NO!" The queen screamed as the guards growled angrily. "Who is out there?!" she cried, lunging at me.

I ducked, and before the queen could figure out what was happening, I rolled onto the floor and jumped out the open window.

"COME BACK!" She screamed after me as I plunged through the sky. Something flashed across her face again, something weird—a strange hatred that looked like it had been there forever, and her wonderful teal eyes glowed red. I blinked, trying to convince myself I had imagined it— the change was merely a trick of the light. When I looked again, the queen returned to normal, angry and defeated. Now I was certain it was just my imagination.

I smirked. I had won the game. But then I remembered how high up the window had been and my smirk turned into a scream as I fell, the ground rushing up, closer and closer to me. I wanted to yell for help, but my mouth wouldn't and couldn't move. Plus, who would help a human anyway? I looked down. The fall wasn't high enough to kill me, but it would hurt. A lot.

The fall seemed to take *forever* before I landed on the grass, hard. It felt like my body was on fire. Too shocked to move, I stayed sprawled on the ground. I tasted blood.

"Carl! Carl, are you okay?!" Jolly hissed from somewhere near me. I looked around, but the world was a blur of green grass, the black night sky, and the gray stones of the palace. I hadn't realized how late it had gotten, but I didn't focus on that. I had a bigger problem at the moment. *I literally just fell out of a building,* I realized. My head was spinning. If the ground was any more solid or the window was any higher, I could have died or broken every bone in my body. *Oh my gosh, I literally just fell out of a building!* Surprisingly, I didn't think I had broken anything, but my whole body stung, and my head, neck, shoulders, and back were really sore.

Maybe Queen Gilly thought that I had been hurt worse than I had. That would be an advantage when I went back into her palace.

I tried to push off the ground and stand up, but the world danced in circles so I sat right back down again. "Yeah… I'm fine…nothing broken… I think." I winced. Were there doctors in the fairy kingdom? Probably not human doctors either way.

"Oh my gosh, oh my gosh, oh my gosh. Okay. It's okay, Carl. You'll be okay." Clover's voice said frantically, trying to convince herself more than me. "Can you stand up?"

I pushed myself off the ground and managed to stand up, although my head was pounding. I tried to orient myself to my surroundings, but the world was still a blur of colors. I didn't see Jolly or Clover. They were probably hiding. That was a good thing. I really wanted to keep them safe, because at this point just being my friend was dangerous enough.

"Back here!" Jolly's voice whispered. I was so surprised I almost fell back down again. I turned in the direction of the voice, but the only thing I saw was a bush. My brain was running in circles so I didn't even stop to think about what that meant.

"A talking bush?" I mumbled. I must have hit the ground harder than I thought. The bush laughed in Clover and Jolly's voices. Then I put two and two together and felt embarrassed.

"Not *a* talking bush, silly, *behind* the talking bush," Clover said, holding back her laughter. I harrumphed. As if it wasn't obvious now.

"I'm so dizzy, I can't even think straight," I muttered defensively, even though I knew that she didn't mean it in that way. In my defense, I was talking to a troll and a fairy on a quest to stop an evil vampire. I guess anything was possible, right? I shook my head, which hurt a lot, and groaned again. "Note to Self: never jump out of a window," I muttered.

"Probably a good idea." Jolly agreed. Clover snorted her agreement. I rolled my eyes, though I was smiling. Those two were no help at all. I limped over toward the bush and pulled the branches apart to find the two of them curled up inside, covered by the green leaves. I stepped through the bushes to hide with them in the meantime. The queen and her guards might assume I died, and if they came by while I was still in plain sight I'd be a goner for sure. I lowered myself into a sort of comfortable sitting position.

"Oh, Carl, your leg!" Clover cried suddenly.

I looked down and winced. The bottom of my leg was covered in blood.

"It's fine, I can wrap it," I said. My leg was kind of numb anyway. I untied the jacket around my waist and wrapped it around my leg to stop the bleeding. That was something I had learned from adventure novels, but thankfully, it worked. You could learn a *lot* just from reading.

Clover sighed in relief. "Can you walk?"

"Sort of," I mumbled.

Jolly sighed. "So what do we do now?"

"Let's go back inside." I blurted. I knew it was dangerous, but for some reason, I couldn't wait to get back inside. There was something interesting about the queen, something that was drawing me to her.

Clover and Jolly stared blankly at me. Then they both burst out laughing. They laughed harder than I'd ever seen anyone laugh before, tears streaming down their faces.

I put my hands on my hips. "Guys! Stop!"

Their laughs shortened to coughs for breath and their faces darkened.

"Oh, you're serious," Jolly said darkly. "Are you crazy?! You just almost DIED escaping that place!"

"That was probably because I jumped out of a window," I pointed out.

"Yeah, and maybe you fell harder than we thought!"

"You can't go back in! You'll go to the troll dungeon!" Clover yelled suddenly. She looked around quickly and her voice softened to what was nearly a whisper. "I was listening from the window. That's what the queen said."

Jolly froze, her green face suddenly pale. She turned to Clover slowly. "The troll dungeon?" Her voice was quiet too, almost like saying the word too loudly was cursed. She shared a worried look with Clo.

"Yeah... What's wrong with the troll dungeon?" I asked, fed up with all of the secrets. "I mean, I get it, it's a dungeon, and all dungeons are bad. But even if I said I was going to a normal dungeon, you wouldn't be this worried."

"One, we'd *totally* be this worried. And *two*, I hear it's the most secure dungeon in the *world* with the highest defenses. The cells are far apart and disgusting, and the guards are chosen from the strongest trolls in the kingdoms. That dungeon is scarier than anything that you think is your worst nightmare, Carl. It's so secure that you'd be foolish to try to escape. You can't go back in there," Jolly whispered, looking around as if to make sure that no one else had heard.

The walls of the palace seemed to laugh at me, taunting me. *You can't even come inside, or you'll go to that awful dungeon*, they said. Well, I'd come this far, and I wasn't about to let some high-tech dungeon stop me. I gulped and peeked around the corner at the doors to the palace, where two guards were standing and talking nervously. I was afraid, of course, but something was calling me back toward the palace. I started limping forward. We went there for help, and that's what I was going to get!

"STOP!" Jolly belted angrily.

I stopped, thinking the whole palace must have heard her. I glanced nervously at the guards, but they were frozen in place, mid-conversation. The whole castle seemed to have frozen in place, actually. I blinked, but everyone was still frozen. I gasped and spun around, tripping on my own feet. The trees had stopped swaying in the light breeze. Even the wind was frozen.

"Jolly…?" I questioned slowly. She was the only other being that wasn't frozen. I opened my mouth, but no words came out. I blinked at her.

"Carl, I can explain… You know what? I can freeze time." Jolly muttered, looking upset.

It took me a moment to process the words before I nearly fell over in shock. That wasn't possible, was it? I mean, again, I was standing in a kingdom of frozen fairies, talking to a troll who claimed to have superpowers. So I guess anything was possible, but that was just… weird. And if it was true, wouldn't she have told us before? There had to have been a mistake, right?

"Could you repeat that, please? I think I misheard you." I said softly. I had to make sure.

"I can… I can freeze time." She repeated the words in a mumble.

It had to have been true, I realized, still processing what had happened. Nobody would lie about that. And it was the only explanation. But how did you react to someone who had superpowers? Pure awe, of course! I felt my face widen into a grin. That was so cool!

"You have superpowers?!" I squealed loudly, not careful to be quiet anymore. No one could hear me anyway because they were all frozen.

Jolly winced. "No, it's not—"

"Why didn't you tell us? That's great!"

"No!" she yelled. "It's *not* great at all!"

I paused to consider that. Of course it was! Why was she being so odd about it? Maybe she was just upset that I still wanted to go back into the palace. Yeah, that had to be it. Well, I didn't know why, but I just had to talk to the queen again.

Suddenly, as I stood there, wondering about Jolly's strange powers, an old legend I'd heard pulled at a memory from the back of my brain. "The… old powers!" I realized. "How…"

According to the legend, the old powers were really rare. Supposedly, only trolls could get them and they included the power to freeze time. I'd read about the powers in a book, but my uncle burned the book, and I'd never heard about them again in any other story. I'd wished that I'd had powers like that to avoid Jean, but as far as I knew back then, it was all a fantasy. The *'fantasy'* must have been written by one of the people who lived in the Fairy Kingdom! That's why there was only *one* story about the old powers.

That's when I realized— most fairy tales had to have been based on life in the Human Territories, written by the people that regretted the mistake of trying to start a fight! Of course, none of them stayed behind, but maybe a few felt bad and wanted to pass on stories. That meant they were all *nonfiction*! *That's* so *cool!* I thought, happily letting my mind make the connections. This was basically my dream!

"My great-great grandma had them," Jolly admitted bitterly. "I didn't think that I would get them, too, but I did… my…my parents…" The words seemed to get stuck in her throat. I didn't understand what she was trying to say, but she just shook her head

I gaped at her. Before I could say anything else, Jolly dragged me back next to Clover. Indignant, I opened my mouth, but Jolly shushed me and flicked her hands. I felt wind on my face, and the grass moved softly in the light breeze. I heard the echoing voices of the trolls that were guarding the palace, unfrozen. The castle returned to its normal, busy self, and the creepy silence stopped. Then Clover appeared behind my right shoulder.

"Carl? You're back? I thought you were going into the palace—I was so worried… How did you get over here so fast?" She asked, looking completely baffled. I turned to Jolly and gave her a look.

"You froze Clo?" I hissed. Jolly glared at me. Clover opened her mouth, but I just shook my head and muttered, "Don't ask."

"Okay…?" The fairy was completely confused. Jolly shook her head and gave me a look.

"Whatever." I said, completely determined. "I'm going back into the palace."

"*I?*" Jolly asked, in a dangerous tone. "*Don't you dare, Carl,*" her glare said.

"Yes. *I.* I'm going in alone," I repeated, trying to make it clear that there was no arguing.

"No. No! We all go, or you don't go at all," Clover insisted.

"No. I'm sorry. It's too dangerous." I started running toward the palace, causing pain to flare like a fire in my legs. But suddenly, I blinked, and I was back to hiding spot where Clo and Jolly were.

Clover still looked totally confused, but she didn't say anything this time. I glared at Jolly.

"We go together," Jolly repeated, not sounding sorry at all.

I took a deep breath, trying very hard not to be mad at her. "Fine. But I have a plan this time."

I whispered the plan in their ears.

"It's risky," Clover said, not pleased with my idea.

"You don't have to help, but it's worth it to me! I need to find my parents," I snapped.

"Slow down, Carl. We're with you. Why here though?" Jolly asked.

"Yeah, why did you come to the fairy kingdom, of all places?" Clo asked.

I explained about Stephanie sending me. "If she sent me, there has to be someone here who can help me," I said. "I trust her." My face burned slightly. Was I stupid for trusting someone I'd just met?

"If you trust her, then I'm in," Clover said doubtfully. We both glanced at Jolly.

"Fine," the troll muttered. She handcuffed me, hiding the key.

"Where did you get those?!" I asked her. They seemed to have appeared out of nowhere! Jolly held me tight but didn't answer.

Clo started to fly after us, but I held up a hand to stop her. She paused. "You're not coming."

She started to argue, but Jolly stopped her. "It's for the best. We don't want Queen Gilly to see you. Remember, you're technically betraying *your kind*," the troll reminded Clover, who looked sad as she watched the troll dragging me along. I hoped that she wouldn't change her mind and betray *us*.

The guards, who had been talking loudly moments before, saw Jolly. They stiffened and shut up immediately. "What are you doing here? The next guard shift isn't for another hour and a half," one of the guards said gruffly. He hadn't seen me yet. They were probably being more protective of who was on what shifts because of what happened with Gerald and Terry, the two trolls who had been standing guard what must have been only a few hours ago.

"So... remember that human boy?" Jolly said nervously to the guards, trying to hide her fear. My heart was running in circles, pounding against my chest. She shoved me in front of her, giving the two guards a clear view of me. Their eyes widened with a dangerously unrecognizable emotion. I winced. "I caught him."

My heart slowed, running the final lap of its tiny race inside of my chest. Everything was going exactly as planned. For the time being. The plan was risky, and a million things could go wrong, but hopefully we were ready. It was an okay plan, I guess, as far as crazy plans go.

I pretended to struggle against Jolly as she shoved me forward. I've learned that acting isn't too hard if you believe in what you want.

"C-caught him?" One of the trolls asked excitedly, studying me from afar like a dangerous creature that had just been discovered. I guess that's what I was to them. A rare specimen. Humans were rarely caught because none of them knew this place existed. And also because of how smart we were, maybe. It wasn't like we were just animals, waiting to be caught. We'd built an existence for ourselves, even without help. But so had the fairies.

"Here, take my shift. I'll bring him to the queen." The second troll offered Jolly a spear.

"I would, soldier. But you know the rules." Jolly bowed her head respectfully.

I looked up at her, wondering what rules she was talking about. She kept a straight face, not meeting my eye. I made a show of struggling against the handcuffs, which were digging into my skin every time I moved.

The guard looked at me with a sneer on his face. "Why did you even come?" he asked, looking me up and down, amused at my 'struggle.' "How did you even find us?"

I tried not to smile, almost enjoying myself. If only he knew.

"Let me go, and I might tell you." I challenged. Maybe they would be scared that more humans would come and attack them, thinking that I was a spy or something. It didn't work. The guard's face twisted into anger instead of fear like I had hoped.

"You don't have a say in this, little boy!" He roared. I fell back.

"Uh, guys!" Jolly interrupted, saving me. "Did you hear the story about that toll troll?"

For a second, one panicked second, I'd thought that she'd meant herself, but nobody knew about that yet, right?

"You mean Bean? I heard that he was fired." One of the guards said. "And banished from the kingdom."

"Yeah. I don't know why he would do that." She shook her head. I wondered what Bean, a random toll troll, had done to get banished from the kingdom. I liked the name, though. Bean. Sounded cool for a troll. Jolly continued. "Being a toll troll seems hard." I looked up for a split second, seeing a sort of sadness in her eyes, and felt bad.

"Maybe so, but toll trolls do get to eat some humans." The second troll eyed me with an evil smirk. "I sort of envy the troll who was on duty when this one arrived. How he got past them is beyond me."

"Sure you do." Jolly muttered sarcastically, quiet enough that only I could hear her. I snickered. Jolly was one of the only toll trolls who did not like eating people, which was lucky for me. If it had been the shift of some other toll troll, I wouldn't have gotten into the fairy kingdom. I might have been eaten.

"What?" the first troll asked suspiciously. "Did you say something?"

Jolly faked confusion and then nodded as if a lightbulb was going off in her brain. It was so convincing that I could have believed her act. She could be an actress. She'd probably enjoy that more than being a toll troll, I guess.

"I just said that being a toll troll has to be very hard work." She covered. "You have to stand in the hot, the cold, and the rain and the snow." She looked slightly upset as she talked about being a toll troll, but thankfully the other trolls didn't notice. Though the guards' jobs must have been hard too, I knew that Jolly's was probably harder. I felt bad. I knew she was hinting at how much she hated it.

"No, I heard that part. After that." The second troll frowned suspiciously. Jolly just shrugged. "Either way, I'm sure it is difficult. How would you know, though?"

"My cousin is a toll troll." Jolly replied. The lie was so convincing that it made me fidgety.

"Which troll?"

I shifted nervously. This was it. The moment where they asked a question that we couldn't answer. The one where we got too nervous and we were found out— and captured if we were lucky.

But Jolly didn't even seem very nervous, like I was. If anything, she seemed calm.

"Crelish." She answered immediately. I looked up, startled. Who was Crelish?

"Oh, Crelish! He's a good friend of mine." The guard smiled. "I didn't know he had a cousin, though."

Jolly just shrugged.

"Waaaiit…" said the second guard suddenly, suspicion creeping into his voice as he dragged out the word. "You look familiar. Doesn't she look familiar?" He turned to his partner.

Jolly froze, eyes wide. She looked funny with wide eyes, like something out of a poorly animated troll movie, but I was too nervous to laugh. I was sweating. My plan could go wrong in many, *many* different ways. The other troll didn't have time to answer because Jolly grabbed my arm. I yelped in surprise.

"You've… uh… probably seen me around Crelish." She covered quickly, and the trolls both nodded in agreement. The queen needed to get better guards. The current trolls were way too easy to fool.

"Well, we'd better get going." Jolly said quickly. That conversation was the first time I'd seen her get really nervous while talking to another troll. She looked at me with an extremely convincing fake smirk. "The queen will want to see you." She turned to the other trolls. "It was nice talking to you two!" Jolly pulled me forward through the castle.

Some of the trolls in the halls of the palace stopped us to congratulate Jolly on capturing me and winning the prize of my capture, or to glare at me or scoff or laugh. I frowned, feeling uncomfortable, like a caged animal that didn't belong. Feeling the guards' eyes on me, I shivered. I didn't fit in—like a giant porcupine in a room of balloons. I could picture that scene in my head, and it wasn't a very happy ending for those balloons. I could almost hear the noise, the kind that would give your cat nightmares for months. *POP!* I sighed. Why was I thinking about balloons and porcupines and cats? I must have been going crazy or something. When we turned a corner and there were no more guards, I finally relaxed.

"Guards, the human has been caught!" A voice echoed down the hall. I stiffened. The voice was deeper, louder, more official.

We ducked behind a pillar and hid. I heard footsteps and peeked in the direction of the voice. A large troll wearing a blue-

and-gold guard uniform was marching down the hall. He could easily have been some leader of the guards. What must have been every single guard in the palace dropped their heavy spears, which clattered to the ground with a deafening sound. They all jumped up and cheered for a "safer" kingdom, for punishment and capture. Jolly didn't move. She just stared at them, looking upset.

I turned to her. Something was wrong. "Jolly?" I asked softly.

"I don't remember them being this merciless and... and cruel! They would never *cheer* for capture," She mumbled bitterly, frowning as she watched the trolls that may have been her friends. She didn't even turn to me as she spoke. She just sat there quietly for a minute, not saying anything. I watched her carefully. Jolly turned to me, and shook her head. It was only then that I noticed the tears in her eyes. "Something changed."

"You say the boy has been caught?" Queen Gilly asked, appearing out of what seemed like nowhere. I winced as she marched down the hall, yet the sight of her filled me with a sort of excitement. She moved quickly on the ground, her tiny wings flapping behind her, as strong, perfect, and stubborn as her.

"Yes ma'am." The words echoed around the crowded hallway, perfectly in unison and on point, as if they had been practiced.

The queen made a suspicious face. "Well, where is he?"

"Um..." Several guards mumbled different answers. Queen Gilly glared. I guess she'd known that something was wrong when she didn't see me with them.

"Don't you guys go around, getting everyone's hopes up without proof! Proof, gentlemen!" She roared. I covered my ears.

The trolls stopped celebrating immediately. They lined up against the walls, halting in salute.

"Where is he?" the queen repeated angrily, turning to a random guard and pulling him toward her with magic. Jolly gasped softly. When I turned to her, she looked troubled, although I wasn't 100% sure why. Honestly, I was more focused on the queen and her guards and the crazy things that were happening.

"I-I-I-I don't know!" He stammered.

She glared. "And you believed that he was caught without proof?" Queen Gilly roared. "Are you that gullible? Or are you just stupid? Where did you hear this rumor from?!"

"H-h-him!" He stammered, pointing to another guard. "He told me!"

The queen just released her magical hold on him and walked to the guard in question. She didn't say another word to the poor troll she'd just grabbed, who collapsed to the ground.

"You know of his capture?" The queen asked. The guard nodded quickly. "So where is he?" She magically pulled the guard toward her, just like she had with the first.

"I don't know!" The guard answered, looking terrified. The queen asked where he heard the rumor from and he pointed to another guard. The queen repeated this with every single guard in the room, and I winced. How could she treat her guards like...this?

"Something's wrong," Jolly mumbled, more to herself than to me. I looked up at her, alarmed. I thought she might have been hurt or something, or maybe someone had seen us!

"What? Are you okay?" I felt my heart pounding against my chest. *Calm down, Carl.*

Jolly could sense my worry and looked down at me. "What? Oh. Yeah. Uh, I mean… no." she said. "It's not that bad. It's just… The queen never acts like this. She respects her guards, and they respect her. She treats them like equals. And she would have normally listened to you, not tried to put you in the troll dungeon. Something's definitely wrong with her. Even her voice is kind of different," Jolly explained. The queen continued yelling at her guards. "There's just… something off." Well, that didn't sound good.

When Queen Gilly got to the last guard, instead of grabbing him, to my surprise, she just put her hand on her hip. It was the guard in the blue-and-gold uniform—the one who had announced my capture before. I figured he must have been some kind of captain.

"Who are you going to blame?" She sighed, with an "*I can't even get anything done around here because of these trolls*" look on her face. The troll, who was shaking with fear, didn't answer. Before, he had seemed so scary, but apparently, the one thing that scared these trolls more than anything was Queen Gilly. Even though she was small, she was powerful. "Where is he?" she asked calmly.

"I-I… I swear I don't know!" He cried.

The queen scowled at and she slapped him across his large, green face. A slap from such a tiny being could hardly do anything, I bet. I wondered how that must have felt. Would it feel like a mosquito bite, or did it feel like being hit with a pebble? Did it feel like a foam bullet from a toy gun? While the queen was too small to physically manipulate the giant troll, she still scared him. She simply had a powerful aura. Anyone could see that. Clearly the queen scared the trolls more than anything else.

She turned away like she might storm off, but simply took a deep breath and turned back to look at the troll as if nothing had happened instead. I growled quietly. Jolly did too.

"Who told you he was here?" she asked calmly. The guard quickly pointed in my direction. For a second, my heart stopped. I thought he was pointing directly at me. But he was pointing toward the door.

"T-the two soldiers by the door. They said he came inside with a different troll. That's all I know, I swear." He said quickly. The queen dropped him, looking annoyed as if this were simply a minor inconvenience.

"Your highness!" I yelled, starting to rise. I couldn't just hide anymore while the queen treated her guards this way. I felt a hand on my wrist, but I shook it off.

"Carl! What are you doing? Get back here!" Jolly hissed. "Carl! Carl!" Every troll in the hall had turned toward the sound of my voice, but thankfully, they hadn't heard Jolly. She grabbed my arm and pulled me down, but I shook my head and wiggled out of her grip.

"Where are you, Carl?" The queen asked, saying my name like it was an inside joke. I could hear the sneer in her voice. I slowly lifted myself off of the ground, sending a sharp pain into my ankle where I had fallen several minutes ago. Immediately, a group of guards ran at me and grabbed me. As if I would try an escape now. I was the one who had revealed myself.

The queen smirked at me "Well," she said. That was all. She was waiting for me to do something. So I did. I started acting, hiding my fear, this time letting my strong anger— which I had hidden very deep inside— show.

"Tell your guards to let me go or I'll make them." I threatened, making a big show of struggling against the guards. "Let me go. I'm warning you."

The queen ignored me, instead getting obnoxiously close to my face. "How? You can't do anything. What is a *useless* human like *you* going to do?" Her words hung over the shining hall like a storm cloud. Her face said it all— *"you're just a helpless little boy."* This time, it was my turn to sneer at her. *That's what you think. And I'll prove you wrong.*

"Let me go and you won't have to find out." I challenged.

She just stared at me with that signature smirk of hers, and I realized that it was the only expression I'd seen on her face. Jolly was right. Something about her was definitely off.

"I don't believe you," the queen said simply, as if that was the end of that. But this wasn't the end. The games were just beginning, and this time I had the advantage.

"You will." I warned.

"All right. Who caught him?" she asked, ignoring my warning. "I promised an award, and an award you'll get."

Now it was Jolly's turn to speak up, stepping from behind the pillar and dipping to a bow. She looked nervous. "Your majesty, I caught him." The queen was smiling proudly as if to say, *"finally, someone competent."* I just stood in front of the queen, who was saying something, perhaps congratulating Jolly, or maybe she was talking to me, but I couldn't hear, and their voices sounded far away. I wasn't listening either way.

Suddenly, power poured over me, coursing through my body, knocking me over. My blood felt warm and my heart was pumping faster than usual. I prepared to reach out and catch myself, but mine were still handcuffed. I screamed, falling toward the queen's feet. What was that? Some tremble from deep within the Earth's core? Had I simply tripped over my own feet? I heard the queen laughing, but it sounded far away.

Then I heard a soft voice harmonizing. *Carl. Come.*

For some reason, I could tell that the voice wanted me to focus on that power, a glowing, calm center in the middle of a wild storm.

Jolly lifted me up by wrapping her arms under mine, as painfully as she could. I grunted. I assumed that she was brutal on purpose, to keep the plan in action, but it still caught me off guard and it still hurt.

"Guards…!" The queen called, sounding more excited and less angry now. She had found her prey—me. Now the guards were coming to get me. I heard footsteps through the halls. The guards ran up with dark circles under their angry eyes, ready to protect and fight for their queen as long as it meant that they stayed alive. I felt bad for them as I saw them line up behind Queen Gilly in salute, looking picture-perfect.

"Remember what I warned you about." I reminded her. "You'd better let me go or you'll have to face a dangerous power!"

The queen just laughed again, not even slightly worried. "You won't be getting out of here with your fake threats. You're just a boy." I rolled my eyes. Yeah, I was just a boy. A boy who survived a vampire and pirates. Plus I'd escaped her palace once already. The queen continued. "If you really have some secret weapon or power, show me. Prove to me that you are special, and I might reconsider taking you prisoner."

I knew it was a lie, but it couldn't hurt to try. "NOW!" I screamed. The guards stared at me for a second. When I blinked, my handcuffs had been unlocked broken off. I knew that Jolly had frozen time and undone them, but the sudden change even startled me.

"What happened?!" the queen yelled.

"Just like I said, my threats are *very* real!" I said loudly, turning to Jolly, who flicked her hands. I smiled. Everything was going according to plan.

But then nothing happened. I stumbled backward. A burly guard launched into a run and sprinted at me. Jolly stared at her hand, and then at the troll who was running at me. He hadn't stopped, and I was still in his way. The queen was watching us expectantly, looking smug, like she knew that "my powers" wouldn't work. Seriously, now of all times? Why weren't Jolly's powers working?

In the midst of my panic, the queen had already composed herself. "So what, you escaped your handcuffs." She scoffed. "If you had any true powers, you could have escaped the vampire and the pirates on your own. You could have saved your parents." I faltered for a second at the mention of my parents. It was all a game, I reminded myself. People who get upset in games always lose. "If you have true powers," the queen continued, "you can escape this guard too." She still had this smug look on her face that made me want to punch someone.

"I *said*, Your Highness, that my threats are very real," I repeated loudly, glancing meaningfully at Jolly. "Obviously I can escape this guard."

Jolly stared at her hands and flicked them again, but still, nothing was happening. This had to be a joke, right? The serious look on her face told me that it was not. "I-I-I-I can't!" She screamed frantically.

That was when I realized my mistake.

"She's with you?!" The queen screeched angrily. "Get him," she told the guard, who nodded and didn't stop running at me. I glanced at him. Either he was really slow or just pretty far away. Probably both, as he wasn't really getting anywhere. Despite this, he was absolutely terrifying and I was too panicked to move. He was getting closer. Queen Gilly's voice rose into a yell. "Get him! GET HIM!"

"STOP! STOP! FREEZE!!" I yelled, closing my eyes. *Please stop. Trip, fall, anything, stop. Please just stop.* I willed silently. I waited for my attacker, eyes still closed. The room was silent. I felt all of the eyes on me. After a while, when I still hadn't been pulled, shoved, grabbed, or attacked, I opened one eye. Then the other. I blinked twice.

"Wha—" My eyes widened to almost twice their normal size. Everyone was staring at me. "Jolly, did you…?" I asked slowly, turning to her. I really hoped she would say yes. She shook her head, eyes equally wide. My heart pounded against my throat. There was no other possible explanation. Only a couple inches away from me, the guard who had been running at me moments before was frozen mid-run.

And I had somehow caused it.

***

Chapter Eight

Legends That May be True

Queen Gilly was glancing quickly from me to Jolly to her guards, although her shocked looks were more like glares. "The old power," she whispered as I gaped stupidly at my hands. "N-no… that's impossible. The powers have only been seen on trolls before. T-that's…" She turned to me like I had done something that was wrong but incredible. "You did that?"

I didn't know what to say. I really didn't know what I had done. Somehow, I had gotten Jolly's powers. I was about to admit that I didn't know what I was doing when I realized that this could actually help the plan. The goal was to prove that I had magical powers, right? Well, now I really did. I took a deep breath and forced the corners of my mouth into a smug sneer. I was actually getting better at acting. Turns out all of this lying had actually paid off.

"Yeah. I did that." I bragged.

The queen took a deep breath, trying to compose herself. It took her a moment, but she managed to turn back to her not-so-normal, smug, self. "*Get. Him!*" She ordered again.

Three more guards ran at me, looking more reluctant now. I flicked my hands and all three were frozen. Three more launched into lunges toward me, now looking absolutely terrified.

"Freeze," I whispered, flicking my wrist at them. They froze mid-lunge.

"NO! GET HIM, YOU USELESS, SMALL-BRAINED TROLLS! GET HIM!" Queen Gilly yelled at the rest of the trolls, who were gaping at their five, frozen colleagues.

My mouth twisted into an unpleasant frown at the corners. "Freeze!" I cried out and all of the queen's guards froze. I felt bad, but they would have captured me in a heartbeat. Well, before I had these powers at least. Jolly backed up and stood behind me, her teeth bared in a scowl, ready for a fight.

The queen glared back at her, before turning her head to me. Her glare faded into her trademarked smirk. She whistled and slow clapped. "Wow," she said. "That was impressive." The hairs on the back of my neck stood up. Her tiny wings fluttered softly behind her back. Her long, golden hair streamed down her back like a river cutting off at a straight edge. Her sharp, mysterious teal eyes gazed into my soul. I shifted uncomfortably.

Suddenly, I heard a growl behind me.

"JOLLY!" I screamed. "WHAT ARE YOU DOING?" The troll had lunged at the fairy queen! Queen Gilly looked displeased, but not worried. If she was an emoji, she would be that sighing one where the eyes are closed and the mouth is in a not-so-pleased straight line.

"So, the traitor really is with you? It wasn't an act, then." An angry sneer took over her face, making her look rather unpleasant. If Jolly was affected by the queen's words, she didn't show it, and neither of us denied it. It was far too late for that. Then the queen's eyes widened like she had realized something. Jolly seemed to be falling in slow motion toward the queen, who now looked very, very angry. "The powers were hers, of course!" She growled. "I promise I'll put you and all of your filthy friends in prison!!"

I heard a scream and looked up. Jolly was practically on top of the queen, just a few inches above her!

"FREEZE!" I screamed, freezing both Jolly and Queen Gilly. Jolly was frozen with her arms extended like she was trying to fly. I walked over to her and dragged her away from the queen. Even for a giant troll, she was heavier than I would have thought. When we were a safe distance away from the queen, I unfroze Jolly. "The queen can't help us." I said, pulling her toward the door. "Let's get out of here!"

Just then, I felt the power inside me weaken, flickering like a dying flame. I felt my concentration on the power shatter into pieces. Suddenly, the queen and all of her guards unfroze and a burly troll lunged at us. I rolled out of the way, but there was another troll directly under Jolly, ready to attack her! Before I could react, the troll grabbed one of Jolly's large, green legs.

"Huh? Fr—"

"I recommend that you don't freeze anyone." the queen said dryly.

"Jolly!! We gotta run!" I hissed loudly, my throat feeling dry. What had just happened? My powers, they... they just stopped working, and everyone I'd frozen before suddenly unfroze and started attacking me and Jolly! I suddenly felt weak and scared. I hadn't realized how much I had relied on the powers until they were gone. They were my one advantage over the queen.

"Carl! Run!" Jolly cried. "Put the pieces of your—MMM!" She started to say something else but a guard muffled her speech by covering her mouth. I started to panic. The pieces of my what, and where? I didn't have any pieces to put together! What did she know? Was it about my... her powers? Was it important?

The guard pulled out his knife and held it way too close to Jolly's face. She whimpered. The queen laughed and gracefully sat down on her jeweled throne. My panic amplified by ten.

Then the queen did the last thing that I'd expect her to; she proposed a deal, and one that I'd never have guessed the subject of. "Listen, Carl. I know there's a fairy with you. Tell me who and I won't hurt you or your troll friend."

Jolly's muffled cries got louder. I glanced at the queen. The offer seemed irrelevant, but it didn't seem like something a good queen would do to keep her people safe, I guess. I didn't know much about being a good queen, or anything like that. The deal didn't seem very realistic, but what if Queen Gilly was telling the truth? I didn't want to throw Clover under the bus, but what if I'd do anything to get out of here with my friends, safe, rescue my parents, and stop Drake? Was that selfish?

"What would you do to her if I told you?" I asked slowly. Not promising I would tell her anything, but letting her know that it wasn't a definite no. What else did one do when his best friend was being threatened by an armed guard?

Jolly must have read my mind, because she fought to get the guard's hands off of her mouth. "Carl, don't! Just go! Put—mmm! Mmm!"

"NO!" I yelled.

The queen waved her hand, and all of her guards disappeared down the hall, except for the one holding Jolly. I kept my eyes on the gleaming silver knife and reached toward her desperately. What was she trying to tell me? Was it about my power, or about the queen? Just then, I saw Clover appear in the window. Oh gosh.

Just in case you're wondering how to make a guy panic, throw in both of his best friends who happen to be traitors, an evil queen, and a knife. That's the perfect recipe for disaster. Let's just say I said a few unkind words in my head. I won't repeat them now.

"Stay away! Stay away Stay away!" I mouthed desperately.

Clover took one glance around the room and gasped. The queen saw me looking and turned toward the window. Clover ducked just in time.

Instead of rushing to the window or trying to attack again (she was smarter than that), the queen turned to me. "Who's that, Carl?" Fake sweetness crept into her voice, like poisoned sugar— appealing but deadly, aimed to harm. That was her strength— brain, not brawn.

"Nobody." I muttered, not focusing on the queen. Instead, I focused on the broken shards of power in my mind. I had figured out that the power was a mental thing, and that was a start.

In my mind, the power looked like a glowing, golden ball of comfort. It smelled like freshly-baked chocolate-chip cookies and it felt like having the sun on your face in summer. I fueled the power with a *lot* of mental energy. I felt the power calling out to me again, and a Queen Gilly-trademarked smirk covered my face, matching hers. Her evil grin faded, and she directed a questioning look at me.

"Freeze!" I tried again. Nothing happened. Again, I summoned up the mental image of my powers again. They looked like puzzle pieces. Suddenly, I understood. That must have been what Jolly had meant! The powers were a puzzle.

Queen Gilly composed herself. "Well?" She waited expectantly for my response, a look of triumph on her face.

"Freeze!" I yelled. This time, the guard holding Jolly froze. I grinned. But that's when I learned not to count my chickens before they've hatched or whatever (it's a saying), because before I could celebrate, the guard unfroze again. Flickering in and out of being frozen, he started to panic. That just made him freeze and unfreeze faster.

"What's going on?" he yelled, voice shaking. This allowed Jolly to slip out of his grasp.

My face paled. Trying to keep the guard frozen was taking up all of my mental energy.

"Carl? Are you okay?" Jolly's voice called. Everything was dark.

"HELP!" I yelled, not sure why I yelled it. Jolly was the one who needed help, not me, but I was trapped under the weight of the power, the weight of the world, trying to keep the guard still for long enough so we could escape.

"Carl? Carl?! Are you okay?" Jolly repeated.

I groaned. "I'm okay," I muttered. "It's fine." My voice was weak and hoarse.

I managed to open my eyes, just in time for me to see Jolly's captor grab her again. Now, instead of freezing entirely, the guard's legs and arms were going limp every few seconds. Jolly wiggled out of his hold. Her eyes met mine, and I gave her a reassuring but fake smile.

The pieces of power were banging around my brain like cannonballs, giving me a terrible headache. I felt the hum of the power, shaking my very soul. I closed and opened my eyes again.

Jolly's lips were pursed together. "Carl?" Then she looked like a lightbulb was going off in her head, like she suddenly understood what was happening "The puzzle... put the pieces together! Focus! Carl, focus!" She yelled to me. Her voice joined the cannonballs in my brain. *"FOCUS!"* I squinted at her. I was trying!

Suddenly, hands wrapped around her. She yelped as the guard pulled her back.

"Stay still," he grunted in a dangerous voice. The knife got closer to her neck, pressing against her rough skin with the sharper edge. She screamed, tears in her eyes. The guard froze again. This time, he didn't unfreeze. But Jolly couldn't move either. She was trapped between his frozen arms.

"Boy, what's going on?" Queen Gilly shrieked angrily. I didn't answer. Instead, I walked over to the frozen guard and shoved his arms out of the way so that Jolly could duck out of his grasp. When she was far enough away, I unfroze the guard, simply because I felt bad for him.

"Let's go," I said to Jolly.

"GET HIM!" Queen Gilly yelled at the guard, who looked absolutely terrified.

"B-but he'll hurt me!" the guard stammered nervously. "I don't want to be frozen again!"

"I don't care! Get them both!" the queen roared. She didn't look pleased that her own soldiers were arguing with her. The guard charged at me with his eyes closed, a horrible battle tactic, and he froze again. I felt kind of bad, but it was the queen's influence making him do this, the only influence that I couldn't stop.

Queen Gilly glared at me. "You little...!" she yelled.

I decided to end this once and for all. "Fr—"

Jolly's shaky voice cut me off. "Come on Carl. You don't need to freeze her. Let's just go." Jolly gave the queen a look and put her hand around me. We turned away from the queen. It was clear that Jolly clearly felt kind of bad for her, or just respected her, which I guess I understood. She was a queen, after all. But she wasn't my queen.

The fairy queen barreled forward into my back with all of her might, which still wasn't much. It felt like being hit with a small rock. I tried to shake her off, but she held on to the back of my shirt with surprising strength.

"You didn't tell me who the fairy who helped you was yet!" She shrieked. I tried to shake her away again, but she was surprisingly strong for her size. Had she lost her mind?!

"Let go," I said through gritted teeth, staring directly at her. Then, I started slowly freezing the queen. First, her arm froze and then her leg, sending her flying across the room. She ended up on the floor near her throne.

She suddenly looked terrified. "Please, Carl..." She managed to get down on her knees in a begging position. "Come on, Carl we can talk about this! You wouldn't freeze a queen, would you? Especially one who knows the location of your parents, right?" She stood up again. I stiffened at the mention of my parents, but I was done playing her games. I was not just a helpless little boy anymore. "Carl! HELP! PLEASE!" She managed to give me a dirty look before she froze in place, right next to her guard. I stared at the frozen queen for a few seconds. And then I ran for dear life, Jolly close behind me.

While I was running, the power in my mind that I had worked so hard to build shattered again. I didn't look behind me to check if the queen was still frozen, or try to freeze her again, because I knew that even if she wasn't frozen, which she probably wasn't, she wouldn't follow me just yet. She had offered me a silent agreement to let me and Jolly go. I don't know how I knew that; I just did.

Outside of the palace in the middle of the night, Clover fluttered down from the sky with the moon behind her, making her wings and her hair seem like they were glowing against her back. She looked upset. "What took so long?!" She shrieked. "Are you two okay?"

"Yes, we're fine." I said quickly. I had a bad feeling about hanging around there. I just wanted to get out of the kingdom. Clover didn't seem to hear me, or maybe she was just ignoring me. She wrapped her small body around Jolly as best she could. I could see the tears in her eyes.

I watched them with a sad smile for a second, and the world seemed to melt away for a moment. My friends were safe. It was just the three of us. I shook myself out of the calming trance-like state. "We need to run." I hissed. "Now!"

I had a really bad feeling. Even though Queen Gilly hadn't come for us *yet*, even though we had that sort of silent truce, she'd probably *still* chase after me. I wouldn't put it past her. The moment the words left my mouth, I heard grunts and shouts in the familiar deep voices of the queen's troll army. Great. Foreshadowing. I groaned in my head. Just my luck.

"She's coming!" Jolly yelled. "We have to leave!"

Clover lifted off of the ground and started flying away hurriedly. Jolly and I dashed after her, though she was twice as fast as us. A mob of soldiers (I counted thirty-five) ran out of the castle, screaming at us. They were clutching swords and spears. Some held fancy wooden bows and had packs of arrows slung over their backs. I gulped. Then, the queen strode gracefully out of her castle with her hair bouncing on her back and her wings fluttering behind her. Five guards marched on either side of her, fully armed and each brandishing a pointed weapon. Five more guards trotted out behind them, blocking the queen from attackers at her back. Fifty trolls and the queen! That was a lot of soldiers. I even recognized some of them. I gulped and sped up even more. The queen and her fifty soldiers marched after us. They were faster and stronger.

"Clo!" I whispered through gritted teeth. "Hide!" The queen didn't know about her involvement, and I didn't intend for her to find out.

But Clover shook her tiny head. She perched herself on my shoulder bravely. "If you get caught, I get caught! I'm not sitting back and hiding again!" I couldn't believe it. She was about to throw away her whole life for me. Words she'd said only earlier that day (it felt like much longer than that) echoed in my head. *I don't have a life here. I don't mind.* I swallowed, suddenly feeling sick. I understood, because I felt the same way. I was tired of sitting on the sidelines, waiting for my parents to come back and get me. She must have felt the same way.

Jolly stood near us, shoving away any troll that got to close to us. "Hurry up, guys!" She hissed, not unkindly. She kicked a troll in the leg. He fell to the ground and scampered back to the queen. I knew he'd be back, and he'd bring company next time.

I couldn't speak for a second, Clover's words still in my head. I didn't know what to say, so I just went with a soft, "Thank you. For everything."

I winced. Fighting off an army of trolls wasn't a great time to bond with your friends.

I looked to the side as Clover perched on my shoulder. Ten of the guards separated from the group and pushed toward us. It was almost like they were dancing around us. There was almost a rhythm to the way they poked at us with their weapons.

Jolly let out an overwhelmed yelp, a strange noise to hear from a troll. Too many soldiers were reaching for her at once. I gave a strangled noise, matching her yelp, trying unsuccessfully to fend them off with my bare hands. We needed weapons. I felt ten pairs of angry, hawk-like eyes on me. Something was strangely suspicious about the way they moved all together as they slithered around the grass.

I gasped loudly. They were moving *around*! Just too late, I realized what the army of trolls were trying to do. I called out a warning to Jolly and Clover, but it was already far too late. The rest of the trolls had caught up with us, drowning us in a sea of pointed weapons.

"It's an attack!" Jolly yelled in a strained voice. "We can fight back, Carl!"

The trolls surrounding us continued their graceful dance. They had clearly practiced. A spear flew at my head. I dodged and scowled at the trolls, trying to figure out who threw it.

I heard that cold, merciless laugh again. It was so familiar but I just couldn't place where I'd heard it before— like a person that you know you've met somewhere, but you can't quite place their name or their face. The sound echoed in my brain, not matching with a face. It didn't match Queen Gilly at all.

"This is no attack. This is WAR!" The fairy queen bellowed, echoing over the large fields of the fairy kingdom. I couldn't even see her anymore. The whole world was a dark muddle of gray and red. Jolly took a backwards step closer to me and grabbed my hand defensively. Clover remained on my shoulder, holding up her tiny fists in a fighting stance as if she could fight off one of the trolls. I knew she couldn't, but I appreciated the gesture. I swung my fist randomly into the crowd of trolls. One guard fell to the ground and got up with anger in his eyes. I felt butterflies in my stomach. I couldn't tell if that was power or nerves.

"I can freeze you in a heartbeat." I threatened. The threat hung empty in the air. The queen was not impressed.

She responded with that same, familiar cold laugh. "You're outnumbered! Fifty-one to two!" The queen argued.

Clover glanced at me. It was the perfect time to reveal herself. I opened my mouth to argue, but nothing came out. I'd agreed to this. Why had I agreed to this? What had I done? I started to panic. But before I could give voice to any of my thoughts, the fairy shot into air and flew through an opening between soldiers, directly into the queen's line of sight.

"Not two. Three!" she called. "Call off your guards, Queen Gilly." She put hands on her hips defiantly. I could imagine the queen's face, red with rage, but also Clover's, somehow terrified and brave at the same time. She was a hero. I tried to peek through an opening in the guards' circle to see what was happening, but I was nearly stabbed when I tried.

"CLOVER?" the queen bellowed, her voice just not right. "I... I know you! I... I saw you earlier!" I could hear the confusion in her voice, but not anger. The betrayal seemed almost forced. Strange. But I didn't have time to focus on that. Jolly pushed the soldiers surrounding her to the ground. I continued punching and kicking at random. Groans came from the trolls as they fell to the ground. Shaking, they crawled back to the queen, but they didn't stop there. They crawled all the way back to the palace. Jolly and I gave a loud battle cry together and fought our way toward the queen.

She wanted a war? Well, she'd certainly get one, because we weren't going down without a fight.

***

Chapter Nine

The Queen's Secret

"CHARGE!" The queen screamed, slithering into the back of her group to hide like the cowardly snake she was. Clover, left out in the open, flew back to me and hovered just above my shoulder. One of the trolls surrounding threw a knife at me, barely missing. He muttered a few curses under his breath. Coward. All of them were cowards. I scowled. My hands started shaking with anger. Just then, ten of the soldiers ran at me and my friends, hollering.

"Freeze," I muttered. I heard a panicked grunt before the ten trolls surrounding us stiffened. I pushed through the circle around me, knocking them down like dominoes. Twenty down, thirty to go.

I heard a battle cry. "ATTACK!" yelled an unfamiliar voice. I gritted my teeth. Another group of ten guards branched off from the group and ran directly at me and my friends, swords raised. Jolly and Clover both ended up with swords pointed directly at their throats. A third soldier ended up grabbing my arms from behind in the most brutal way possible. I started to panic for a moment, before I remembered my powers again.

"FREEZE!" I screamed loudly. The soldiers did just that, mouths open mid-holler and swords raised high. Thirty down. The other twenty guards gasped and raised their weapons higher, circling their queen in a protective shell.

"Well? What are you waiting for?!" The queen snapped at her guards, although there was a slight quiver in her voice.

"You wanted a war, that's what you'll get!" I called, hoping I sounded much more confident than I felt. When I glanced to my side, Jolly was standing there alone, frozen in shock. One of my friends was missing. "Clover?" I whispered. I felt something on my shoulder, and I found her resting on it. I tilted my head to see her better.

"Y-yes Carl?" she whispered back. She was shaking like a leaf. I know she said she didn't care, but I still felt bad for her. What on Earth was I doing?

"I don't have a life here," her voice reminded me in my head. I shivered and shook my head. Now wasn't the time to think about that.

"Do you think you could maybe… grab us swords?" I asked her quietly, pointing toward the frozen trolls. "We need weapons."

She definitely wouldn't be able to lift those heavy swords, but I'd seen the queen lift things with magic so I assumed Clover could too.

She just stood there for a moment, trembling. "S-swords?" she asked in a small voice.

I suddenly realized what I was asking. My face softened and I bent down. I caught her staring into the eyes of one of the frozen. I could imagine her trying to recognize them, probably thinking, *they'll never forgive me.* Then I heard her words in my head again. *"I don't have a life here."* I couldn't stop hearing them. They were haunting my thoughts for some reason.

I glanced to the side again. Jolly was fighting a troll with her bare fists, looking tired. She was wary, but if she was feeling the same way as Clover, she didn't show it. I grabbed another attacking troll and pushed him away, scowling as well. I looked back to the fairy in question. Now wasn't the time to be thinking this way, to be talking with my friends. This was war. But I needed her to know that she wasn't alone, that I knew how she felt.

I dodged an attack and muttered, "Freeze." The attacking troll went stiff. Clover winced, maybe hoping I wouldn't notice, but of course I did, and I felt bad. I didn't want to do this anymore than she did.

I sighed. "You won't have to hurt anyone, Clover." I said softly. "You don't have to hurt them." I nodded toward the army of trolls.

"I-I…. I don't?" she asked quietly.

I sighed again. "No, of course not."

So she inhaled and puffed up her small body. She nodded, though her face was unreadable, and she flew toward the troll army. She pulled the sword out of a frozen troll's hand using magic. She checked to make sure that no one had seen her before used her magic to tug a second sword free. She grunted with the effort and bit her lip. The tiny fairy checked both directions one more time and then started to dart toward us. Unfortunately, she missed *one* pair of eyes following her. The queen had seen her.

Queen Gilly dashed after Clover and tackled her. I yelped, a strangled noise stuck in my throat. Next, several things happened at once. One of Clover's swords clattered to the ground and her face paled. My concentration shattered in my head and all of the frozen guards unfroze. Then they charged at me and Jolly. I panicked.

"CARL, CATCH!" Clover hollered, using the last bit of her energy to fly upwards and magically toss two swords at me before Queen Gilly grabbed her ankle and pulled her back down again. I caught the swords and narrowly avoided slicing one of my fingers off by accident.

The queen tackled Clover again. The two fairies fought hard, tackling, shoving and kicking. I had never imagined two small fairies fighting, ever, let alone like this. I gripped the hilt of one sword. The hilt was smooth and made of ruby. It had a nice feeling and weight to it. I turned to the side and threw the other one to Jolly. She immediately started slashing with it, using it as if she'd been holding it the whole time, knocking the guard that she was fighting straight to the ground. As Jolly slashed away with her weapon, she muttered a few disrespectful things under her breath. Again, I won't repeat those.

I turned back to Clover, who was still fighting the queen. The full moon glowed behind them ominously. The remaining trolls awkwardly stepped away to either side of them, whispering to themselves as they gaped at the fighting fairies.

I started to move forward in protest but Jolly pulled me back and put her large green hand on my shoulder. She spoke in a shaky voice. "Let them be. This needs to be settled."

And so, the fight went on.

Queen Gilly dodged a kick that landed very close to her face. Clover dodged a swift punch that missed her by a few inches. I winced, once again tempted to run to the center and stop it all. I felt Jolly's hand on my shoulder. A quiet warning. *Don't. Let them be.*

"YOU TRAITOR!" Queen Gilly spat, pouncing on Clover's right wing. "HOW COULD YOU BETRAY YOUR QUEEN?" Clover pulled the queen's hand off of her and aimed a punch at the queen's head. Thankfully, she didn't aim it very well. In response, the queen threw a pointed kick.

Clover was shaking, and I couldn't tell if she was angry or scared. When she turned, her eyes were wild. Angry, then. But there were also tears forming in the corners. Maybe a mix of both. "I don't have any friends here. Carl is my friend! No one here understands me! Carl, he… he gets me." Clover snapped, slamming her fist down and missing the queen's head by an inch. "And I get him! I don't have a life here, and he knows—" BAM! Her fist slammed down again. "How—" BAM! "IT FEELS!" CRACK! This time, her fist landed right on the queen's nose, which started to bleed. The queen looked furious, and Clover looked horrified.

"MY KINGDOM ISN'T GOOD ENOUGH FOR YOU? I SHOULD HAVE BANISHED YOU YEARS AGO." Queen Gilly roared, grabbing Clover's ankle again. Clover shook wildly, trying to escape. This was not going well so far. At least Clover managed to stand up for herself.

Suddenly, a knife flew past my head, startling me out of my trance. The weapon missed me, but just barely. The remaining trolls were running at me, so I protected myself, slicing and blocking with my sword, occasionally freezing somebody. One by one, they ran to the back of their group, covered in blood and dirt.

Suddenly, I heard a clicking noise and some rustling, and I looked up. A fairy had apparently heard the screaming because a light went on in a nearby mushroom. She was a sleepy-looking fairy with curly brown hair, lime green eyes, and freckles. She flew out of her tiny mushroom home and blinked. She was wearing a lacy sky-blue dress. She looked around with her mouth wide open, clearly too shocked to speak. She glanced at the queen, who was on top of Clover with her fists up. She glanced at the many armed soldiers, most of which were frozen. Finally, she glanced at me, and that seemed to startle her out of her trance. She screamed, and she didn't stop for several minutes.

As she continued her screeching, two more fairies flew out of a single mushroom, one a grumpy-looking grandma with a gray bun and one a happy-looking fairy who seemed to be about five years old. She was humming an unfamiliar song to herself. "What is going on here?! It is the middle of the night! My granddaughter is sleeping!" the older fairy demanded in a loud voice. She glanced at the humming fairy and corrected herself. "*WAS* sleeping, thanks to you…!"

The grandma stopped when she saw me. Her face was blank with shock, as if the fact that there was a human in her kingdom wasn't registering properly in her brain. She stared into my eyes for a moment, her granddaughter babbling happily beside her. I stood there as still as I could, worried that any sudden movement would send them into another fit of screams. Suddenly, a spear whizzed past my head again, narrowly missing. I somehow managed to catch the weapon and twirl it between my fingers, thinking the word *freeze* repeatedly. The soldier who had thrown the spear at me stiffened immediately. All of the fairies (minus the granddaughter) started to scream again.

I stopped moving suddenly. I felt like a monster. What I was doing started to register in my brain. I started moving forward. I didn't want this.

Jolly pulled me back again, looking tired. "Carl..." She warned. But I didn't stop. I shook myself away from her grip. She didn't have a chance to grab me again since she was distracted by another soldier. The two began to fight. I didn't look back. My world was spinning. *I don't want this. I don't want this.*

I moved forward, past frozen trolls, toward Clover and Queen Gilly, who were still fighting at the center of the "war." As I walked, I looked around. A soldier was slashing at Jolly with a sword. Clover aimed a kick at her own queen. The two older fairies kept screaming as they watched the chaos ensue.

The usually peaceful kingdom was full of chaos. I shuddered. *Eyes ahead, Carl,* I told myself. Don't *look back.*

"Amy! Come back!" I heard the grandma screech from far away. I looked back. The younger fairy clumsily started to fly toward me. Amy hadn't gotten very far before she heard her grandmother's voice and stopped. She glanced back at me, curiosity written all over her face. She looked hurt, as if she was wondering why everyone was fighting. I felt terrible. I was really a monster to them.

"Stay away, little fairy," one of the trolls ordered Amy, blocking her path to me with a sword. The tiny fairy burst into tears at the sight.

"Now you get that sword away from my granddaughter!" the grandmother yelled. At the same time, a guard lunged at Jolly. Jolly slashed his sword away with her sword. Amy flew to back to her grandma, sobbing loudly now. Suddenly, it was as if the whole kingdom had woken up. Hundreds of fairies were sleepily beginning to slowly flutter out of their homes, hearing all of the shouting. Now I felt the eyes of the whole kingdom on me— children, men, women, everyone. Suddenly, I felt a thousand times worse. Everything felt far away. I was in a dream-like state, but I was having a nightmare. The kingdom erupted into chaos as all of the fairies yelled and screeched. I couldn't take it anymore.

"STOP!" I shouted helplessly. "I didn't mean to cause all of this!" The whole world around me looked like it had frozen. If you didn't know any better, you may have thought that I had used my powers by accident. Everything was silent, and everyone had stopped moving to stare at me. You could hear a pin drop. You could hear a fly buzzing.

The queen just grinned evilly, as if she had expected this. She knew I would be too soft to watch the chaos. That smile… it was so familiar… like a predator trapping prey. Something tugged at the back of my mind. Oh, yeah! That was a Drake-trademarked smile, I thought to myself. *One step ahead.* It was a mistake to come here, just like it had been a mistake to get on Drake's boat in the first place. What had I gotten myself into?

"Citizens, please remain calm. Tonight NEVER happened. Return to your homes. That is an *order.*" Queen Gilly said, clapping her hands in a brusque manner.

All of the fairies stared at her for a moment as if she had grown another head. She might as well have. I was just as confused. How could she expect everyone act as if nothing had happened? We had literally just fought a whole war! But suddenly, as if waking up from a dream, the fairies yawned, turning back to their mushrooms one by one. I relaxed a little, but I knew from experience the queen was up to something. She always was. Slowly, the glowing kingdom went to sleep. One by one, lights flickered off in the mushrooms all around the kingdom. It was as if the world had gone dark. Even the insects and birds seemed to have gone to bed, for they were all silent too. The queen's guards remained by her side, in salute.

Queen Gilly turned to the rest of the trolls with a slight smirk on her face "Carl, would you please unfreeze the rest of these guards so they can go rest?"

I obeyed. Murmurs ran through the crowd of trolls.

"You may go rest," the queen told them They looked extremely confused, but also grateful, and they didn't question their luck. They practically ran off to the castle before the queen could change her mind. They didn't care what happened after that.

When the last troll was gone, the queen turned to me and my friends. The silence was creepy. The queen just stood there, grinning evilly. I opened my mouth, then shut it. I didn't need to ask the question we were all thinking— *what happens now?* The queen snorted with smug laughter, breaking the silence. Then, without missing a beat, the queen suddenly flew over to us and grabbed me by my wrist. Somehow, her perfectly cut nails managed to dig into my skin. I yelped.

"Let me go!" I cried, my voice echoing helplessly into the black night sky. She started dragging me toward the palace. My friends yelled and grabbed onto my legs and started pulling but ended up being dragged along behind me. There was no way the queen could be this strong. She was just barely bigger than a rock! Suddenly, the queen's pretty teal eyes glinted a familiar shade of red. I froze as something clicked in my head. A flash of light blinded me, coming straight from… Queen Gilly's face? Silver and blue sparkles swirled around her, forming a familiar face. A *way* too familiar face, one that I'd know anywhere. My breath caught in my throat. My heart pounded against my chest, and I felt my eyes widen.

"Y-you…? B-but—" My voice barely came out above a whisper. I started shaking uncontrollably, stuck in Drake's iron grip yet again, surely being dragged to my doom— for real this time. My friends didn't seem to notice the sudden change, struggling to free me from her—no, his—grip. This was how the "queen" was so strong. This was why "she" didn't really care about the fairies or the trolls. How long had Drake spent researching the two kingdoms? I glared into the red eyes, holding my gaze for as long as I dared. "You monster…" I whispered.

Drake smiled evilly again, winking at me. I squirmed in his grip. The silver moonlight shimmered above us, cruel like Drake as it smirked down at me. My head was spinning

"You're just like your parents. Look where that attitude got them." He tutted, shaking his head with mock displeasure. I scowled. Drake got so close to me that I could feel his rotten breath on my face. "Listen, Carl, I may be a monster…" He hissed in my ear. "But no one will ever know." A hideous grin formed on his face.

I tried to escape his grasp, but he started to drag me away again. Suddenly, his face was covered with blinding blue light, and his face was Queen Gilly's face again. All of Drake's features had disappeared. I struggled against Drake—no, now he was the queen again. He snatched Clover's tiny wrist with his free hand, then switched his hands so that he was holding both of us with one hand. I screamed.

"No! Run!" I cried out. Clover pulled against Drake-as-Queen-Gilly, but we continued to be dragged away. I knew as well as Drake that Jolly was way too loyal to leave. She would follow us all the way down to the dungeon if she had to. I struggled even harder, but again, Drake's magical grip was like steel claws wrapped around my fist.

"You can't escape this time!" Drake called in Queen Gilly's high-pitched voice. In my head, her—no, his—teal eyes kept flashing that dreadful red. I shivered, gritting my teeth.

Drake's face swam in my head. My parents' faces, trapped, swam in my head in front of him before being overwhelmed by the bright red eyes. I was stuck with the vision in my head. I screamed, though I couldn't tell if it was in my head or out loud, and then the tears came. *Focus, Carl!* The logical part of my brain insisted. *You're the only one who can stop this!* I knew it was true. But what if I just couldn't do it? It would all be my fault. I started shaking violently.

"FREEZE!" I screamed desperately, but I couldn't find the pieces of power I needed or the right amount of concentration. It was like when I was stuck on a puzzle, I couldn't find the pieces, and just didn't have enough brainpower to figure it out anymore. Drake continued marching us toward the castle. His laughter was dark, empty, and cold, and grew louder and louder as we got closer and closer to the doors of the palace. A place that had once seemed peaceful, but now seemed daunting.

"NO! Freeze! Freeze! *FREEZE!*" I felt tears forming in my eyes. I could feel small bursts of energy bouncing off of Drake, bouncing around in my head.

"Weak!" Drake-as-Queen-Gilly jeered.

He was right. But I refused to accept it. I focused harder, my head pounding.

"NO!" I screamed helplessly as we walked into the palace. My voice got louder as my panic grew, sending more bursts of freezing energy. All were weak and had no effect, bouncing right off of Drake's magical vampire shell or whatever it was that protected him. I sent more, tears in my eyes. "FREEZE! FREEZE!"

"Weak, weak... Even weaker." Drake taunted as my magical attempts continued failing.

I growled. When he laughed, the queen's beautiful face still showed traces of the evil man behind it. It made me want to punch something. As he dragged us down several flights of stairs, his smirk widened and my fear grew, if either were even possible. We went down, down, down... closer to the dungeon I had heard so many horrifying things about.

"Listen," I got closer to his ear and spoke in a quiet voice. "Nice acting, but you don't need them. You know it's me you want. You're not their queen. You know that as well as I do. Just let them go. I'll stay here, in the dungeon. Do whatever you want with me! Just let them go, Drake!" I was almost begging. I took a deep breath to compose myself.

Drake simply laughed. His face just said, *"Predictable."*

"You're just like your parents, Carl. Too loyal." He spat, like the word was vermin.

How dare you? How dare you mention my parents like that? I thought, shaking. I really, *really* wanted to punch him right now.

"You won't leave anyone behind. You'd sacrifice yourself for them!" Drake continued in a gleeful tone that didn't match his words at all. "That's your weakness. It makes the whole 'job and legacy to kill your whole family' thing so much easier!"

Wait, *"'Job and legacy to kill my whole family' thing*?!" What was that supposed to mean? Was he being forced to kill my family? Was he being payed to do this, or had he come up with the idea of killing my family himself? Did his whole family have a history with mine, or just him? What had they done? What had he done? Why? My world was spinning and my thoughts were racing. I couldn't breathe. Just hearing the words sent a chill through my spine.

"Job and legac—" I started to ask.

"Yes, yes, that's not important right now." Drake interrupted brusquely.

I mulled over his words as I was dragged along. Did that have something to do with his history with my parents? Or was this about something else? Why didn't my parents tell me about all of this? What did they know that I didn't? I pulled away from Drake's face— his breath smelled gross. *Focus, Carl,* I told myself sternly, taking a deep breath.

I frowned. "I'm assuming that means you won't let them go," I said flatly, trying to keep my annoyance out of my voice.

Everything was quiet for a second, before Drake started talking again. "Before I finish killing off your family, I intend to hit you where it hurts. This is the revenge I have been waiting for! Your dumb grandfather will pay for what he did to mine."

Of course. Instead of answering, Drake was talking his nonsense again, targeting my confusion and frustration. Like, seriously. Revenge? My grandfather? What on Earth was he talking about, and why was he trying to kill off my family? Where was the rest of my family, my parents and my brother? How did I get myself and my friends involved in this crazy mess? I furrowed my eyebrows in confusion.

"So—"

"Yes. Whatever you're thinking, I can tell it's correct." Drake interrupted me again. I scowled. I wasn't sure which of my many questions I was going to ask, but it definitely wasn't a 'yes or no' question. He continued anyway. "Plus, if you try to escape, I'll use them like bait, like I did before." He smirked, like this whole thing was funny. "You're going down, and your family is going with you. Don't make your friends go too."

So down we went, both literally and figuratively, but this time I kept quiet. When he said down, he meant it. There were so, *so* many flights of stairs with what could have been hundreds of steps in each. My legs were growing tired, and the queen's nails (or Drake's nails, I guess) were definitely going to leave a mark.

As we walked deeper, I saw a large, chained wooden door. Pinned to it was a sign that read *Fairy dungeon.* I peered through a crack in the wood. All types of fairies dejectedly shook the miniature bars, trying to escape. Drake yanked me away from the door and we went down another flight of stairs. The further down we went the colder and sharper the air got. Down, down, down some more... At the bottom, there was another door, exactly like the first one, but this time the sign read, *HUMAN DUNGEON* in painted red letters. When I looked through the door, confused-looking humans leaned against the metal bars with wide eyes, clearly not understanding where they were or how they even got there in the first place. I bet they were also wondering why everyone around them seemed to hate them so much. Their dungeon was so cramped that I almost wondered how it was legal to treat prisoners like this at all. *Almost.* Jolly's story was still haunting me. The humans in the dungeon seemed dull, lost, with their hands shaking and eyes unblinking. For a moment, they brightened, seeing me, but as I got farther away, the dull look of no life returned.

We continued down toward the worst dungeon of them all. The scent of sweat and tears and pain and rage and hate seemed to drift up the stairs. I kept trying to pull away from Drake—who was still disguised as the fairy queen—struggling against him with all my might. I could see Clover doing the same, but Drake, even as a tiny fairy, was still too strong.

As we walked— or I guess I should say as we were dragged— deeper and deeper I mulled over Drake's words, trying to think of a way out of our current situation. Maybe even just for my friends. I would stay if need be. They didn't deserve it.

"Please." I hissed to Drake. "Just let. Them. Go."

Drake didn't answer. Instead, he turned around and punched Jolly in the face with his free hand. She groaned, slumping forward. When she straightened up, she glared at Drake, as bold as she dared against her own "queen."

"Hey!" she yelled. Drake pretended not to hear her. He definitely did, he just didn't care.

Jolly chased after us to catch up. I wished she didn't. I wish she just fell behind and stayed behind. She could still escape. Maybe Drake was right. Loyalty could be a weakness too.

We walked up to a big, heavy door, even heavier and harder than the first two. Everything reeked of must. Drake threw the door open, still laughing like a crazy person. He *was* a crazy person.

"Drake! Let them go!" I cried out as loudly as I dared, tears now streaming down my face. Drake, still laughing maniacally, tossed us into the cell closest to the entrance. The air was damp and cold and tasted rotten, and everything was so gross and terrible that I can't even describe it. And then, just like that, Drake was gone.

I looked both ways, in every direction around me. The prison was filled with trolls sitting in their jail cells— skinny trolls, burly trolls, tall trolls, short trolls, you name it. Most looked angry. I had never seen so many trolls in one place. That was a sentence I never thought I'd say. I peered into the cell next to us. Inside was a giant troll with huge muscles. He was definitely the largest and strongest-looking troll in the dungeon. I wondered what he had done to end up in prison. Maybe I didn't want to know. I was surprised that he wasn't trying to escape. He looked like he could bust out of the cell in about two seconds, bending the bars easily. So why didn't he?

"Hello?" I called, to see if any of the trolls in the dungeon would answer. I caught our dangerous-looking neighboring troll staring at me. "Um...hi...?" I greeted, suddenly timid. I took a deep breath. The troll snorted gruffly. "Uh... Why don't you try and twist the bars open? You look... er... very strong...?" Some of the other trolls seemed surprised that I would even dare to speak that way.

"You calling us weak, newbie?" his gruff voice asked. "You don't think we've tried, eh?" The words had an edge to them. I didn't want to get on this troll's bad side. I didn't mean to judge a book by its cover, but he'd already been locked up, and he looked dangerous. *What has he done to get thrown in prison? I* wondered again. I didn't ask out loud, thinking it might be rude, although now that I thought about it, there were probably no manners in a dungeon. After all, the other trolls seemed to all be so blunt and gruff and... even dull, lifeless.

"No, no, of course I wasn't! I was just... um...."

The troll snorted again, and similar snorts came from other surrounding cells. "You're just, um?" The same troll echoed in a mocking voice. "Okay, then. Relax newbie, it was a joke."

Oh. I tried to laugh too, but my mouth felt dry. Jolly elbowed me in the side.

"Heh heh, um..." I tried a fake laugh, but I wasn't great at those. The troll didn't seem to buy it either, but he just leaned against the metal bars.

"What would a human like you be doing' in our nasty little space down here? Don't humans get their own dungeon?"

"And what's the fairy doing here?" A different troll drawled. He had a strange voice, a heavily accented type of snarl.

In response to their questions, I just shrugged. "Don't know," I replied, even though I did know. I was trying to act casual, almost bored, just like them. "The queen said this dungeon had more security. She really wanted me here, said I was more sneaky and clever than the others." I decided not to mention that the real queen was who-knows-where, and the person—or vampire— who was disguised as her was a psychopath who had a grudge against me and really wanted me dead. I knocked against the bar again. "Um... but why can't we all just escape?" I wondered out loud. I knew it was a stupid question, but still.

"Magic, duh," the troll said quietly, bitterness in his voice. "Those bars are tougher than they look." He turned away and didn't say anymore, leaning against the walls. I shook the bars, but the troll was right. They were rough and heavy, clearly made by magic, impossible to break down. I looked to Jolly and Clover, who seemed to be frozen in shock. *We may as well get comfortable,* I thought to myself. At least for now...we were stuck.

***

Chapter Ten

The Trio in Troll Prison

I looked around at the other trolls in the dungeon as they leaned against the bars or sat in their cells, rocking back and forth. I observed their expressions. They looked angry and trapped, like they were wondering when they could just get out and get it over with, which made me even more nervous to be near them. I was stuck wondering what they'd done wrong. The cell belonging to me and my friends was right next to the door, but it still seemed so far out of reach. I studied the metal key ring, which hung against the wall directly across from our cell, and sighed. The keys jingled softly as they dangled below it. I pulled on the bars with all of my might, banging on them. I even convinced my friends to help at one point, though they were doubtful. I even asked Clover to try to fly through the bars, but when she tried there was a flash of light, and what seemed to be an invisible force field stopped her. So instead I banged on the bars again and again. It was a good way to get my anger out.

"Cut it out," a troll on the other side of the dungeon called in an annoyed voice.

"It's loud," another added pointedly, leaning against the bars of her cell. "And annoying."

Yet another troll said, "You've been trying for an hour. It's never going to work."

"I know." I said, shaking them harder. "Isn't it worth another try though?"

At that, the trolls in the dungeon shared a collective groan.

"Definitely not. Don't you think we've tried?" That was our neighbor, the first troll that had spoken. "This dungeon is so secure it would be foo—"

"Foolish to escape." I finished and turned away. That was what Jolly had told me. But I couldn't give up. I really needed to escape before Drake tried something. Suddenly, I heard a voice behind me and turned to see a familiar pair of evil red eyes watching me from outside of the cell. How ironic. I snarled.

My friends each gave me a weird look that clearly said *"Who is that?"*

I waved them away and focused on Drake. *"I'll tell you later."*

"Poor little Carl, and his poor little friends," he sang. "Trapped in a cell. You do know that this is all your fault, right Carl?"

I looked away. "Leave me alone, Drake." I snapped, ignoring the short pang of guilt. I couldn't help but feel that he was right.

The vampire smirked again. "Hmm, let me think... Nah, it's way more fun to make fun of you." He laughed. Drake pressed his face against the bar, uncomfortably close, and his voice slipped to a giddy whisper. "Before I kill you."

I shivered and inhaled again, staring the creepy vampire in the eyes. "What do you want, Drake?" I asked, trying to sound confident. I needed to escape before Drake did something bad to me or my friends.

"Tomorrow, I have permission from the queen to go on a little... *walk* with you. There's some stuff we need to discuss," he said in his normal voice. He grinned his evil grin. I shifted uncomfortably.

That's what you think. I will find a way out of here. I glared at Drake.

Drake stared back at me, a smug look on his face. "See you tomorrow." He grinned, and then he waved, bending each of his fingers. He then snapped his fingers, and suddenly he was gone. The prison immediately broke out into a fit of whispers.

One troll asked, "Who was that man? What did he say? Where did he go?"

"What did that human do to get in here?" asked yet another troll.

"Nothing," I wanted to say. Instead, I kept quiet.

"He seems like trouble," muttered a fourth troll

"He definitely is, if he's here." That troll gave me a look. I shifted uncomfortably

"Did anyone notice there's two others in his cell? A fairy and a troll?"

"Yeah! But I can't see them. What are they doing here?" The troll bent over to see. I buried my face in my hands.

Jolly put her hand on my shoulder, and I looked up. "Ignore them," she said, and that was all. Her voice was oddly quiet, softer than usual, so only I could hear her say, "I used to have to deal with them all of the time. They'll leave you alone if you ignore them." Her voice broke.

I looked up at her. Her eyes were teary and haunted, much like mine. She had bad memories of this place too. Maybe that was why she seemed so worried when she heard that I was to be sent there. I put my hand on her shoulder. "You… you used to work in the dungeon?" I asked quietly.

She sat down on the floor, legs crossed, and rocked back and forth with her eyes closed. She didn't answer for a moment.

"Yes," she finally answered as she buried her head in her hands. Her voice was hoarse as she continued. "You should have seen them, yelling at me, cursing me, throwing things at me… and I couldn't do anything to help them." She looked down again. Backward…forward… backward… "You know, I didn't want to work in the castle. I didn't want to be a toll troll either. I did it all for my family," she continued softly.

I sat down next to her. I didn't know what to say, but thankfully, Clover flew over, interrupting us with questions so I didn't have to say anything at all. "Who was that man?"

Jolly looked up at that and tilted her head, looking at me pointedly.

I shook my head. "Nobody," I said flatly. I felt something light on my shoulder again, and it took me a few seconds to realize it was Clover's tiny hand, trying to comfort me.

"Carl," the tiny fairy pressed softly. "Was that—"

But I shook my head again, firmer this time. "Nobody," I repeated. Even I heard the hard edge in my voice. I was snapping at my friends, though they'd done nothing wrong. It *was* none of their business… but everything that had happened to them was still my fault. I buried my head in my hands again. *This IS your fault*, a familiar voice in my head said. *You're a terrible friend.* The harsh words made me wince. It took me a while before I realized that it was my own voice. This whole situation was definitely messing with my head. I felt tears in my eyes.

"I'm sorry. It's just… this… it's… everything that has happened to you both has been because of me." I said softly. Drake was right. "It's all my fault."

"Carl, it's not—" Clover started softly, reaching for me again. I pulled away from her, turning so she wouldn't see the tears in my eyes.

"It is!" I cut her off, staring longingly at the key hanging across the hall—so close but so far out of my reach. I sighed to myself. It was like an adventure story: the main character and his friends are trapped in a prison. But suddenly, he gets freed by a spy or tricks the captor into escaping. I waited for a moment, imagining if one of those things would really happen. It seemed childish, I knew. No spy was coming to save me. I had no tricks left up my sleeve. Just because my life had somewhat become an adventure story recently, it didn't mean that there was always going to be a happy ending.

Suddenly, I heard a ringing bell, metal clanging, and the now-familiar flutter of wings outside of the prison. But it wasn't Drake again, disguised as the queen. Instead, a small fairy with a ponytail of long, wavy black hair and tired, silver eyes flew through the door. She was wheeling in a cart of troll-sized dinner trays using the same telekinesis-style fairy magic I'd seen Clover and the "queen" use earlier. I'd learned to just roll with it.

My stomach growled. I realized I had lost track of time. I hadn't realized how hungry I was. It must have been morning already, I guessed. That meant it was time for breakfast.

The food on the trays looked bumpy and weird, but the other trolls were watching it with hungry eyes. It smelled fine, so I guessed it would be okay to try. Would Drake feed me something that could poison a human? Nah, he wanted to kill me himself.

Suddenly, Clover darted toward the front of our cell, a strange look in her eyes. She tried to push through the bars again, but she was stopped by the weird force field thingy again. The fairy with the food picked up one of the trays, struggling under its weight, but when she saw Clover, she was so startled that she put it right back down again. "C-clover?" She asked softly.

I turned to Clover and tilted my head, but she was already rushing forward joyfully. "Abby!"

The other fairy, Abby, flew through the bars and tackled Clover in a tight bear hug. Several trolls grunted in protest, still waiting for their food.

Who is that? I wondered. *And how did she get through the force field thing?* Maybe she worked in the castle. She did bring food for us, after all. But she seemed to know Clover.

"Oh my gosh! Clover! I'm so happy to see you!" Abby said tearfully. "I've missed you so much!"

Clover hugged Abby back. "I've missed you too!"

"Wait—" Abby pulled out of the hug and her face shifted into an angry scowl. She looked around the cell, and her eyes landed on me. Her scowl deepened. She turned to Clover again. "HOW COULD YOU? YOU BETRAYED OUR KIND! YOU HURT OUR QUEEN!"

I covered my ears. "Uh, what if I told you that… that wasn't actually your queen that she hurt?" I offered timidly, trying to be helpful.

They didn't seem to hear my actual words—just my voice. Abby whirled towards me with a wild rage in her eyes. "No one asked you, *human!*"

"Chill, Abby," Clover said, holding the other fairy back. "He's my friend. He's really nice." She looked directly into my eyes and nodded.

"Oh, yeah," Abby said sarcastically. "It's so 'nice' how he landed you in jail!"

I winced, but Clover hugged Abby, laughing and crying at the same time. "You're amazing," Clover said softly. "I love that you care."

Abby started whispering in Clover's ear. I leaned into listen. While it seemed as if Abby didn't want *me* specifically to hear her words, it definitely wasn't something personal. That wasn't the kind of thing you share in a dungeon surrounded by criminals. So I listened:

"Look, Clover. If you need to escape, I can let you out."

Wait, what? Abby was willing to break the laws of her own kingdom? She seemed like such a rule follower! But still, that was great, because that's what I wanted! Clover could escape and go back to her family and friends.

Yet she looked doubtful. "But—"

I groaned out loud and marched toward them. Abby glanced at me warily, but she let me talk. Perhaps she knew that I would agree with her. After all, Clover needed someone else to convince her. "Oh, come on, Clover! That's great news! You do not deserve to be here and I can't let you stay. Please go with her? For me?" I begged, lowering my voice. Abby looked annoyed that I'd eavesdropped, but for once she seemed to agree with me. Clover clearly didn't.

"Carl, I can't do that." She sighed, turning to me. She turned back to Abby, who was practically shaking with anger. "Abby, it's just..." She sighed. "Carl's my friend. My only friend besides *you*, Abby. He helped me, and now he needs my help. I can't just leave him." She perched herself on my shoulder where she fit so perfectly.

I sighed. She really didn't belong with me. It was far too dangerous. But I guess she didn't belong in her own kingdom either. Could I really convince her to save herself? She didn't know what plans Drake actually had for us. Even if she did, would she still stay? I started to speak again, but grouchy voices from the other cells quickly cut me off.

"This reunion is lovely and all, but quit the chatter! We're hungry!"

Several other prisoners shouted their agreement, so Abby decided to hurry up.

"Okay... whatever you do, Clover, just remember... I love you." She sighed and squeezed Clover's hand. "And... I'm sorry."

She flew back through the bars and grabbed two dinner trays. When she knocked on one of the bars three times, the bars magically shifted open, creating a gap just big enough for the trays to fit through. I stared for a moment. I'd learned not to question anything, but seriously, *how did she do that?* She handed one tray to Clover and one to Jolly. She gave me a look but flew past me without handing me one. I guess I deserved that. Either way, I'd probably get one later. Besides, food wasn't exactly on my list of priorities at the moment.

Abby then flew around, handing out meals to all of the other trolls with her magic. She passed our cell again and looked like she was about to leave.

"Wait! Carl didn't get a meal," Clover called.

Abby stared at me. I stared back at her, and my stomach roared again. I hadn't had real food since I'd eaten those sandwiches with Jolly on her bridge—before I knew how much of a mess this would be. My stomach growled again, dragging me back to the moment in the jail cell, where Abby was looking back and forth between me and her last lunch tray.

"B-but... he—" She blinked. She looked like she was seriously considering leaving me without food, but she saw Clover's glare and hurried over. The bars magically parted so she could bring the tray into the cell and slap it into my hands. I almost dropped it, but I caught it just in time.

Abby hugged Clover one more time and whispered something else in her ear. I leaned in to eavesdrop but couldn't hear anything. I didn't want to disturb them, so I sat down on the floor and picked at the weird-looking food. It was no Golden Gaile sandwich, but it wasn't half bad either.

Abby was probably still trying to convince Clover to escape with her. But when Clover shook her head and Abby glanced at me, pouting again, I knew it was no use. Abby grabbed Clover's hands and held them close. Before I could say anything else, Abby quickly flew away, leaving us with our dinners. Clover sunk to the floor, looking sad.

I waited a moment or two before gently asking, "Clover, why didn't you go with her?"

Clover blinked rapidly, trying to hide the tears that I knew were there. "You know why, Carl."

"Okay, but who was that?" I bent down gently to see her better.

She looked away from me. I thought she might not answer, but after a moment, I heard quiet words.

"She's... She's my stepsister."

Her words took me a couple seconds to fully comprehend. When I did, I was speechless for a moment. "Clo, I—"

"No, it's okay. Really, it's...fine. Really." She stared at the floor.

I stared at the back of her head. I still heard her quiet sobs. She didn't seem fine. It wasn't fine at all. But there was no right thing to say, only an infinite amount of wrong answers.

"Uh... She didn't seem to like me much." I commented lamely, still totally flabbergasted. There was no answer. "Oh... Clover, I..."

"Carl, I'm serious. I'll be fine."

I hesitated, staring at my feet. I remembered my brother, and how much I'd missed him. I'd never even told my friends that he existed, but I remembered every detail: his honey-colored eyes, his fluffy, chocolate-brown-hair, his innocent laugh... but he was gone. He was with my parents on the boat. Unless Drake got him too... but that would be worse than any other outcome—a tortured, haunted life.

"I'm really sorry, Clover," Jolly said, speaking up for the first time in a while.

I felt a pang of guilt. Even though my friends had said otherwise, I still felt like it was all my fault. If I'd realized that the queen was actually Drake sooner, we wouldn't be in this dungeon.

"Me too." I said softly. "I'm so sorry." Even though I'd meant the words for Clover, I realized that the words had come out for both of them, Jolly and Clover.

"It'll be okay," Clover repeated, more to herself than either of us. "I'll be fine."

"You could have taken her offer," I said quietly. "I wouldn't have minded. You could be free. That's what I want. I want the best for you. Go back to your family, your friends."

"No, Carl, you don't understand. I don't have many friends. I guess I was a little...different when I was young," Clover said quietly. "I was clever, but never popular. My birth dad ran away. My stepdad is nice, and so is my mom, and I have Amy, but..." She looked down. "That's it. You *rescued* me, Carl, not the other way around. You helped me, you saved me, and... you care. I need to stay with you." She closed her eyes. I stared down at my feet.

"It's not your fault, Carl," Jolly whispered to me so that even Clover couldn't hear. It was like she'd read my mind.

"I'm sorry." I repeated, unable to think of anything else to say.

But it looked like Clover didn't want any more apologies. "I'm *fine*."

She just stared at her food, waiting on its shiny tray. I decided to give it a rest. She definitely wasn't fine, but I knew that I would only make it worse.

My food suddenly seemed bland. The only sounds I heard were some trolls talking quietly on the other side of the dungeon and loud chewing. The prison was always quiet and always terrible. I curled up into a little ball, and started rocking my body again, back and forth, back and forth. I leaned back against the cold cell wall and kept rocking, my eyes closed, back and forth, back and forth.

Finally, I heard a whisper. "Hey, Carl?" I looked up to see Jolly sliding closer to me.

"Yeah? Everything okay?"

"Oh, yeah, I just wanted to ask you a question." She smirked. I tilted my head, surprised.

"Oh. Okay. Anything." I smiled at her, even though I was kind of confused.

"What has to be broken before you can use it?"

A riddle? A classic one too. I rolled my eyes, but before I could stop it, a playful smile covered my whole face. "I don't know, what?"

Jolly grinned back at me. "An egg!" she answered. Despite everything that had happened, I burst out laughing. Jolly started laughing as well.

"Okay, okay. My turn," I said, grinning, racking my brain for my best riddle. Pretty soon, I was laughing harder than I'd laughed in a while. Clover remained quiet, just watching us, but pretty soon, she couldn't hold it in anymore, and then she was laughing too. It almost seemed impossible to be sad in that moment. It seemed so easy to forget the bad stuff.

So we did. We tried to forget that we were in prison, forget how sad everything was, and just forget. And it was so easy to just hide from everything because we had found a little happiness to share. It restored some of my faith in humans and fairies and trolls, and it restored my belief in the possibility of our friendship—I'd been losing more and more of it since I heard the story of the war with the fairies. Even some of the trolls in nearby cells heard some of our jokes and started laughing too. The jokes and riddles spread through the dungeon like wildfire. The jokes were passed around the prison and pretty soon, everyone was laughing! Some of the trolls were even sending jokes back to us!

***

Just then, Abby flew back into the prison in a huge panic.

I seemed to be the only one who saw her, so I held up my hand. "Everyone shush for a moment!" The laughter died down almost immediately. I gave Abby a thumbs up and a smile that she didn't return. She looked pale and terrified.

"The prison is on FIRE!" Abby yelled. "EVERYBODY EVACUATE THE PRISON NOW!"

Then, I heard the screams. I looked around and saw a golden flame in the corner of the prison, getting larger and larger. I smelled smoke. I screamed and immediately regretted it. I shouldn't have wasted the breath. The smoke was breaking through and choking everyone. I coughed, feeling the heat on my face. Everyone else was panicking.

"What?!" Jolly yelled. "What—How? Someone would have had to set the fire. But who? Why?" I had one guess: Drake, for sure. I guess he wasn't waiting to kill me after all. He'd changed his mind yet again.

I heard complaining from the other cells:

"Help!"

"Let us out!"

"What's going on?!"

"It's hot!"

"Fire! Fire in the dungeon!"

"Are you going to come help us or leave us to burn?!"

This seemed to knock some sense into Abby. "Uh... just hang on, guys!" She darted from cage to cage, opening doors and freeing trolls. Only a few thanked her. Most of them just stampeded past her, screaming things like:

"Freedom!"

"Run!"

"Fire in the dungeon!"

When all of the trolls were free except me, Clover, and Jolly, Abby zoomed straight past us to the huge prison door and slammed it open with the remainder of her strength. She began to slide through, and that's when I realized that she had completely forgotten us. Whether she left us on purpose or by accident, the flames were getting closer. The smoke went up my nose and in my mouth. Clover coughed, and I heard her whimper. Abby winced and stopped, but she didn't turn around. The terror in Clover's eyes was too much. I needed to call out to Abby, even if I used up all of my remaining air. Drake really needed to make up his mind as to whether I would end up dead or alive. I wasn't about to give up after all I'd been through.

I took a huge deep breath and shouted, "ABBY".

***

Chapter Eleven

Jailbreak

Abby turned around and glanced at me harshly. I burst into a coughing fit.

"Abby, you forgot us," Clover managed to choke out.

"Clover, please," Abby pleaded, her voice strained. "I'm under strict orders to leave that…" She paused, and hesitated. "…boy here."

I wasn't surprised, but Clover clearly was.

"Orders? Orders from who?" The tiny fairy grabbed my sweaty hand.

I think I already knew. "Was it orders from your queen?" I asked quietly. "She's… she's the one that set fire to the dungeon?"

Abby looked down and didn't answer. Clover looked up at me in shock. She then shook her head slowly, but it looked forced.

"How did you…" Abby hesitated, looking startled. Then she sighed. "If you must know, yes."

Clover started shaking, her eyes wide. "No, the queen wouldn't do that. The queen would never."

Even Clover sounded doubtful. She didn't trust her own queen anymore. She didn't even trust herself. And it was Drake's fault, as well as mine, she didn't know who the "queen" really was. Her statement remained unanswered. Now wasn't the time to tell her. I didn't know if I ever could tell either of them. Even though they knew about Drake, if they knew that he was pretending to be their queen the entire time… I mean, it would certainly clear some things up for them, but I didn't want them any more involved with Drake than they already were.

I turned toward Abby. "Look, Abby, I know I'm hu—"

"Save it!"

"We can set aside our differences…"

"No, we can't!" she yelled. She lowered her voice again. "I'm sorry."

Now she seemed to feel guilty. I knew she really was sorry. And I realized that she was right. We couldn't set aside our differences. It wasn't her fault. Humans betrayed her kind, and she couldn't trust me, because of who and what I was, what I'd always been. I guess the real queen just didn't want her people to get hurt all over again. Abby couldn't betray her queen, and she wouldn't. It wasn't her fault that she believed Drake. I had trusted him blindly too. And now my friends were in danger of getting barbecued. I started shaking again. I was a villain to them just because of what I was. But a villain is just a victim whose story hasn't been told yet, right?

Right?

"Guys—" Clover started.

"Clover, you could come with me!" Abby said, cutting her stepsister off.

"Only if you let my friends go too!"

"Clover, please!" Abby yelled. "You know I can't do that!" She looked down and her voice came out as barely a whisper. "I'm not allowed. I can't betray the queen. I'm not like you! I'm not... brave."

Clover smiled sadly for a second. "Abby, you are the bravest person I know."

They stared at each other, smiling for a moment. The moment was over when Clover sighed and looked down.

"Clover, go with her. Please," I begged, hanging my head.

The tiny fairy shook her head stubbornly. "Only. If. You. Come. With. Me!"

"I... I can't." I said, tears forming in my eyes. I coughed again. The smoke was coming for me and my friends, threatening to suffocate us all.

"But why?" Clover asked softly. "Why not?!"

"The queen wants me dead." I said, but that wasn't exactly the truth. The words suddenly sounded lame, empty, hanging in the smoky air around us. Just from the way I said that it seemed obvious that the queen wasn't what was troubling me.

Clover seemed to notice the emptiness in my words. "She's not *your* queen! Why should you listen to her?"

"Because *that's not the queen*!" I shouted suddenly, the words bursting out of me like an erupting volcano. It felt so good to admit the truth. I don't know why I didn't tell them sooner. I just couldn't bring myself to explain. It would only endanger them more. I'd been horrible to them, I know. I'd been lying to them. But now that the jumble of words had started, I couldn't stop. "I *have to* listen. He'll find me. He always does." I rambled. Now I was shaking, on the edge of a total breakdown. My friends stared at me. "I just found out. It's my fault. I shouldn't have… I'm sorry guys!" I choked out.

"What—who?" Jolly asked. She hesitated. Her voice came out hoarse. "If it's not Queen Gilly… who… who is that?"

"Th-the man with the red eyes, disguised as the queen! He's… a vampire, who wants…my whole family dead!" I confessed. Once I'd started, I couldn't stop rambling. I quickly spilled out what I had known but kept secret, feeling so free but also trapped at the same time.

"Wha…" Clover looked confused. "Drake? The guy you told us about?" I nodded.

"I knew she wasn't acting like herself!" Jolly said triumphantly. She was trying to bring up the mood, but we all knew that her words were only half-hearted. She sighed dejectedly. "Sorry. Bad timing."

"Anyway…" Abby said uncomfortably. "Clover, please. I have an offer for you!"

Clover looked toward me, questioning, as if to ask whether she could listen to Abby's offer was or not. I was startled for a moment. I hadn't realized that I was the leader of our little group. I guess it kind of made sense. So I nodded. The answer was of course! I wanted her out of this prison, didn't I? I watched the flames out of the corner of my eye. The fire was moving very slowly, like Drake was taunting us, but the smoke was all around us already. We had to figure something out quickly.

"What's your offer?" Clover asked reluctantly, looking from me to Abby. She was a loyal friend, but almost too loyal. I really was just trying to help her.

"Come with me! Leave your friend…" She hesitated. "…and the human," She added

I grunted. I was her friend too, and Abby knew it. She would take any chance to mock me, wouldn't she? I took a deep breath. I knew that I shouldn't let it bother me.

"You should go, Clover. It will be okay." I said quietly.

"It's her choice, not yours," Abby snapped.

I gritted my teeth. I'd made it clear that I was on her side. I'd already proven that I was different from other humans, and that I hadn't really fought with the actual queen. I turned back to Abby and blinked at her. "Why do you hate me so much Abby?" I just had to ask. I'd tried to ignore it, since I knew the answer as to why she hated *humans* as a whole. But I was different, and she knew it. There was just no good reason to hate me specifically.

She hesitated for a moment, clearly caught off guard by the question. "I... I just do." She answered, looking away. "Anyway, Clover, what do you think?"

It will be okay, I thought, leaning against the cold, stone wall of the cell. I was trying to direct my thoughts at Clover, like if I thought them hard enough, they'd be true. *It will be okay. It will be okay.* I looked back at Clover. *It will be okay.*

Clover glanced at me, hesitated, then nodded sadly. "Okay," she whispered sadly, closing her eyes. "Goodbye, Carl." She gave me a sad smile, hugged my finger and flew toward the bars of our cell.

"You made the right choice," Abby whispered, grabbing Clover's hand. "Thank you, Clover. I wish I could be brave like you."

Clover didn't respond. A spark of magical electricity flew between their hands. I realized that the magical sparks of electricity were probably magic switching from Abby to Clover, and that was how they got through the bars of the cell. Clover was silent as she flew through the gap in the bars. Neither stepsister said anything else as they left, and Jolly and I couldn't do anything other than just helplessly watch them leave.

Not long after they had both left, everything got worse. The fire wouldn't wait much longer. It was consuming everything that remained in the other side of the dungeon, which was nothing but ashes now. I collapsed on the floor. My vision blurred. I pushed myself up and looked around desperately for something, *anything* that could get us out. But I couldn't think or even see. Everything was red hot pain rushing to my head. The smoke curled around my lungs, and my face felt hot from the heat of the flames.

"Jolly?" I rasped. I saw the dark, blurry blob that was Jolly, looking around through the thick layer of smoke.

"Carl, are you all right?" she asked in a low voice. Obviously, trolls could hold their breath longer than humans. I guess that kind of made sense. But it sounded like even she was running out of air.

My heart thumped against my chest. "No. But that's not our biggest problem right now. How are we going to get out of here?"

"I think I can help with that!" a very familiar and cheerful voice said as the door to the dungeon swung open. A tiny, blurry speck fluttered into my vision. I squinted into the smoke. Wait... I gasped loudly, even though it sent sharp pains through my throat.

"Clover?" I called in a hoarse voice. "You came back for us!"

I heard another gasp from behind me as Jolly moved closer to see her. The tiny speck that was Clover flew toward us.

"Of course I did!" she said cheerfully. "I could never abandon you two. I was thinking... and then I suddenly got an idea! If I escaped, you could escape too!"

"Oh my gosh! Clover, you're a genius!" I cried out. Why hadn't I thought of that? It was the perfect plan. At that moment, I really wanted to hug her.

"I could never leave you!" the tiny fairy declared.

I smiled to myself. "Where is your stepsister?" I asked. "Does she know you're here?"

The tiny fairy looked down guiltily. "She's at her house. She invited me over. She's... making breakfast. I... asked her if I could go clean up. She had a room already prepared for me and everything, but I..." she sighed. "That should give us enough time to" —tears filled her eyes—"escape."

"Oh." I pursed my lips, regretting asking at all. I decided that it would be best to change topics as soon as possible. Of course Abby wouldn't let Clover come back for us. Had I really thought otherwise? "Well...Thank you, Clover. You're the best!" I told her softly, smiling. She perked up again.

"Can you help us?" Jolly asked.

"Why do you think I came?" Clover grinned as she flew across the dungeon. Using her magic, she lifted the key hanging on the grimy stone wall. She squinted with obvious struggle and she grunted.

I picked up on that immediately. "Clover? What's wrong?" I squinted into the smoke.

"That key... is really heavy!" Clover grunted.

"Okay, but... you've got this, right?" I asked with concern.

She coughed. "I don't know, Carl. Even magic has its limits."

And she was right; the key was meant for a large keyhole, a troll sized one. And it was made of really heavy, solid metal. Not meant for a fairy, even one with telekinesis.

"Oh, come on, Clover!" I rasped. "You... can... do...it..." Clover coughed again and grunted with determination. She slowly fluttered to our cell, still holding up the key with her magic. She magically slammed the key into the hole in the lock of the heavy cell door then flew over to grab the key in her tiny hands. She twisted it and yanked on the key until it turned and unlocked the door with a click. Jolly and I pushed on the now unlocked door. It swung open.

The three of us sprinted to the dungeon's door. My legs felt like jelly, and red-hot pain pounded in my head, but I still ran. I couldn't stop. My shoes fell off of my feet and tumbled down the stairs, leaving my feet bare, but the fire was coming quickly and they would probably burn fast. Anyway, I didn't have time to go and get them. I'd just have to be barefoot for a while. I could get new shoes *after* I saved my friends, and hopefully my parents.

The rest of the prison was eaten by the fire, and suddenly, I had an idea. I knew that the smoke was messing with my brain, but I just stopped running from the fire. I turned back to the bright red and orange flame as it devoured the castle, wondering if I could stop it before it hurt anyone else. My friends immediately started protesting, but their words didn't reach my brain, and I didn't turn back around and run away.

"Freeze," I rasped, as bold as I could be, staring directly at the fire. It immediately stopped its creepy, taunting dance toward me and my friends.

As we were running up the stairs, I tripped and collapsed at the top. I tried to get up, but my legs wouldn't work anymore. I looked over my shoulder. I know I lost my concentration but the fire stayed frozen somehow. *Ha!* I thought to myself. I smirked into the darkness that was slowly surround me, picturing Drake's angry face, growling in defeat, and my grin got bigger. But even a small victory is a victory nonetheless. Take that, Drake.

Then, my world faded into gray and black.

***

"Carl! Carl!" Familiar voices called out to me. They seemed like they were coming from far away, muffled as if I were underwater, and for a moment it almost seemed as if I *was* underwater, drowning in a sea of black and gray. It was calm and peaceful— no attacks, no hate, and no Drake—the kind of place where you could forget who you were. I couldn't remember my own name. But rough hands shook me, calling out to me again, so I opened my eyes, blinking.

Suddenly, everything came rushing back into my head. I was Carl, on a journey to save my parents, hated by everyone, wide awake once again. I looked down the stairs of the fairy palace, worried that the fire would come raging up, devouring everything in its path, but somehow, it was still frozen, and everything remained calm for another minute. Then I heard noises behind me. Heavy footsteps pounded up to me.

"Who are you?" the deep voice spoke from behind me, making me and my friends jump. "What are you doing here? And... what on *Earth* is wrong with that *fire*?" I could tell that the person behind me was a soldier. He sounded suspicious, which made sense, of course. My heart was pounding, and my hands were sweaty. I stuffed them into my pockets so he wouldn't see.

"I'm... a messenger." I lied quickly. My friends nodded approvingly. "I'm delivering a message to Queen Gilly." I took a deep breath.

He didn't seem to be buying it. I didn't want to turn around to face him, because I wasn't sure if he would recognize me or not. I quickly peeked over my shoulder, and decided to risk it. He didn't look familiar. Maybe he hadn't been on shift last night. He studied me for a second, and I held my breath. He frowned, but I let out the breath I'd been holding. At least he didn't seem to recognize my face.

"What's your name?" The soldier sniffed suspiciously. My heart was pounding so hard that I was surprised he couldn't hear it thumping against my chest.

"Name? Of course, my name!" I rambled, trying to buy some time. The soldier tapped his foot impatiently. "My name is... uh..." The soldier's eyes were staring into my soul, into my lies. "Uh..." My world was spinning, and I felt dizzy. "Uh... Jean!" I yelled suddenly. "My name is Jean!"

That was first name that came into my mind? *That's just great,* I thought, annoyed with myself. Why was I even *thinking* about him?

The soldier just raised grunted. He still didn't sound convinced. "And you're a messenger… Jean?"

Perfect, I thought, *now I'm Jean, named after my horrible uncle, in an unfamiliar kingdom where I'm likely to die.*

***

Chapter Twelve

Crelish

Unfortunately for me, it was too late to change my lie, so I stuck with it. "Yeah... I'm a messenger!" I said. "And my name is Jean, because, uh, why wouldn't it be? Yep, *Jean*, that's me..." My voice was high and weak, but I was smiling a huge, fake, nervous smile. "Um, so... I'm delivering a message! To Queen Gilly. Um, so—"

"Yeah, right!" The soldier interrupted, glaring at me. Suddenly, he was chuckling, but it wasn't a happy sound. He made a face before continuing. "You're a... human!"

"Yes, I am, but—" I tried. But he didn't let me explain—just like Abby, just like the queen, just like everyone else. I was getting really tired of that.

"We're at *war*, in case you forgot!" he yelled. "Besides, there's a human named Carl who's sneaking around here somewhere. What if that's you?" The guard scoffed, looking ready to call in reinforcements.

Thankfully, Clover flew forward, calmly placing herself in front of me. "He's with me, and he really needs to deliver an important message to the queen," she explained calmly. "And I'm sure you would not like to get in the way of royal business."

The guard still didn't look convinced. "Miss, I have no intention of 'getting in the way of royal business.' But *he* is clearly terrible." He looked me up and down and scoffed again. "How he even convinced you to help him in the first place is beyond me."

"He didn't." She put her hands on her hips defiantly, glaring at the soldier. "I made my own choice. You cannot judge someone by how they look, and you cannot tell me what to do."

He snorted again. "*Suuure*." He rolled his eyes. "You've got some attitude." He smirked down at the tiny fairy. "What's your name, miss?"

"I'm... Abby." Clover hung her head.

The guard raised his eyebrows. "Well, *Abby*, I was going to suggest joining our team of fairies here in the palace, but I've heard your name around. And your shift is over now. So if you don't leave and take your human...Jean... with you, I'll have to remove you myself." He then opened his mouth to call out to the other trolls.

Just then, Jolly marched in front of me, less calm, shoving Clover out of the way. "No, sir, as I'm sure any *fool* like *you* can *see*, he's with *me*!" She roared, glaring at the guard. His mouth snapped shut immediately. I'd never seen Jolly get this angry. "Doubting your safety around him is doubting *us*. Now please let him be so he can deliver his message!" The guard froze; he didn't answer or move.

"And, of course, keep in mind that we will *not* hurt you." I chimed in.

"*I* may." Jolly said in a loud and not-helpful-at-all voice. I pushed her out of the way.

"Honestly, I'm just here with news about the war, honest. *WE*"—I glared at Jolly—"are not here to hurt you." I told him kindly. Jolly snarled at me, but I barely noticed the menacing sound.

"Yeah. Yeah. News. War." The guard said nervously, nodding quickly. He was clearly afraid to mess with Jolly any more.

Jolly put her hands on her hips and gave the guard a death glare. He nearly fell over. "So we won't have ANY TROUBLE?" she asked, her voice rising.

The guard quickly shook his head like his life depended on it. "No. I-I mean... well, yes, b-but—" he stammered.

Jolly pounced immediately. "So we will have trouble?" The guard shook his head again.

I shivered, imagining what would happen if Jolly decided to betray me. I wouldn't be able to escape then. She would never do that, I reminded myself, so there was no point to these thoughts at all. She cared. She didn't like eating humans. She understood me. She'd betray her own kind to help me. I shivered again, this time for a different reason.

"No! No, no, no! Not at all! It's just... it's just that the queen, she... she's not here right now." The guard squeaked. "She went to look for the other human boy, um, I'm sure she just didn't know you were coming... and, uh... well, you can wait for her to get back, or..." He suggested.

"No, that's okay!" I interrupted. "I'll just write it down and leave it in her room, if that's okay?"

"Yes! Uh, of course, sir, her office is that way." The soldier pointed to a fancy door in the long hallway.

"Okay! That works just fine." I smiled at the soldier. "Thank you for your help!" I called, dragging Jolly away. The guard quickly turned around and left the hallway,

"Thank you for your help," Jolly mimicked mockingly, with a huge eyeroll for dramatic effect. I elbowed her gently in the side. She turned to me, but she was grinning now.

We turned around and ran out of the palace. The lush green grass was soft and comfortable under my bare feet. The sky was still bright orange, light blue, light purple, and pink, blinding me. I had gotten used to the darkness. I closed my eyes. It was so peaceful. Most lights that had come from mushrooms the day before had been turned off, and the whole kingdom was silent, sleeping peacefully.

Suddenly, I heard a high-pitched voice, far behind us, coming from deep within the castle, echoing through the kingdom. "CARL!"

I gulped. That was Queen Gilly's voice! Drake knew I had escaped. "We have to hurry," I said quietly. So, we picked up the pace and ran all the way out of the Fairy Kingdom and to the bridge. Jolly took the lead with Clover behind her, and me hidden behind them.

Suddenly, a young troll stepped into our path. He seemed to be a couple years younger than all of the trolls I'd seen. In our hurry, we had forgotten about the toll troll! The troll stared at us, looking Jolly up and down. Luckily, she was the one in the front so he couldn't see me or Clover. I gulped.

"Do you have permission to—" He started, and then paused. Jolly's face lit up, and so did the troll's. Maybe they knew each other. Maybe Jolly could talk him out of eating me.

"Well *that's* something I didn't see coming! It's *you*!" Jolly grinned back. I hesitated again. Just because he knew Jolly didn't mean he wouldn't and couldn't hurt me, I reminded myself. But Jolly could at least try to stop him, and maybe, just maybe, he would listen. I didn't know if he had heard about all of the things I had done, but even if he hadn't, humans were still illegal and classified as evil throughout both the fairy and troll kingdoms. I felt like running back into the Kingdom to get away from the new toll troll, one who might not be as nice as Jolly. But knowing there was a vampire- disguised as a queen with an army and a whole kingdom under his control, made me feel sick. I decided that one troll was less scary than a whole army of them. I hid behind Jolly. At least he hadn't seen me yet.

"Jolly!" The young toll troll said, his silly grin growing bigger. He started laughing.

"Hey, Crelish," Jolly responded, not seeming worried at all. "What's up?"

Wait… *Crelish*? That was the name of the toll troll who Jolly had mentioned when talking to the guards. She had lied about being his cousin!

"I'm great! Better than great, actually. My first week of being an ACTUAL toll troll! I never thought they'd pick me. You were so much better at it. I've been a toll-troll-in-training since we were kids!"

"Are you kidding? Congrats!" Jolly said excitedly, sounding truly proud. "I didn't realize you got the position! That's amazing!"

"I still haven't seen a human yet though," Crelish said, frowning a little. I raised my eyebrows. Thankfully, Jolly still didn't seem worried.

"You'll see one soon, for sure." Jolly promised Jolly lowered her voice. "Real soon," she muttered. *Well, that's my cue.* I thought.

The young troll's eyes lit up. "You think so?" he asked hopefully.

"I know so," Jolly said sincerely, winking. "One sec, Crel."

Jolly turned back to me, still grinning. Her smile was almost contagious. I was starting to smile for some reason. I'd never seen her this happy, and seeing her so excited almost made me excited. Even though I didn't know who the other troll was, and I was nervous that he might eat me, I trusted Jolly.

"Who's that?" I asked.

"My brother, Crelish!" Jolly replied.

I tilted my head. "I didn't know you had a brother."

"Well, you don't know everything about me!" she replied with a laugh.

I frowned for a second, but the statement wasn't rude, just joking. "I guess not." I laughed. "You don't know everything about me, either." I added, in a mysterious, joking voice. She chuckled, then turned back to her brother.

"Hey, Crelish?" Jolly called out, tilting her head. "Can I ask you something?"

Crelish tilted his head too, still grinning. "Sure. Anything!"

"Well... I have some... friends." Jolly replied carefully. "And they need to cross this bridge. It's just... you know one of them, but the other one is kind of... *different*. Can you help them?" Jolly asked.

Crelish nodded instantly. "Of course! Any friends of yours are friends of mine," he claimed.

Jolly turned around and eyed me worriedly. "Clover first," she whispered. "He already knows her and trusts her. He may not like you as much."

I grunted, slightly offended, but I agreed. Jolly tapped Clover on the shoulder and whispered something in her ear. Clover nodded, flew out from behind Jolly.

"Crelish!" she exclaimed with a huge smile. I raised my eyebrows.

"Clover! I didn't know you knew my sister!" Crelish said.

"I only met her a little while ago," Clover replied, shrugging. "Thanks for your help, Crel."

"Anytime, Clover." Crelish replied happily, hugging Clover by cupping his hand around her. They must have been friends back in the kingdoms. Jolly cleared her throat. Crelish sheepishly pulled his hands away and Clover flew to his side.

"Hey, Crelish, I have one more friend," Jolly said. "I'd like you to help him too, if you can."

"Ooh, of course! Who is it?" He asked excitedly, looking around with interest. "Do I know him?" I took a deep breath.

"Uh, no, Crelish. Not exactly. See, this is the... other friend I told you about, the one that's..." She hesitated. "Kind of... different. Don't overreact." Jolly warned, and stepped aside, so Crelish could see me. He gasped loudly.

"A HUMAN! I'VE NEVER SEEN A REAL HUMAN!" he shouted. His eyes sparkled. I winced. But that's when I realized that he wasn't angry or scared like the other trolls I'd met... he was *excited* to see me! I hesitated for a moment. He seemed nice enough, though.

"Shh!" Jolly whispered urgently. "No one can know that he's here!"

"Sorry. I've just never seen a real human before!" Crelish said in an excited whisper. He stuck out his big, green hand. "Hello… uh…"

"Carl," I told him, shaking his hand.

His eyes widened. "That's *such* a cool name. Humans are *so* awesome!" he exclaimed.

"Thanks." I smiled at his enthusiasm. No one had told me that I was cool in a while. "You seem pretty cool too."

Crelish looked as if he might faint. "A human just smiled at me! The *human* called me *cool*!" He seemed more excited to see me than anyone had been in a while, especially after my experience with Drake the vampire, the whole fairy kingdom, Mason the pirate, and even my uncle Jean, which made me feel really good.

"Well, it's nice to meet you." I gave him a thumbs up.

He shrieked with excitement. "Oh, can I have an autograph? Just to prove that I've seen a human? The other toll trolls are always making fun of me because I've never eaten one." He made a face, pulling out a rough roll of paper and a blue ink pen out of a pocket on his spotted blue shirt. He handed them to me. I wasn't sure that the trolls wanted to see an autograph, and they'd probably make fun of him even more, but I still felt kind of bad, so I took the cap off of the pen. Maybe the autograph would be something he'd look at for the rest of his life. The scroll had a wobbly-looking stick figure human without a face that Crelish must have drawn himself on it. I laughed and gave the figure a face, my hair, eyes, nose, and a smile, before signing my name. I still felt awkward for being treated like a celebrity, especially by a troll, but Crelish looked so excited that I couldn't refuse.

"Sure, here you go!" I handed him back the signed paper then turned back to my friends. Jolly was smiling fondly. "Wait, how are we going to get out of here?" I looked out over the bridge. Clear blue water stretched out in every direction. Even more water. There was no way to get away from the island, and I certainly couldn't stay at the kingdoms, because both were convinced that I was a criminal who wanted to kill their queen (and perhaps all of them too) when it was really the other way around.

"We can take that boat." Crelish answered like it was no big deal, pointing to a red and white striped paddle boat that almost reminded me of a candy cane.

"Won't you get in trouble if you just *take* it?" I asked as I followed him across the bridge, grabbing a wooden paddle on the way.

Crelish just laughed, not in a mean way but like he thought I was joking.

"Stealing isn't as much of a deal here as it is to humans, because fairies and trolls only steal when they need to—never just to take things." Jolly explained.

I guess that made sense. I was starting to doubt everything I knew about humans. Life in the kingdoms was so… peaceful. It was the humans' faults that everything went wrong. Jolly got in the boat, and I followed her. My past didn't define me—especially a past I was never part of, I reminded myself. Except it somehow always managed to interfere. Clover hovered above the end of the boat. Crelish started to get in, too, but I stopped him.

"You're...coming?" I asked. It was the same thing I'd asked Clover before she left with us. Both Jolly and Clover snorted at the exact same time.

"Dude, you need to stop asking that." Jolly said with a laugh.

"Well, people I barely know keep offering to risk everything they have for me!" I pointed out.

Clover just shrugged. "It's not like I had much. You just need to accept a little help sometimes. The more the merrier, right?"

"Not when it comes to danger!" I said, my voice rising slightly. Why weren't they listening to me?

"Come on! Just let him in the boat!" Clover insisted.

I realized I was blocking Crelish from getting into the boat. Embarrassed, I melted back into my seat.

"It was his idea in the first place. He wants to help us." Jolly's voice broke. "Please let him come, Carl. I can't leave him behind!"

I looked at Clover, who hesitated. "Well, it's up to Crelish, remember that," she said. "I think it's dangerous, and I want to protect him. He's my best friend, after all. But he's old enough to make choices for himself.

Crelish was staring at me, pleading in his eyes. "Please, Carl? Come on, this is the adventure I've always been waiting for."

"So… you are coming?" I asked again.

Crelish nodded confidently. "Yes! I've never been on a real adventure, much less with a real human! It'll be fun." He seemed super excited. He had no idea what he was getting himself into. I felt bad. "Besides, the next shift will be here soon. About"—he tapped his chin—"Right now." He'd barely finished the sentence when another toll troll walked out onto the bridge and began scanning the area. I immediately ducked into the boat. Clover, Crelish, and Jolly quickly copied me.

"Creepy." I muttered under my breath.

"Yeah, I know. They're never a second late," Clover whispered.

"It's so weird. For some reason, I always find that when it's my shift, I end up on time—not even a second late. Even if I'm about to oversleep, even if I was about to leave the house a minute late, if one thing is about to go wrong, something pulls me in the right direction and everything goes right. It's like magic!" Jolly told us. "In fact, now that I think about it, it probably is." She laughed to herself.

I laughed too. I guess it would be nice to never be late again. I dipped the paddle in the water, creating several ripples, and I started pushing the boat forward

"Where are we going, Captain?" Crelish asked.

I smiled to myself. I kind of liked being called 'captain.' "I don't know. But we can't stay by the Fairy Kingdom," I said. "We'll go wherever feels right. Maybe something will work out. This whole world is based on magic and chance, isn't it?"

Crelish nodded. He seemed to understand, even though I wasn't sure if I did.

We'd find our own way. I kept paddling forward.

***

I had paddled for what seemed like ages when the sun began to dip on the horizon. I yawned. I hadn't slept well in days, and it was getting late. But I had to keep paddling. I pushed the wooden paddle into the water again, though my whole body was screaming in protest. My eyes drooped.

"Hey, Carl, you seem tired. Why don't you take a break? I can paddle," Jolly suggested, reaching over for the paddle.

I covered another yawn. "It's fine." I lied. "I can do it." Jolly ignored my response and snatched the paddle anyway. I protested sleepily.

"I insist," Jolly said.

I relaxed a little bit in my seat. I wanted to sleep, but still, I had to help out my friends. "I can do it," I argued, still feeling so, *so* tired.

"See, that's the thing, it doesn't look like you can." Clover pointed out. Of course, she was still trying to get me to "*accept more help"* or whatever. But what if something went wrong?

"Don't be silly, of course I can!" I insisted. "What if something happens to you guys? I can't sit back and rest. I can handle this!"

The two girls shook their heads in unison. "C'mon, sometimes it's important to accept a little help." Clover said again.

"I do!" I argued. "Sometimes. I let you two come and help me, didn't I? And Crelish is in the boat. These are *my* parents we're trying to find, and *my* enemy after us. I need to help you guys!"

"But those were *our* choices. We *want* to help you. You can't fight a vampire on your own," Clover insisted gently. I could tell that she felt slightly bad for me, and I didn't *need* her pity *or* loyalty. I realized, she was right. She had given them to me out of kindness, proving how good of a friend she was.

"I promise I can handle this, Carl," Jolly said, dipping the paddle into the water.

Suddenly, I heard Clover's voice in my head, telling me to relax, that Jolly could handle it. I wanted to argue, but my senses took over, telling me to let everything go and sleep. But I couldn't! *Come on, Carl. Take a break! Jolly, Clover, and Crelish can handle this,* one part of my brain said. *You're wrong,* said the other part. I shook my head and tried to sit up straighter in my seat. I was tired, but still! What if something bad happened? What if Drake came? The possible what-ifs were bouncing around in my head like a storm. *What if... what if?* Whose fault would it be then?

"Asking for help isn't as bad as it seems, Captain," Crelish said in a gentle voice. I studied him for a moment. It was funny how much he liked humans. After being treated like vermin for days, I finally had friends. Maybe he felt the same way. And now I had one more—one that understood, one that was funny, one that thought I was really cool, and didn't judge me for what I was. "We will have things under control," he continued.

Sleep did sound good. But what if Drake attacked? What if he hurt me or my friends? I wanted to yell. But I was so tired... Just a little while, right? It couldn't hurt, could it? What was the worst that could happen? Creative scenes of Drake doing horrible things filled my mind, and I shivered. I was the only one who could at least *try* to freeze him for a while... but then I remembered how that didn't even *work* last time. We would be defenseless either way, and my friends could handle themselves, right? I couldn't even do that much... but still, I wanted to be there for them!

It was hard to fight the delightful idea of sleep. My hands balled into fists. We were vulnerable, floating in the middle of the ocean! But my brain was in control, and it needed sleep. I wanted to fight, to protest, but I couldn't. I just had to mumble, "If you insist. Wake me if you need help." And then everything faded into a peaceful black.

***

Chapter Thirteen

Memories

"Carl? Carl, wake up!" A voice from far away, maybe Clover's, called. Large hands were shaking me, bringing me back to reality.

I groaned sleepily, rolling on my side. *What is going on?*

"Carl!" Another voice was calling out to me, Crelish's this time. Hands shook me again, but I couldn't do anything, I was too tired, enjoying the dull, peaceful darkness.

"Five more minutes," I grumbled.

"Carl! We need you! We need your help!" Yet another voice called out, maybe Jolly's.

That woke me up. I knew I shouldn't have gone to sleep. I *knew* something bad would happen! This was all my fault! I was awake, but all of my thoughts were jumbled, still half asleep, mixed with my rising panic.

"I'm awake! I-I'm awake!" I mumbled. "What's wrong? What… what happened?" *This is all my fault… I shouldn't have gone to sleep; I should have helped!*

I forced myself to open my eyes and look around. Everything seemed normal. The sky was a dark gray, and freezing water sloshed at my bare feet. Wait, what? My brain was startled awake by the cold liquid. "What happened?!" I yelled again. I looked around the boat and noticed a large hole in the side. We were sinking! Oh, no, oh, no, oh, no! *This is all my fault. This is all my fault.* "Why are we sinking? What… who did this?" Had Drake come? Had we hit a rock?

"I don't know! It was terrible. We heard an evil laugh… a flash of light! A shadowy figure stabbed a hole in the boat!" Crelish exclaimed. "All I saw was a pair of bright red eyes."

That gave it all away. He found us. He found me.

"Drake," I said in a low voice. We all shivered just hearing the name.

Jolly hugged the pieces of the broken wooden paddle. It had somehow been destroyed and snapped into two halves. *Seriously, Drake*? How had that happened? I hadn't even realized. We had no way to steer, and the boat was broken. Perfect. Even worse, Drake was nearby!

Suddenly, there was a flash of light and an island appeared. It seemed like it was growing, stretching up to the dark, eerie sky. I squinted into the distance. The sand was dark and the grass was wilted. The water around it seemed murky and gray. The whole island was just plain creepy. It gave me the chills.

Just then, there was a strong blast of wind. The wind seemed to be pushing us forward, leading us to the island. "WHAT'S HAPPENING?" I yelled.

"We have to get to that island!" Jolly cried.

"We won't make it!" Clover screamed.

Crelish clung to his sister. "What are we going to do, captain?" He glanced at me worriedly. My heart broke. I had no answer.

"LET US GO DRAKE! I KNOW YOU'RE HERE!" I screamed. But there was still no response. The boat was shoved forward. Maybe, using the wind to our advantage, we could get to the island before the boat sunk. The wind sped up. I paddled forward through the water using my hands. Jolly used one half of the paddle to help me. She handed me the other half, the part that was just a wooden stick, and I used that instead. We were going just a little faster now. Maybe we could make it.

The boat hit the sandy bottom of the spooky island and we all got out. I was shaking as I looked around. The whole place seemed pretty empty. I decided to explore. Maybe I could find Drake. The damp, gray sand was pretty gross: chunky and rough against my feet. I handed Jolly the other half of the wooden paddle and started moving forward toward a dry patch of grass. The sand tickled my bare feet.

"Carl..." she protested.

"Nope!" I held up my hand, cutting her off. "Thank you. Thank you all, for everything you've done. But I can't let you come with me now. This is my fight, and I have to face him myself. I can't risk losing you. I'll be careful, I'll come back for you, whatever you want. But please, just stay here."

"Carl, don't be an idiot, you know we can't let you do that!" Jolly said.

"There's no way we're letting you go alone, Captain." Crelish continued.

"We don't want to lose you!" Clover added in a begging tone.

I ignored them and climbed onto the patch of wilting tall grass as it swayed in the soft breeze, making my feet itch. I looked around the small island. As creepy as it was, it seemed fairly normal, and Drake was nowhere in sight.

Suddenly, hands grabbed me, interrupting my thoughts. My first thought was to pull away. But then the hands wrapped me in a huge bear-hug and lifted me up. I started to pull away, flailing my legs, but when I turned my head, my eyes met a pair of gray ones. I sighed in relief. It was Jolly. Even under such dark circumstances, I had found such good friends. But hadn't I made it very clear that I didn't want their help right now? Wasn't it my fight?

There wasn't time to think about it because just then a dark, creepy voice echoed around us. "Welcome. We have been expecting you."

I mulled over the attacker's words. *We*? That meant there was more than one person on the island. My friends ran forward, stopping around me in a protective circle. This time, I didn't protest. They were going to help me whether I wanted it or not. If I was being honest, I could really use their help, although I wouldn't admit it. I wasn't being rude or anything, I was just trying to protect them!

I decided to follow the voice. As I walked forward, I looked back at my friends. They were still standing in a circle, looking expectantly at me as if waiting for a signal. I hesitated, before motioning for them to follow me deeper into the mist of the island. Clover gave me an approving thumbs up.

"Who are you?" I called out.

"No one and everyone," was the only reply. Well, that wasn't very clear. Who or what is nothing and everything? Who even says confusing things like that? Someone magical, probably, I thought, running through possibilities in my head. Where even were they, whoever they were?

"Come out! Show yourself!" I commanded, trying to sound confident. "What kind of creepy old stranger hides on a creepy old island, anyway?"

I heard a deep, evil laugh. "My dear Carl, I am not a stranger." I froze, but my friends noticed too late and crashed into me and then each, causing a domino effect. Soon, we were all on the ground.

The hidden being (or beings?) laughed again. Maybe they were watching us somehow. How did they even know my name? Drake's words rang in my head again. Always one step ahead. I growled, picking myself up and dusting myself off. Stupid Drake. Stupid island. Stupid *"one step ahead!"* None of it made any sense. *Nothing* made sense anymore.

"How do you know my name? And how are you not a stranger if I have never met you?" I asked, my voice shaking. I helped my friends up.

"But you have." The shadows curled around me, forming a dark dome around me, and I heard footsteps coming out from behind a small group of trees in a remote corner of the island. Just then, a man with chocolate-colored hair and a matching beard appeared. His eyes were dark like mine, wide with terror, and his face was very pale. He had shadows wrapped around his wrists, serving as handcuffs. He was a prisoner, then, to the bigger force on this island, the one with the dark voice.

I looked up into the man's face and I recognized him immediately. My face paled. My friends let go of my sweaty hands and looked at me, clearly concerned.

"Carl? Are you okay?" Clover asked. "Carl, hello?" She waved a tiny hand in front of my blank face, but I didn't really hear her. I was focused on that one man, the one man I'd wanted to see for years, the *one* man I was looking for. I started shaking. My mouth could barely form the words I needed. I wanted to reach out to him and collapse into his arms. My mouth formed a circle, feeling dry, and a sound finally came out.

"D-d-dad?" The dark eyes met their match. The man's mouth also formed an *O*, gaping at me. My world was spinning. That man. That one man. My dad.

"Carl...?" His eyes flashed with recognition, shining with tears. "You... You shouldn't be here! Run! *Run*! Ru—" My dad's legs collapsed beneath him and suddenly, black shadows poured out.

Dad? I wanted to call out, to reach for him, to run for him, but my dry mouth wouldn't move. My jaws were glued together.

"NONSENSE!" The voice was back, but now it was coming out of my dad's mouth. "There is no need to run. Your dad is not here." My friends backed away slowly.

I wanted to lunge at my dad and hug him, tell him it'd be okay, to hurt the one who would dare to hurt my father. I would *kill* the one who would dare to hurt my father, the one who ruined my life! I prepared to charge at the man, but my friends held me back. There were tears in my eyes, but not tears of sadness. Perhaps they were tears of fear. But I wouldn't be held back by my pain. This monster needed to suffer! My fear was gone immediately, replaced with pure, red, hot rage, burning through my vision, coursing through my body and burning up everything. Whoever was in the shadows had kidnapped my dad. Whoever was in the shadows had ruined *everything*.

"WHO ARE YOU? WHAT ARE YOU DOING TO MY FATHER?!" I roared, shaking out of my friends' grips, screaming, crying, kicking, and punching. My dad became my only focus. I was ready to hunt. The black shadows danced around me, teasing, taunting, like all of the other villains I'd faced. *One step ahead*, a brand new voiced jeered, haunting my thoughts, invading my brain. "GIVE ME MY DAD BACK! GIVE ME MY FAMILY BACK! YOU TERRIBLE, HORRIBLE, LIFE-RUINING, NO GOOD..."

"Now, now, Carl. That's no way to talk to your father." My father's face laughed in the villain's voice. I growled. I wanted to end the villainous being, but instead I took a deep breath. I could be clever. I could be cunning. I could play these games all day. I'd done it before. This villain thought they could control me? I waited another minute, hiding my rage behind a calm mask.

"You just said my father was not here though, didn't you?" I pointed out mockingly, trying to shove my bubbling anger back down. I was surely more clever than whoever was hiding behind their magic, right? I had beaten people at games like this before. Drake used that tactic often. How strange. I was starting to see a bit of Drake in everyone, especially on the creepy Island of Darkness.

"Ha, you're good." The voice said. "It's a good thing your friends stopped you, for I would not hesitate to end you, Carl. Enough of this." The shadows parted and an equally shadowy figure waved its hand aggressively. A large burst of wind knocked me to the ground. The shadows closed around me and my friends again, quickly swirling around us.

I picked myself up, scowling into the shadows. "Come out, come out, wherever you are and show yourself!" I called. "Stop hiding behind your magic tricks, and your prisoners. You're just like all of the other villains I've faced. Cowardly, hiding behind your stupid games, acting smug, messing with my head. Well, game over. Stop playing your games." I took a deep breath. *Be smug. Be clever. Be better. Be one step ahead.* "Because I play them better."

"YOU INSOLENT FOOL!" Thunder roared through the shadows, snarling with the voice, getting louder as the voice got angrier. "You know nothing about 'true evil' or true pain. There's no such thing as a good person."

"I know more about pain than you could ever imagine." The shadows whirled around me, unsettled as if startled by my bravery and courage. "And yes, there are good people, noble people everywhere, if you really look." I pointed out, looking into my dad's blank eyes. "My parents." I swallowed. *One step ahead.* "Me." I tried not to doubt my own words as I searched the shadows.

The creature in the shadows was enraged. "You think you're so innocent? You've done bad things to get to where you are today, Carl. You've stolen, you've brainwashed, you've broken in, you've broken out, you've lied. I've been watching you, and you're not as innocent as you think you are. Don't play the victim. Your parents did things too. Why did they end up here today? They've lied, Carl. To you. To me. They've done bad things, and worst of all, they had no idea how much it hurt *ME*!" My dad's body said in the angry, deep voice that wasn't his own. My dad's pain became the creature's pain, which became mine. More shadows swirled around us, getting faster with the now extremely loud thunder and the angry snarling voice. "Everything, everyone, at some point in their life does something bad, no matter how hard they try to cover it up, no matter how good they say they are. You clearly know nothing of the world, Carl. You clearly know nothing..." the voice paused dramatically, and I almost thought that it wouldn't say anything else. "Of me."

But that was the thing, I didn't. I knew nothing about the hidden creature in the shadows. I took another shaky deep breath.

"Of course I know nothing about you. You won't show yourself because you're too scared. To me, you are nothing, because I see nothing, know nothing, and nothing is how much I care. I've never met, heard of, or faced you. So please, show yourself if you *truly* want me to know anything of you."

"Why would I need to show you more? I have your family, and I will not let them go unless you do exactly as I say." The eerie voice responded, using my father's mouth. I looked the stranger in my father's eyes.

"Family? No, I doubt that. You only have my dad." I taunted, really hoping that was true.

"Oh, really?"

My heart sank. I immediately knew I'd messed up. It wasn't a lie. The shadowy creature was too confident. They probably had my whole family, or whatever remained of it anyway.

A woman appeared next to my father. She had long, wavy, light brown hair like me, and honey-colored eyes, which were blank like my dad's. She stared straight through me with no recognition in her eyes at all, like she'd never even seen me before. My heart shattered into pieces all over again. I reached out to her, a helpless child once again, before the sadness mixed with the anger, clouding my judgement and blinding me with hot, dark-red anger and pain.

"Mum!" I screamed to the woman, my mother. But she didn't hear me, didn't see me, didn't remember me, didn't call out to me and wrap me in her arms, reassuring me like she should have been there to do for my whole life. She was already too far gone. "MUM!! MUM!!" I was ready to run forward and save her. My friends had to grab my arms to hold me back again.

"Carl, calm down." Jolly hissed in my ear as she wrapped her hands around me. "Seriously. He's not worth it. He's trying to trick you. We'll save your parents, I promise, but you need to stay calm." I barely even heard her. She was far away, along with the cries of my other friends, and I didn't need her help. She was the one holding me back. I was angry. Angry at the world, angry at Drake, angry at my parents, angry at my friends, and angry at the shadowy stranger. I growled, barely recognizing the sound. I didn't need nor want *anyone's* help.

"Mum… MUM!" I yelled, tears in my eyes as I pulled against my friends, seething with rage. There were no words to describe how I felt. I turned back to my friends and growled at them. "Let me go." When they didn't listen, I turned back toward the shadows, fire in my dark eyes. "Let them go! Leave them alone! DAD! MUM! MUM!!!"

"Your mum isn't here either. Only me, remember?"

My blood boiled and my fingers curled into fists, my nails digging into my hands. "Hurt them and you've lost everything." I warned, trying to unclench my fists, which were starting to become white and sore. Staring at my mum and dad, who were in terrible condition, I ended up stuffing my hands into my pockets instead.

"Listen, and I'll let them go." The stranger countered. "Make the right choice, Carl." The voice echoed into the swirling, dark fog. I heard a loud sound, like snapping fingers. and my parents' eyes were human again. Normal again. Well, normal but wide with tears and pain. They looked like they were waking from a nightmare. They screamed, writhing with pain before they collapsed onto the ground, squirming, hurt, and broken.

"NO!!!" The rage felt like it would break me too. "WHAT ARE YOU DOING TO THEM?!" I broke free from my friends' grasps and light flashed in front of my vision. The shadows whirled around me, dizzying and sickening, and a familiar pair of evil red eyes, glared through the shadows straight at me. I froze, and my world started spinning. *Him.*

"Drake?" I froze in place, almost forgetting my rage in the shock. The familiar vampire stepped out of the shadows, dusting off his drab black clothes.

"Yes, it is I." Drake said, still using the grand but creepy voice that he'd used before when he was hiding in the shadows. He cleared his throat, correcting himself and going back to his normal voice. "Hello, Carl." He rolled his eyes. "Honestly, doing the voice is quite a hassle, you know. Not my taste. And the shadows... *so* last century. You know I appreciate a grand entrance, though."

Something clicked into place. My rage came back again, coursing through my body. "It is you. It was you!" I screamed. "It always was you." My rage poured out.

Drake shot me a confused look.

I glared back at him. Surely he knew what I meant. "It was you the whole time, wasn't it? You... ruined my life! You stole the boat and sank it! You always knew where I was going to be! You messed with my head so that everything would go as planned. When you threw me off the boat, you didn't want to kill me. Otherwise you would have. You *planted* your boat near the pirates so that Stephanie would rescue me and send me to the fairy kingdom. You put me in prison, then set the prison on fire! But it wasn't to kill me, was it? It was so I ended up here. You tricked everyone! But *why*? *Why* do you want to *ruin my life*?!" I roared. I could see my surprise at myself reflected on the faces of Drake , my friends, and even my parents. "Forget being one step ahead! You had magic… that's definitely cheating! For all I know, you're the one allowed Ivy to have that vision about my parents in the first place! You manipulated me and everyone around me!"

Drake threw up his hands, clearly as annoyed as he was surprised by my outburst. I had surprised myself. But I wasn't afraid of him, and I never would be again. All of the pieces were coming together in my head. Drake wouldn't manipulate my life any longer. Drake performed a kind of mini shrug, rolling his eyes. "Yes, I did, but you already knew that deep down, didn't you Carl?"

As he spoke, my friends caught up with me, trying to pull me away from Drake, but I dodged them. They were just trying to protect me, but I didn't need their protection anymore. I was confused as to why he even bothered to tell me these things. He just loved to talk and talk about how great and evil he was. Now he was saying something along the lines of, "You see, the thing with magical manipulation is that I had no idea if some of it would work or not—"

"You've been chasing me down! YOU'VE RUINED MY LIFE!" I screamed, cutting him off. I'd had enough, because seriously, *who cares, Drake?*

Drake winked smugly. "Yep, that too. Glad you noticed." He laughed sarcastically.

My fists were still white and clenched, and even though they were still kind of sore, the rage bubbling up inside of me sort of numbed the pain. I was glaring so hard that if I was a cartoon character, lasers probably would have shot straight out of my eyes. I'd never felt so angry, I realized, ever. There was rage buzzing in my ears. My heart was hammering against my chest, full of hate for Drake the vampire, my enemy. All I saw was Drake's face, one I just wanted to punch. I wanted to break him, make him hurt like he'd made me hurt. All I heard was his voice and mine, everything else was drowned out, such as my friends cries to stop, to get back, to run. And even my parents' cries of agony, calling for me to run, reminding me how dangerous Drake was, were all lost to my rage.

"Did you ever think about how I felt?" I spat out my burning question. "Why do you hate my family so much?"

Drake hesitated for a bit, and for a moment I thought he wasn't going to answer. "Well, have you ever heard the story of the day your grandfather fought with a vampire, the day he danced with death?" Drake was scowling at me.

Something clicked in my head. Sure, I'd heard the tale many times when I was little, but I'd thought that it was just some ridiculous bedtime story that my grandfather had made up. I tried to recall the exact details of the story. How did Drake know it, and how was it relevant? My grandfather knew nothing about Drake or the magical world at all, otherwise he would have told me, right? I refused to believe that my grandfather had anything to do with Drake. He was just so funny, so jolly, so *normal*, with his white hair and his gray beard. I still missed his laugh—an honest, true laugh that you couldn't fake for a million dollars. His laugh was a laugh that could make the saddest person alive join in.

I took a deep breath. "Yeah, so?"

"You really never considered that it was true?" Drake snorted, looking amused for a moment. Then he adopted a more solemn expression. "I expected better from you, Carl. We were hungry, starving, cold. We would eat anything. Including a human. We sent my grandfather out to hunt... and he never came back, Carl." His voice got louder. "AND *DO YOU KNOW WHY, CARL?*"

I swallowed. Hidden behind the mask of smugness, there were tears, the face of a little boy, completely crushed and destroyed. I almost felt bad before I saw my parents, and my anger churned in my stomach.

"I get that my grandfather killed yours, but yours attacked mine first! Why do you need to hate *me* so much?" I spat, my voice rising as well. "I did *nothing*."

"My grandpa and I were very close. How do you think what your grandfather did to mine affected my family? I was just a young bat!" Drake yelled.

"But how is that my fault? I understand what it's like, but seriously, Drake. Think about this, really. *Why*? It makes no sense. Revenge is never the answer!"

Drake just shrugged. "My whole life, I was taught that revenge is the *only* answer. Like you said, it's not you," he said, as if it were that simple, as if I would just lay down and die so his revenge could feel fulfilled. I stared at him. If only he could hear how ridiculous he sounded.

"I know it isn't me, it's *you*. I know my grandfather hurt you. But he's not me, and that doesn't change how wrong what you're doing is."

"Wrong… or just wrong to *you*?!" Drake spat. "I'm doing this for my family!"

"By harming mine!" I argued. "That isn't fair! That isn't right!"

"Who are you to talk about 'right' and 'wrong', Carl? What would *you* know about *'fair?'*" He took a deep breath. "Do you know how much pressure is put on a vampire? How much pressure was put on me?"

I shook my head.

"Do you want to know?"

I wasn't even sure whether I wanted to know or not, but my curiously got the better of me and I nodded, still glaring at Drake. "This won't change anything, Drake."

"Fine. I'll show you what you want. Just don't try anything."

***

There was a flash of pale pink light, blinding me for a moment, and I looked around. I wasn't on the island anymore, and I seemed to be alone in a creepy, old house. The walls were all painted gray and the floor was made of dark wood. On the wall was a shelf that had a skull on it, along with a book titled, "A Vampire's Guide to Unlocking His Powers" and a photo of an older vampire with gray hair and a long black cloak. I sighed. The drab home seemed exactly like somewhere where a vampire would be happy—someone like Drake.

"Home sweet home." A dry voice said from behind me, and I spun around to see Drake.

"Where are we?"

"In my memory." Drake said simply, as if that was normal.

"What?" I asked loudly, panicking just a little bit.

"Relax, it's not that bad. Only you can see and hear me, and only I can see and hear you, so it won't ruin the memory. But don't worry, we can't harm or touch each other here." Drake rolled his eyes as if I should have known all about vampire magic

Suddenly, the door slammed open, banging against the wall. A sad-looking vampire walked in, wearing a plaid uniform and a blood red backpack. I stared at him, almost expecting him to stare back at me. But, of course, he didn't notice us watching him.

"I'm home." The younger Drake called, sliding his backpack off of his shoulder and throwing it onto the floor. The zipper popped open just a bit and a black notebook slid out of the bag. It seemed like he'd just gotten home from a bad day at school.

I turned to the older Drake. "Where did you go to school?" I asked him. To be honest, I was slightly surprised that he had gone to any school at all.

He rolled his eyes. "Don't be so surprised. I had to learn stuff too, you know." He shook his head. "I went to an academy for young witches and wizards. The Magical Territory is right next to the vampires', and since ours is so small, we don't have a school here. That's why I got made fun of—because other vampires just skipped school entirely. No one cares about us vampires, so we do what we want. That's just how we were raised."

"Oh." I said miserably, trying hard not to feel bad for him. There was no excuse for his actions toward my family.

"Hey, kiddo!" Another vampire, the one who was in the picture on the shelf entered the room dramatically, slamming the door open with a huge smile. "How was school, Drake?"

Drake's grandfather. I swallowed.

"Bad. Like always," the younger version of Drake said. Annoyance was clear in his tone. He bent down and started rummaging through his backpack. It seemed like he was looking for any excuse to avoid eye contact.

"Oh?" Drake's grandfather frowned as he spoke, showing his sharp teeth. He slid a gray cloak off of his shoulders as he walked slowly across the room toward the young vampire. "And why is that?"

"The other kids always make fun of me. Because I'm a vampire. I'm different."

"Being different is good," the old vampire pointed out.

"Not when you're me. Plus, they all have strong magic, and… I haven't even been taught to use mine yet, Grandpa."

"I'm sorry, Drake. You're too young." Drake's grandfather shook his head sadly, patting his grandson on the shoulder.

The younger version of Drake gritted his teeth. "Don't patronize me."

I looked over my shoulder and raised my eyebrows. The current Drake winced visibly.

"Oh, little bat, they just don't know how amazing you are."

Young Drake pulled away. "That's what you say every time. How are you so fine with the vampires' unfair treatment? I just wish I was like everybody else."

"I know, I know." Drake's grandfather sighed.

Young Drake threw his arms around his grandfather's neck. "Grandpa, am I... am I broken?"

My heart shattered at that exact moment. I heard a choking sound and I turned around to see Drake with tears in his eyes. For just a second, I wanted to reach out and tell him that it was okay. I didn't. It obviously wasn't okay, and he was still evil. Even so, I almost felt bad. I could see Drake's grandfather from his point of view: a kind, caring, loving, funny angel on Earth.

Finally, Drake's grandfather sighed, rubbing Drake's back. "Hey, it's okay. Of course you're not broken, kiddo. If you really want, I'll teach you your powers. But only if you're *really* ready."

"I am!" Drake said immediately, almost desperately, nodding his head repeatedly. He looked like he couldn't believe his luck, so thankful toward his grandfather, his hero. "I am ready! Please, Grandpa?"

Drake's grandfather sighed again. "I guess it's about time. You should learn to defend yourself. But you have to promise to use them for the greater good, please."

"Yes sir." Young Drake saluted, smiling foolishly.

His grandpa just smiled a bit. "As you know, magic is all in your head, so follow my instructions *very carefully.*" Young Drake nodded. His Grandpa continued. "Focus on the universe. All of the powers in the world. Imagine them as puzzle pieces. Put the puzzle together now." Drake's grandfather instructed. The younger Drake tried his best to focus on those directions, and I felt the familiar rush of power with him. The young vampire gasped in awe. It was exactly what I did when I wanted to find my freezing power, except slightly different because I focused on only the freezing power. He focused on *every power in the universe.*

"How do you feel, Carl?" the adult version of Drake asked from behind me.

I couldn't even answer. I don't know how, but I felt what Drake felt. I felt him being overwhelmed. The power was stronger than anything he'd ever felt. He'd never been good at puzzles, but this was different. This was a beautiful, safe, dizzying feeling.

"Now close your eyes," Drake's grandfather instructed. The younger version of Drake obeyed and gasped.

Curious, I looked back at the current Drake. He nodded. "Go on, Carl. Close your eyes."

Not knowing what else to do, I closed my eyes. What I saw was the most beautiful thing I'd ever seen. A huge chart with every single power in the universe listed on it, was glowing in front of my eyes. It existed only in the imagination of vampires, yet it was very real. I could feel how it took all of Drake's concentration to even look at it. I could feel how it became even more difficult to keep all of that power pieced together.

I opened my eyes and watched Drake's grandfather smiling softly. "You see it. Good," he said. "Now imagine choosing which power to use. Look through the whole chart and pick an easy one. Focus."

I closed my eyes again. Drake didn't know what to pick, overwhelmed by the many choices, so he landed on a spell that allowed him to shoot a blast of ice out of his hands. The glowing chart disappeared, and Drake's thoughts faded into darkness. I opened my eyes, feeling faint because the chart had taken up so much of Drake's energy. He created a thin line of ice around the room.

Then, more quickly this time, he reopened the table in his mind and chose a heat manipulation power and melted the ice. I could feel his pride, but also his exhaustion. He knew he had done well by his grandfather's grin.

"You are going to do great things."

Young Drake bowed respectfully. "Thank you, Grandpa."

"You're a quick learner, Drake," the older vampire said. "Just take it easy. That's a very complex spell for a beginner." He put his hand on Drake's shoulder.

I was startled by Drake's voice from behind me. I had been caught up in the memory. It was like watching a movie in 3D. "So, Carl," he prompted. "Such is the responsibility dumped on a young vampire. *That* is real magic. Not whatever you have been shown. Now you know."

Then the pale pink light flashed again, and the first memory was over.

The second memory was in the same room as the first one, but this time, the younger version of Drake was crying. He wiped his tears away and walked through a door, disappearing on the other side. The current, older Drake started following his younger self, before he paused, turning back toward me expectantly. I hesitated before following him. He couldn't hurt me in his memories, anyway. At least, that's what he said. We followed the younger Drake through a dark, drafty hallway to a large bedroom with a door made of dark wood.

"Hello, Mother." He said, bowing down respectfully to the figure in bed. Hidden under the blankets was a vampire with long black hair, gray eyes, and a pale face. His mom coughed, and tears filled the young vampire's eyes again. I felt sad too—like I wanted to sit down and cry. But those weren't my feelings, they were Drake's, I reminded myself. It was getting hard to sort out which ones were which. Drake was in a black shirt with a white button-down jacket. His mom seemed sick, and his grandfather was already gone. He was full of anger, resentment, hate, and judgement. Drake's mom muttered a bunch of incomprehensible nonsense. Her mind had been slipping too, it seemed.

"Do you need something, son?" She murmured to her son, coughing again.

Surprisingly, Drake just burst into tears. "I just want Grandpa back!" The little vampire sobbed. "I miss him. And I know it's not your fault, but I miss you too."

He seemed to know that he was pretty much talking to himself.

His mom muttered some more of her nonsense. "I'm sorry," she mumbled to her son, the words soft and almost incomprehensible. Suddenly, the woman froze up, surprising her son.

Younger Drake panicked. "Mother, are you okay?"

Her words were abruptly clear and understandable, but dark and evil. "You want your grandfather back, yes?"

Younger Drake nodded carefully. "Yes, Mother."

She grabbed her son's shirt and pulled him close. "Kill them all. All of them."

Drake was shocked. "Kill them?" he repeated. "Kill who?"

"The family of the man who killed your grandfather," his mother mumbled, speaking so fast that she was hard to understand.

"Revenge is the only answer. You know that. That's what I've taught you. Kill them. Can you do that?"

Young Drake hesitated. I tried to sort out his feelings. He was curious, but full of regret. No matter how bitter he was, he didn't want to kill anyone. But then again, if he could show his power by killing these foolish humans, maybe his mother would be proud again. He would never be made fun of again. He was also hopeful. Maybe if he worked hard enough, he could bend the universe and bring his grandfather back to life.

"Mother?" Drake asked. The woman looked up. "I'll do it."

She just smirked, before she went back to her muttering. The pink light flashed again, and the second memory was over. The present-time Drake grabbed my hand. Instead of seeing a third memory, I saw flashes of Drake's other memories. I saw Drake and his grandfather at the table, eating cold cucumber soup. I saw Young Drake sitting outside as other kids used their magic to throw rocks at him. I saw a teenage version of Drake, sitting outside all by himself. I felt a whirlwind of emotions, all belonging to Drake: rage at the world, judgement for others, judgement for himself, loneliness and misery and grief and loss, hope for the future, disdain for the past, lust for power, and fear for what he was becoming. The pink light flashed again and again and I started to feel sick. Suddenly, we were back on the island. I looked around wildly. My friends were staring at us.

"I... didn't know all of that," I said softly. I didn't have anything else to say.

"I know..." Drake replied quietly. He was shaking.

"I know you're angry and sad. I know you judged yourself. I can feel that little boy inside of you, one who just wants the support of others, one who just wants to fit in."

"You know nothing about me." The vampire snapped. His voice quivered with rage.

"I do. I know how it feels to be hated and alone, to lose a loved one. I know, Drake."

"I know," Drake said again, his voice rising.

"You don't have to do this, Drake. We can work together. I can't make up for what my grandpa did. But we can, together. You don't need to be judged. You don't need to hurt me! You don't need to kill my family."

"I do." Drake said slowly. "It's for me. For my family. For my mother."

"No, you don't. You don't have to make me suffer like you suffered," I said softly.

"No, Carl. I've made up my mind." The words were cold.

"Your mom didn't mean what she said. No one in their right mind would want to kill a whole family because of what one man did to protect himself," I blurted suddenly.

"I know," Drake repeated one more time. "But you're going to die."

"Please…" I begged, but he wasn't listening anymore.

Drake didn't sound sorry anymore. He *wasn't*. He felt like he didn't need to be sorry to anyone, not ever again. He'd made his choice, and his choice was to be the villain.

He took a deep breath, glaring at me— his rival. I just stared back at him, wondering why he had to be this way.

But he'd made up his mind. He took a deep breath. "Carl, you have two seconds to decide whether you want to die or die."

***

Chapter Fourteen

Death or Death

I immediately took a step back. Drake had countless powers, all of the powers in the universe! I'd just seen the whole catalog. I only had two options: death or death. How was that a fair choice?

"What?! No! Of course I don't want to die! We can work this out," I repeated. I was mostly stalling. My two seconds to decide were already long past up, and Drake knew it too.

"We can't, actually, and since you didn't answer, I'll just assume that you're going to die." The vampire yanked a knife out of his pocket. "But... I should at least give you a chance." He snorted. "I'm not a monster, after all."

I rolled my eyes, but I was relieved. A chance would be perfect. A third choice, hidden between the lines, one that involved saving my family and going home. That didn't seem very likely, but it was worth a try. I was clever. I'd tricked Drake before. Maybe I could do it again.

Drake flicked his hand and there was a flash of pale blue light. Suddenly, pain ripped through my brain. It stopped as quickly as it had come.

"What are you doing?" I asked with annoyance, clutching my head. How was *this* giving me a fair chance?

"Well, Carl, today and only today, you can use any two magical spells— just two— and do anything you want with them." Drake explained, sounding bored. "It just seems more fair. And more fun. Consider this a test. Winner takes all."

I rolled my eyes again. Drake continued. "Just open your mind to the universe and put together the puzzle pieces. I assume you already know how to do that from your surprising development of the old powers. And, of course, you saw it in my memory. Try not to be too overwhelmed." He wasn't even paying attention to me anymore, because he was examining his knife. What a jerk.

What if it was a trick? Actually... no, there was no way it was a trick. That didn't seem like something Drake would do. He just wanted to play. I didn't know what to do, so I did what he said, feeling the exhilarating rush of power. Elemental powers, transformational powers, memory powers... there was no way I could beat Drake with any of those. After browsing through spells for several minutes I was about to choose a random spell and accept defeat when I had the perfect idea! I opened my mind and searched for the correct spell, one that did everything I needed it to. Just when I thought I wasn't going to find one, it appeared. I could have sworn that it hadn't been on the chart two seconds ago, but it was there now, and it was just what I needed. The whole process was very overwhelming but almost calming in a way.

I opened my eyes again, focusing on the island around me. Drake was waiting, smirking at me, still holding his sharp, gleaming weapon. He snapped his fingers and suddenly, pointed vines covered with many thorns crawled out of the ground. Drake definitely had some nasty tricks up his sleeves, surely the first of many, although I didn't know what vines could do to help him.

Then, I heard a muffled sound behind me and, just too late, I realized what was happening. The vines stretched backward, wrapping around my mum, my dad, and all of my friends, tying up their arms, their legs, and even their mouths. I screamed and ran over to them, but I couldn't untie the twisted vines. They were stuck.

"NO!" I yelled, my eyes wide as I turned back to my opponent.

He was just laughing, shaking his head with amusement.

"Why did you do that?!" I asked angrily.

"Sorry, Carl, but this battle is just between the two of us." Drake didn't sound sorry as he spoke. "Your friends can't help you now." The vampire shrugged.

I growled.

"CARL!" My parents both screamed at the same time, but the vines around their mouths muffled most of their words. "CARL, RUN!"

"Hey, let us go!" Crelish cried, struggling against his magical restraints.

"Carl, run! He's trying to trick you!" Jolly yelled, pulling at the vines. "Don't you dare let him kill you, Carl!"

"Carl, Jolly's right," Clover yelled. "He's a liar and a cheater! He's just messing with your mind! Do you think he's actually going to let you beat him in a fight? He's lying! You'll never win, no matter how clever you are. You know that! Just stop before you get hurt!"

Drake mocked being hurt by their words, clutching his chest with fake pain.

"NO!!!" I screamed, tears stinging my eyes. I turned back to Drake. I needed my spell to work more than ever now! But what if Jolly was right and Drake had lied? What if I failed? What if this had all been for nothing? My parents and all of my friends would be held prisoner, or worse, they could be killed, just like I probably would be! I shook my head to clear my horrible thoughts, angry at myself as much as Drake. No! The spell would work! It had too. Plus, Drake wouldn't have been able to fake the whole chart, right? Or could he? He had infinite powers, didn't he? I shook my head, annoyed with myself.

Just like I'd seen young Drake do, I selected the spell I wanted, and waited. It seemed like nothing had happened. There were no flashes of light or spikes of power.

I was so disappointed that I wasn't even thinking about the consequences, until Drake spoke again. "Aw, Carl, that's just kind of pathetic." Drake gave me a fake frown. His voice was mocking now, a baby voice. "But I guess not bad for your first try. It doesn't seem like much happened though. We'll just have to see if it worked."

I stared back at Drake, trying hard to resist the urge to punch him. "It did," I said, trying to sound confident. It must have. At least, I hoped it did anyway. I was secretly worried.

"Sorry, Carl. I've never seen a spell with no light, and I didn't feel any effects." Drake explained. He still didn't sound sorry. "If it did work, you'd have to have created a spell, which is almost impossible. It requires really strong magic, years of training, and the universe bending *itself* for the spell to work. Even I have never created one. But it's very unlikely for the universe's powers to bend because of one powerless, little boy."

Was he right? Was there no such spell, and I had failed? Or had I really created a new one? I knew I had chosen a spell, but if Drake had never heard of it, maybe I had more power than anyone knew! Or, he was tricking me, which seemed more likely. Meanwhile, Drake was still talking about death and magic and legacies and "stupid little boys" and blah blah blah as he continued sharpening his knife. I tried not to let him get into my head.

"Just stop, Drake." I cut him off after a while. His talking was getting annoying. "We all know good always wins." Recently, my life had become a bit of a fantasy story itself, although I knew that didn't mean that I would have a happy ending. Maybe, just maybe, if I could survive everything I'd lived through so far, I could beat a vampire.

"Who says you're the 'good'?" Drake asked, raising his eyebrows. His words caught me off guard for a moment.

I shook my head. I needed to focus. I wouldn't fall into his trap this time.

"Well, hmm, let me think... How about everyone here that you've *captured*, everyone here that you're trying to *KILL*?" I suggested hotly, looking around. "Good people don't harm others for revenge, Drake. You know that!"

"It wasn't my idea. I didn't kill my grandpa."

"No, your grandpa killed himself when he attacked *mine*!" I yelled.

"Well he attacked yours because we were *starving*! We had nothing! Magic doesn't make people's lives perfect, Carl. It hurts people and tears them apart!" Drake yelled back, surprising me. The ghost of the crying, younger version of Drake showed in his eyes, for just a moment. "All I want is my grandfather!"

"Drake, you can't erase the past, but you can change the future! I know you will regret this! Please, don't make this mistake!!" I pleaded softly. "You're about to do something that you really don't want to do!"

"No! I *want* to do this! It's not a mistake!" Drake snapped, although his voice quivered with doubt.

"Please Drake. I don't want to die. My family doesn't either."

"Too bad! You don't get a choice!" Drake said, his voice shrill. "I can't stop. Not now."

"Would your grandpa want this?" I blurted. "What about that promise you made?"

Drake froze before shaking his head. There it was, that fear, that sadness, hidden behind his cruel attitude. That wasn't just any fear. That was fear for what he had become. "No, Carl, he wouldn't have, but if he was still here, I wouldn't be doing this!" Drake screeched. He finally calmed down, just a little bit. "Look, Carl, maybe if I show my power by killing you, to prove to everyone that I *can* bend the universe, maybe I'll be able to create a spell of my own," he said softly. "I would go back and save my grandpa." His face lit up with rage again, and his voice got louder. "And if it didn't work, if the universe STILL rejected me, like everyone else, I'd at least have my revenge." The vampire laughed like a maniac.

"Drake, you know that won't work. That could throw off the balance of the whole universe!" I said, panicking a little. If I'd learned anything after so much reading, it was that that the *number one rule* of magic was to never go back in time. One small change could destroy *everything*. But if the vampire knew that, he didn't really seem to care.

"It *will* work. I'd be the most powerful person in the world!" Drake screeched. "Don't you understand, Carl? Everything would be *perfect* and normal, and I'd have my grandfather. You're just trying to scare me!"

I groaned.

"Again, don't take it personally, Carl," Drake added.

"How could anyone *try* not to take this personally?" I asked heatedly. Drake ignored me. Instead, he put his knife back in his pocket. The movement was so swift and sudden that it made me nervous. He was up to something. He was always up to something.

"Carl, I assume you know who's missing here."

"What do you mean?" I asked, almost afraid for the answer. Instead of answering, Drake snapped his fingers and the vines carried out a boy, definitely a few years older than me. He had my mum's honey-colored eyes, but my dad's perfect, chocolate-colored hair. He was unconscious and stuck in the vines. His face was twisted uncomfortably like he was having a nightmare.

Instantly, I forgot everything else. "Louis!" I screamed, running toward him. Drake didn't even try to stop me. No, no, no. This wasn't happening. It couldn't be happening. Of course Drake had my brother. What was I thinking?! He'd said that he had my whole family, not just my parents. I hadn't even thought about what that meant. I turned around slowly.

"I thought he would want to watch you die." Drake snapped his fingers, and my brother woke up, looking like he had been slapped awake from a nightmare. His eyes darted around nervously, but he froze when he saw me.

"Carl?" he asked. "CARL!"

"Louis!" I tried to untangle the vines and free him. "Louis, it's going to be okay!"

"No, you don't understand! Run!" Louis yelled, shaking against the vines that were holding him in place. "RUN!"

"I'm sorry," I whispered, wiping tears from my eyes.

Another vine grew out of the ground, grabbing me and dragging me away from my brother, back toward Drake. I didn't fight it. Drake swiftly pulled his knife out of his pocket and studied it carefully. I winced, but I didn't run away. I stared into Drake's red eyes.

"No! CARL RUN!" My dad had clawed the vines off of his mouth. I winced again but ignored him. This had to be settled.

Drake grinned.

I silently prayed for the spell I had used to work.

Drake threw the knife at me. I braced myself for extreme pain. It hit my chest in slow motion. My whole body felt like it was on fire, and it knocked me off of my feet.

I looked down. Oh my gosh. There was a literal *knife* in my chest.

Before I knew it, I was on the ground. The pain was almost too much to handle, but I realized that it wasn't as bad as it should have been. Maybe my spell had worked after all.

The world was fading, everything was darkness mixed with pain. I felt like I couldn't breathe. I tried to sit up, but I couldn't move.

"CARL!" Crelish screamed, sounding like he was far away.

I looked calmly at Drake. "Just remember that I gave you a choice."

The words took all of my breath and sent sparks of pain all over my body, but that was when I realized that the spell had worked after all. My friends screamed. I wanted to reach out to them, to tell them I was okay, but I wasn't okay, I reminded myself. I was *"dead"*.

Drake was laughing. He didn't know how badly he had messed up. Everything was sort of numb. I closed my eyes.

"NO!" All of my friends and family were screaming at the same time, overlapping, but I could barely hear their voices. I was clinging to a magical white light deep inside of my soul, one that probably had to do with the spell. "CARL!"

"Who volunteers to die next?" Drake asked, waving a hand at my family. I wanted to get up, but it all hurt. I made sure not to move.

"You monster!" Jolly roared.

"How could you do that?!" Clover screamed.

Their voices overlapped and intertwined, mingling with the terrified cries of my family.

"Don't worry, you three won't remember any of this. After I finish with Louis here, then their parents, I'll erase your memories. You'll wake up back in your kingdoms, in your houses, with your regular queens who, of course, won't remember any of this either. No one in the kingdom will remember the war, the fire in the dungeon, or Carl ever coming in the first place. Everything will be normal, at least for you guys. Look on the bright side. You won't be traitors. The kingdom's already forgotten me. Only you and the queen have not. But you will, soon."

I wanted to growl or yell out, but I kept quiet. My friends reacted just as badly.

"What? NO!" Clover yelled immediately.

"That's just disturbing." Jolly put in. "You can't do that!"

"Oh, is that so? Just watch me," Drake muttered, checking his knife again, eyeing Louis. He was ready to pounce. And Louis didn't see. I didn't know what to do because I had to stay on the ground. Everything hurt.

No. No. I couldn't lose Louis again. *No.*

Suddenly, I heard someone call out, saving my brother. "LOUIS!" I suddenly felt like I couldn't breathe. Drake froze. Everyone was staring at me.

And then I realized. The voice had come from me.

Oops.

It was too late, anyway. I pushed myself up.

The gasps echoed in my ears. I forced the pain to fade. Drake was wrong about me. He thought I was just a powerless boy, but I would prove him wrong again. I had power, more power than anyone knew. I chose the second spell I wanted to use in my head. Everyone was staring at me, and I realized I was smirking.

"Carl?" Drake asked loudly, confused and scared. I knew I'd just pulled a trick out of *my* sleeve, one he'd never seen before.

Then his eyes doubled in size, and he laughed nervously. "Carl, my old friend. You wouldn't hurt me! Right?" Drake begged, shivering with fear. Drake took one big step backward. Then another. He was getting dangerously close to the edge of the island.

"You ruined my life." I said. "You tried to kill my family! You tried to kill *me*!"

"Carl, please, I—"

"You hurt my friends." I interrupted. "I'm tired of your excuses, and I'm tired of you, Drake. You can't always just get what you want. I offered you a chance to change, and you didn't take it."

"But... b-but... I—" Drake tried to argue weakly, but I cut him off again.

My hands glowed dark red. "You were wrong about me, Drake. I did create a spell of my own, and the effects are some you can't feel. Because I didn't curse you like you thought that I would. I didn't take the bait, Drake. Because *I* am one step ahead." I pulled Drake's knife out of my chest, revealing that there was no wound, not even a scratch. "But I'm sure you know of this spell." My hands were still sparkling with a red glow.

Drake's eyes were wide. "Please, no," he pleaded. "Not that spell! *Any* spell but that spell, Carl. Even *I've* never used *that* spell."

I knew it was dangerous. I didn't even really know what it did. All I knew was that it did what I needed it to do, and I knew that it would work. Drake shook his head as if he knew exactly what I was thinking. "Believe me, I know you, and I know that you'll regret using that one."

"I don't know if you deserve this Drake," I said flatly. "I take no joy from this. I'm not that kind of person. But I have to do this. I gave you a choice." I took another step toward him. I could have used the spell then, and I was just about to, but I didn't. I couldn't. I hesitated. "Do you feel guilt for what you did to me? Do you regret it all? Do you have any sympathy at all? Answer honestly!" Drake looked like he was about to answer, but he paused. He knew that there was no changing my mind, and he knew that lying would only make it worse. And he knew that I would believe him because I had learned to think how he thought. I was *finally* one step ahead.

"Not really," he admitted, hanging his head. "Not enough. But please, Carl! You. Cannot. Use. That. Spell."

The red on my hands glowed brighter. "Oh, is that so?" I said, using Drake's exact words from earlier. "Just watch me." I flicked my hands at him.

He looked like he was being pushed backward by all of the forces on Earth, all at once.

"NO!" He yelled as he flew backward. He hit the ocean behind him *hard* with a loud splash. He flailed around. I turned away but didn't say anything.

"HELP!" Drake screamed when he finally managed to get his head above the surface of the water. "CARL, YOU DON'T UNDERSTAND WHAT YOU'VE JUST DONE!"

I think I understand just fine, I thought, but I still didn't look at him. He tried to push to the surface, but a red glow kept pushing him down, pushing him back.

"YOU FOOLS! I'LL BE BACK!" He screamed. Even though he was underwater, his voice echoed loudly around us all. It must have been magic. He raised his black cloak above the surface and disappeared with a flash of murky gray light.

"NO!" I yelled, the tears rising to my eyes. "He escaped! He'll be back for me." I ran toward the water, but he wasn't there. "NO!!!" Strong hands held me back, and I didn't look back see who they belonged to. I pushed forward, but they wouldn't let me go. My rage had already melted away. I turned and collapsed into the arms that were holding me tightly. It didn't matter who they belonged to. "He will be back for me," I whispered. No one answered. They just held me tighter. I suddenly realized that it was okay. I could handle it. I wasn't just a little boy anymore. More importantly, I realized that I wasn't alone anymore.

Maybe I'd even realized that I finally had a family.

***

Chapter Fifteen

The Royalty of the Magical Kingdoms

With Drake gone, at least temporarily, all of his magic faded. The island immediately seemed livelier. The vines bowed down and then disappeared into the ground. My parents and my brother fell to the ground. I ran to check on them.

"Mum! Dad! Louis!" I slid into the sand. My parents wrapped me in a hug. "Oh, I'm so glad you're okay." I said. Normal kids my age would have pulled away from the hug, but I didn't. I just leaned into my parents like a little kid. I felt a hundred feelings at once. I couldn't believe this was really happening.

When I finally pulled away, I offered Louis, my older brother, a hand. He grabbed it, but instead of pushing himself off of the ground, he pulled me down with him into the dirt and tackled me in a hug, like he used to when I was little.

"Carl! I thought you were gone! The vampire—Drake?—told us that you were dead! Then you showed up and saved us all!"

I smiled. "I thought you were gone too. That boat… everyone told me that I would never find you again…" I trailed off, not wanting to ruin the moment. I had found them, after all, and that was all that mattered.

Next, I ran to my friends. "Clover! Jolly! Crelish!"

"Carl! I'm really glad you're not dead!" Crelish said cheerfully.

My brother, Louis saw my friends. His mouth dropped to the ground. "Is that… a troll? No, two! And… a fairy?! Best! Day! Ever!" Louis jumped from foot to foot, smiling like it was his birthday. As a kid, he was super inventive and loved to explore. He was pretty much a supernatural superfan. He barely had any space in his bedroom because all of the space was taken up by monster posters and photo collages. His dream was either to explore the world or catch a real ghost. He had a copy of every book ever written about monsters and he followed at least seven different blogs about Bigfoot on our family's computer, which got kind of annoying at a certain point. He took out a small camera from his pocket. He used to bring a camera everywhere. I bet he had it with him on the day the boat sank. I was surprised that its camera still worked after all these years, but I just smiled as he took some photos of my shocked friends.

Crelish was just as excited to meet my brother. "Whoa, another human! This must be my lucky day! What's your name? What's that?" he asked, pointing to the camera.

I laughed. They both looked like they were meeting their heroes.

"Oh my gosh, Carl. I still can't believe you're not dead! How are you not dead?" Jolly cried, wrapping me in a hug so tight that I couldn't breathe.

I laughed again. "I guess you could call it *magic*."

"Carl!" Clover flew up behind me, wrapping my smallest finger in a hug. "You're amazing!"

"No, you're amazing!" I hugged her by cupping my hand around her.

Before she could respond, I heard a creaking noise, like old wood, and a platform climbed out of the ground, supported by a vine with golden roses on it. The blossoming vine carried the platform safely to the ground I heard a throat being cleared. Someone was on the wooden platform, watching us. I whirled around in surprise. At first, I didn't even see anyone, but then my eyes landed on a familiar face and widened.

"Your highness!" I sunk into a bow. My friends followed me. It was Queen Gilly, the queen of the fairies. Of course, Drake had to get her out of the way in order to disguise himself as her and take over the Fairy Kingdom without raising suspicion, but I hadn't even considered where. She'd been trapped there, on that island, the whole time!

"Carl, who's that? Another fairy?" my brother asked. Then he saw her jeweled crown, and his eyes doubled in size. "Is that—"

"The queen of the fairies, yeah." I finished for him.

He dropped into a bow behind me. His mind must have been having a field day because he looked like he was about to explode. I smiled fondly to myself. The queen didn't speak. She just made a "hmm" sound and flew away while lost in thought. As she was in the sky, though, I could have almost sworn I saw her wink at me. But, no, probably not.

My parents didn't move. They just watched in shock as the queen flew away.

"I bet she's really mad. I'm sure Drake would have told her… well, everything that happened in the kingdom," Clover guessed with a shrug.

I nodded. Oh, well.

"Let's go home," I said. My family, all members, including my friends, who were about as close to family as you can get, nodded.

"How will we get home?" Louis, my brother, asked, skipping happily at the thought of home. The thought of home also made me feel happier than I'd felt in years, and I wasn't thinking straight. I remembered my parents' old house; always warm and cozy, with its smell of dust and cooking dinner. It smelled like a home. I was almost giddy with joy.

"My friends and I had to take a small boat to get here. We can try to get back on that." I replied, leading them across the island. Without Drake, the island already seemed much brighter. The flowers bloomed, the sand was white and pure, and the water surrounding the island was crystal clear and perfect. The shriveled-up trees grew and spread until they were bright, covered by blossoming flowers and fruits.

Jolly pulled me aside, so only I could hear her. "Carl, wait." I looked up into her suddenly worried face. What could possibly be wrong? We defeated Drake. We were going home.

I shook her away. "What's wrong?" I asked. "Don't you want to get home?"

"Of course! But you have to understand. I'm worried." She grabbed my hand as I started to turn. "Like, I can already see two possible problems with your plan to get home, Carl."

"Such as?" I asked. I was trying to remain calm, but I was desperate. I just wanted to get off the island. "We really need to get going, Jolly."

"Where will I go?" Jolly asked.

I froze. I hadn't expected that question. I hadn't thought about Jolly.

"I… I don't know. You...could go back to the Troll Kingdom." I turned away. "Or maybe hiding in the human world wouldn't be so bad?" I suggested, with a small, hopeful smile.

"That wouldn't be… terrible." Jolly said, although I could tell that she was smiling as well. "But there's another problem. The boat was sinking before." That completely killed my good mood. The boat couldn't have survived long since it had been destroyed.

I shook my head. "Yes. It was. But maybe it was part of Drake's magic like the island's curse or the vines. I'm sure it will have faded with him." I replied, trying to be positive as we turned toward the water, getting closer. I squinted into the distance. I couldn't see the boat...

"No, Crelish specifically said that it was torn apart using a weapon, not magic," Jolly reminded me. "Although, technically, if what you said was true, it would still be a problem because the boat would be fixed, but in the middle of the ocean."

I groaned. What if we really were stuck? As we reached the edge near the water, I saw that Jolly was right. No boat. There were a few damp boards and moldy wood. The little boat was gone.

I turned to my family and the rest of my friends, holding up the broken board. "We have a problem." Everyone stared at me. "What do we do?"

Clover did a facepalm. Jolly shrugged like "*I told you so.*" My parents shared a look. My brother stared at the broken pieces of wood floating in the water like he was wondering how he could fix them. I didn't know what to do!

I dipped my toe in the water. Freezing cold. We would have to swim for days, and we'd freeze to death or drown by then. Plus, we wouldn't be able to carry any food from the island, so we'd starve. Swimming was a no, then. Too many ways to die. So, what did we do? Stay on the island, living off of fruit? That wouldn't last long either.

I sat down, put my head in my hands and groaned. "What do we do?"

"Is… is there anything we *can* do?" Clover asked weakly.

"It's unlikely," Jolly replied. "We're stuck."

I buried my face in my hands. "Okay. But even if we're stuck on an island and probably won't last long, at least we have each other, right?"

My mum put her arm around my shoulder and gave me a bittersweet smile. "I missed you, Carl."

My brother shook his head with determination. "It's not likely to work, but we can at least try... together."

I picked a bright red apple from a nearby tree, splitting it with my group as we half-heartedly tried to figure out a plan. We sat in a sort of circle in the sand. I slid closer to my parents.

"Could... uh, Clover fly home and get help?" Mum suggested. We all looked at the fairy.

"I could, but it would be a bad idea," Clover explained. "It would take too long to get back to an island belonging to humans. This area of the world is full of magical creatures, and magical creatures only, and not many magical creatures would even be willing to help one of you, no offense. You'd be dead by the time I got back. I could get home, but..."

Wonderful. That idea was a bust.

"We could build a of a raft or small boat out of materials from the island." My brother suggested half-heartedly. He loved building things, and he was *really* good at it.

"With what?" My dad asked desperately, looking around the blank island. No one had an answer, not even Louis. "There's not enough materials. Plus, we wouldn't all fit."

My brother Louis could always find a solution. Not this time, it seemed.

"Aw man, this is hopeless," I said, hiding my face in my hands. A bird flew by, probably wondering why we were on the normally empty island. I picked off a part of my apple and tossed it to the bird, which chirped gratefully before flying away. I wished I could fly, like a bird. I'd fly away from the island, maybe fly away from my life. I sighed and curled into a ball.

"Carl..." My mum said softly, gently putting a hand on my back. It was like she read my mind. "It's not—" I looked up at her before she could finish.

"It *is* my fault," I said. "I just wanted to rescue you guys, and I even failed to that. I beat a vampire, sort of, and I can't even get my family off of some stupid island. I'm a failure." I stared down again. That time, no one said anything.

Hours went by. We kept trying to think of ideas, but it seemed as if none of them would work. At least I finally found my parents. That was all that I'd wanted, right? The sun started to dip lower in the sky, filling the air with shades of gold, orange, yellow, pink, purple, and blue. Small, cold waves licked my bare feet. The orange sun blinded me as it set low in the sky.

I opened my dry mouth to speak. "We should get some rest," I croaked. Everyone agreed with me, so I made myself a bed of sand and grass, hidden in a tall bunch of plants. "Goodnight." I whispered to my family and friends.

My dad squeezed my hand. "You're a good kid, Carl. Heck, you're growing into a great young man. Good night."

I gave him a weak smile, then curled up in my little bed. I closed my eyes and the world went dark. I was prepared to lose myself in a sea of nightmares, but my dreams that night were different, to say the least.

I opened my eyes, but I was sure that I was still asleep. I was in a golden room. The floor was made out of glass. I looked down. Beneath the glass there were... clouds, as if the golden room was floating up in the sky! I was too shocked to scream. At the end of the room, there were five jeweled thrones in a line. The first throne was much smaller than the others, and the second was much bigger. I squinted then gasped.

"Queen... Gilly?!" I immediately dropped into a bow. The queen laughed, standing up.

"You don't have to bow Carl," she said, smiling at me. I straightened up awkwardly. The queen was exactly how I remembered her, with her golden hair, perfect teal eyes, and her delicate wings. She was even *more* perfect than Drake's version of her. She was wearing a long, white, flowing gown that blew gently around her ankles. And of course, her jeweled crown. She looked beautiful, like she always did. What was she doing in my dreams? Or was it even a dream? Probably not. I'd heard of communicating through dreams before... in fiction. I didn't know whether to be surprised or not anymore. Magic was confusing.

On the throne next to her, a troll wearing heavy armor and a silver circlet that matched his silver eyes was sitting calmly in the largest throne, smiling at me. He had brown hair with gray streaks. Next to them, a pretty girl with a pink flower in her strawberry blonde hair, wearing a green dress with a white belt was sitting on another throne. She seemed young, excited, and full of energy. Her ears were pointed, and her eyes were sky blue. Sitting on the fourth throne, an old man with wise, kind eyes and a pointed wizard hat and a gray beard was sitting, smiling, his eyes closed. He was waving his arms like he was… casting a spell, maybe? His robes were dark purple, like midnight, and he was wearing a sparkly amulet.

"Carl, meet King Javyn of the trolls." Queen Gilly introduced, pointing to the troll next to her. He gave a small bow. "And that's Queen Elise, of the elves." She pointed to the pretty girl wearing the green dress.

She bounced up and down like a child… or like someone who'd had way too much caffeine. "Yes! Carl! We've been trying to contact you all night," she said happily.

King Javyn, the troll, motioned for her to sit. "Thank you, that's enough, Elise." He was smiling, though.

Queen Gilly continued. "And that is Master Alaric, the wizard. He is in charge of the Magical Territory, home to all beings who practice magic," The fairy queen gestured toward the fourth throne.

The wizard gave me a welcoming nod. "Hello, Carl," he said. He didn't stop waving his arms. A trail of golden dust was following his hands. I noticed that the final throne was empty.

"Is… is this a dream?" I asked. I certainly didn't see all of this there when I fell asleep, but I'd learned that nothing was impossible.

"It is all in your head, yes, but that doesn't mean it isn't real," the old wizard said simply, as if that was something everyone knew.

I blinked twice. "Ohhhh-kay…" I said, dragging out the word.

"What is a dream to one is reality to another," Master Alaric added, as if that explained everything.

"Huh, I guess that makes sense," I said, not sure if it actually did.

"What he means is, yes, it is in your head, and yes, you are currently sleeping, so technically, yes, it's a dream. But we are actually talking to you using magic," Queen Gilly said, rolling her eyes. She turned to Master Alaric. "You don't always have to make your magic so complex."

"But it is," Master Alaric said, looking puzzled.

"Okay..." I repeated slowly, still trying to wrap my head around how irrational it all was.

"We had to wait until you were asleep so we could get to you," Queen Elise explained excitedly. "We've been trying to contact you all night."

"Is there a problem, or something I can help you with? We're kind of stuck on an island in the middle of nowhere." I told them. They all hesitated.

Then I looked at the empty throne. There were five species. One was missing. I remembered what Jolly had told me about the magical world. Vampires, I realized suddenly! There was no vampire in the room.

"Does the problem have something to do with vampires?" I asked. Master Alaric was so surprised his arms dropped. The dream flickered, then went black. Suddenly, I was having my usual nightmare, one about my parents and Drake. What happened? Where were the leaders of the magical kingdoms? Suddenly, golden light filled my dream, and I was back in the room with the thrones. Master Alaric looked pale.

"Sorry, Master Alaric accidentally cut off the magic." Queen Gilly explained. "Not his fault... you gave us quite a scare."

Just because I mentioned the vampires? I wondered. *Why was that so bad?*

"About the vampires?" I asked out loud. Master Alaric nodded.

Well, I didn't know much about the vampires. I'd only ever met one.

"How did you know?" The wizard asked worriedly.

In response, I pointed to the empty throne, the one on the far-right side. "The king or queen... well, the ruler of the vampires. That throne is empty. There's nobody there."

"Ah, good eye, Carl! You're even smarter than we thought. Queen Gilly told us you were clever, but we didn't think you'd figure that one out." King Javyn praised me, clearly impressed.

"Is it bad that I know that?" I wondered out loud.

"No, it's just... concerning. Plus, it was a lucky guess," Queen Gilly explained.

"You knew Drake, correct?" Queen Elise asked. I remembered the creepy, red eyes and looked back at Queen Gilly, who nodded reassuringly.

"Oh. Um, yeah." I admitted carefully

"Okay. You shoved him into the water, did you not?" She asked patiently, carefully, talking as if I was a child. She was trying to get me to admit something. There was more.

I took a deep breath. "Yes."

"Okay. Do you know where he went?"

"No. But I'm... I'm sure you do." I stammered honestly. All of the kings and queens and master looked startled. I took another deep breath. "I mean, you guys have magic, right?" Can you tell me why you want to know?"

They shared a look.

"Uh, Carl, it's not as bad as it sounds... and now remember, it's not your fault," King Javyn reminded me. Uh, oh. It was definitely my fault then. "See... and, uh, don't take this the wrong way, but, the, uh, vampires seem to think that we hired you to attack Drake."

"What?!" I yelled indignantly. "He's been trying to kill me for years! Before I even met him! Before I was even *BORN*!"

"We know," Queen Gilly assured me. "We know. But they don't. I doubt they even care. It's just... if we don't figure it out quickly... and this is the reason we called you... it's just... the vampires are convinced we did it. And if we actually had, it would have broken a peace treaty of ours... and they would declare war," she said quietly.

"WHAT?!" I yelled again, louder this time.

Queen Gilly winced. "Look, it's no big deal."

"No big deal? How could you say that?!" I asked loudly.

"We don't even know why they think that or ever would, but now that you've said that on official record, we can fix it. I promise. Don't worry about it." She flashed her reassuring smile again.

"Are you sure?" I asked wearily, already thinking that it was my fault. I really needed to work on that. "If I can help..."

"No, it's fine. We just wanted to make sure you knew," Queen Elise assured me. "To be honest, the vampires are probably just looking to start a fight."

"Elise," King Javyn warned her with a glare. She shrugged apologetically.

"Ah, okay..." I said slowly. "Anything else?"

"Yeah!" Queen Elise said suddenly. King Javyn sighed, but he was smiling and he didn't try to stop her. "I just wanted to say: you're a hero, Carl. No one has ever stood up to a vampire and no one has ever cheated death. You are totally welcome in our kingdoms at any time."

Queen Gilly held up her hand to stop Queen Elise, but she was grinning as well.

"I would totally come visit," I said, grinning widely. "It's just that... I'm kind of stuck on this island here. Can any of you help with that?"

Queen Gilly smirked at me. Suddenly, the dream started to flicker. "We have to go!" she said. Her voice almost sounded... mocking. Was she mocking me? The dream was still flashing. Bright. Dark. Bright.

"Goodbye, Carl," King Javyn and Master Alaric said.

"Good luck!" Queen Elise called over the flashing chaos. Bright. Dark. Bright. Dark.

"No! Please..." I begged, looking for an excuse to stay. "Please stay! I'm not ready to do this on my own! I could help you! Wait!" Bright. Dark. Bright. Dark. "If you don't come help us, we'll die!"

"If you can cheat death once, surely you can do it again, Carl." Queen Gilly said. She was still smirking at me. Did she seriously find my life funny? "Bye!" She waved cheerfully.

"NO! Wait, stop!" I yelled, kicking the air. Instead of the imaginary wall, I felt plants, the ones in the real world, on my beautiful island prison. "I don't want to wake up!"

I felt myself rolling over in real life, proving that I was too close to reality. My life was a nightmare, and I was safe in the dream. Bright white light blinded me, and I saw Master Alaric slowly dropping his hands. *NO!!!* I thought, the word stretching out in my brain like a rubber band. I was falling through a black and purple swirl. "YOUR HIGHNESS, WAIT!" I yelled into the darkness, sitting up.

The sky was a dark purple and filled with stars, slowly filling with light. All of my friends were staring at me.

"Uh, Carl? You good?" Jolly asked slowly.

I exhaled. "I'm okay. Sorry, guys."

Oh well. I guess the rulers of the magical kingdoms weren't going to help us this time.

***

Chapter Sixteen

Happily Everyone After

I curled up into a sleepy, comfortable ball near my friends, sharing a bunch of hand-picked grapes from the island with them. The golden sun was coming up behind us.

Just as I was getting comfy, I heard voices echoing over the water. A familiar voice… one that I'd heard just that night. Familiar *voices* of old friends. Water was splashing and I saw a shape growing in the distance. I squinted.

"What is that?" I asked.

"Who are they?" Crelish asked, pointing. There were two human-shaped shadows resting against the front of the huge, dark shape. And then there was a loud sound, so loud it nearly knocked me and all of my friends off of my feet.

"Hey!" I shouted, nearly falling back. As we started to recognize it, our eyes widened. The shape grew closer, and it got less blurry. My friends' mouths dropped to the floor. It started getting bigger and bigger as it got closer to the island. Wow, it was beautiful.

"All aboard!" There was the call again. It took me a moment to realize what was going on. I was almost giddy with joy. No. Way!

Queen Gilly! The real one! I gasped. The queen of the fairies was floating above the front of a huge, silver, multi-leveled cruise ship!

"Where did she get that boat?" I asked my friends. Clover and Jolly were staring at the boat like it was a million dollars, with silly grins. They must have recognized it from somewhere because they seemed even happier than I was! "Hello? Uh… guys?"

"That's the troll's army boat!" Jolly said excitedly. I could tell that she was trying to keep her cool. "It's used by the best soldiers in the Kingdom!"

"Almost no one has even seen it in person," Clover added with wide eyes. "It's very special! Everyone knows about it."

"And you said the queen was mad at me!" I said in awe, staring at the boat. Clover didn't have a response to that. Why would she have brought that to help us? To help *me*? Queen Elise's words bounced around in my head. *"I just wanted to say: you're a hero, Carl. No one has ever stood up to a vampire and no one has ever cheated death. You are totally welcome in our kingdoms at any time."* The boat must have been super special to the whole Fairy Kingdom, and all of the trolls as well. But so was I. I was special too. That explained Queen Gilly's weird behavior in my dream.

"Wow..." I breathed.

"I thought you guys might need some help!" Queen Gilly called out, winking at me.

I beamed. "Thank you!" I called back as the boat pulled up and stopped next to the island.

Ivy and Stephanie, my friends, greeted us as we walked up. How had they even gotten there?

"Welcome!" Stephanie said, walking over to me once we were on the boat. "It's nice to see you, Carl!" As she walked toward me, her dark hair bounced, glowing in the light of the setting sun. It was still neatly tied into braids, now with pink highlights in it.

"Thank you," I said, wrapping my arms around her. I introduced her and Ivy to my friends. "You dyed your hair. I like it!" I told Stephanie.

"Thank you, Carl." She smiled, blushing at the compliment. "I have to go prepare some more things for your arrival, but we're going to need to catch up later. I want to hear everything!"

I grinned. "Okay. Talk to you later!"

After she walked away, I walked over to Ivy. "Hello, Ivy. How have you been?"

"I've been okay. And you? It's good to see you."

I inhaled. "I-I.... Look, Ivy, I just wanted to thank you for all of your help. You're an amazing friend, and I've never told you how much I appreciate you. I've... I've missed you."

She stared at me, speechless. Without thinking, I kissed her on the cheek. Her face turned bright red. My face burned as well. I pulled away. "I'm so sorry—" I started. I couldn't breathe. It felt hard to talk.

"I—" she tried to say something but closed her mouth. "Thank you, Carl." That was all she said. We hugged awkwardly. Then, she walked away.

Soon after that, the boat started making stops. Everyone on the boat had a big decision to make. Eventually, each person decided that they wanted to follow their dreams. I was going home with my parents. That was my dream. It had been for years. Now I had an even bigger family.

My brother was going to explore the magical world. Queen Gilly had even given him a backpack full of magical things to help him! I didn't want him to get off the boat, but his dream was important to him, so it was important to me. There were many tears and hugs goodbye that day.

Clover, Crelish, and Jolly were going to buy a house in the human world and live together as roommates. I was sure that Crelish would love being around all of those humans, and Clover and Jolly could finally be happy.

Queen Gilly was going to go back to her kingdom, of course. Before she left, she told us all, "Come visit any time."

Ivy had received an exciting offer to move her tent into one of the biggest cities in the world and become a fortune teller there. "The letter said they'll make me famous!" she'd told me excitedly. I was excited for her, of course. I'd really miss her, though.

Stephanie was going to live in the human world as well, to have fun and explore. She was done being a pirate, done being controlled. I'd even heard rumors going around the boat that she was going to try a career as a singer. Apparently Clover, who was staying in the room next to hers, had heard her singing to herself and said that she was really good. I was sure she'd be amazing.

I was just as happy for all of them. I hoped they had fun living their dreams. But I'd miss them a lot. They'd all gotten off of the boat at different times: First Queen Gilly, then my brother, then Ivy, then Clover, Crelish, and Jolly. I had told all of my friends or family the same thing as they got off, "Don't forget to visit, or just write!"

The next few days were made up of hugs and tears and whispers. It had been hard to see them leave, but everyone was so happy. Well, sad yet happy at the same time. Or... not happy. Hopeful. Yeah, just hopeful. Like a dream. But it was all real.

I was smiling. I hadn't stopped in days. I was sitting with my parents on our couch, watching a movie. The movie was a cute, colorful, animated movie—my favorite movie from when I was little. Despite the fact that it was kind of stupid, it was funny. We were sharing bowls of snacks, like popcorn and candy, and we were all snuggled together under a blanket. Just like a normal family. One that hadn't been separated for years. One that didn't know that there was a whole other world of magic out there. One real family. It was nice to have a home. Nice to have a family. After I got home, I was sad to find out that our old house had been sold. Maybe that was for the best. We were starting a new life. It was kind of awkward at first, since my parents had to get to know a whole new me, but it was wonderful. Everything seemed perfect, because everything was perfect. Even if Drake was still out there, my friends were all following their dreams. I was following all of *my* dreams. I had all of my friends and family. I finally had parents. And a brother. And so many friends—something I'd never even known I needed or wanted. My adventure had been amazing, even though it had been dangerous. It had helped me learn many things, and it had taught me things I wouldn't have even known I wanted to learn. Special things, like how to know yourself, and know others, to always be grateful, and to be helpful but also to accept help. My smile grew bigger, which no one would have imagined was possible. My cheeks were starting to hurt from my grin. I felt...different. Like I was part of something. I felt like I could do anything. In that moment, I knew that I could. Why? Not because of my family. It was because of me. Not because happily ever after had been real all along, but because I'd made my own—a special ending—one for everyone. A "Happily Everyone After." And because of me, that was our ending.

***

Acknowledgements

I'm pretty sure that many of you, as the readers, have seen this seen this sentence in the acknowledgements of almost every book you've ever read, but a book cannot be created without the help of many people. In my case, this phrase could not be truer. Now that I have reached the end of my journey as a writer and you have reached yours as a reader, I owe a lot of gratitude to the many people who have helped and supported me throughout this journey of writing my first book. Like many writers, I also worry that I will forget to mention someone by name, so bear with me here.

First and foremost, I would like to offer infinite thanks to my parents who have supported me throughout the two long years it has taken me to write this book. From encouraging me, to helping me edit and publish my writing, they've been there for me since day one, literally, and they are truly the best parents I could ask for. Thanks Mom and Dad; I really love you guys!

Next, I would like to thank all of my many family members and friends. Believe me, if I could mention them all by name, I would. I'm really grateful that they let me talk endlessly about my writing without getting annoyed. I've even managed to encourage a few of them to write their own incredible stories! It doesn't matter where I met you or how long I've known you for. All of you are amazing, and I appreciate all of the love and support.

Up next, my amazing editor, Gina Kammer. Though I did not get to know her too well, I am endlessly grateful for her help, time, and support. She made great changes to my work, especially considering the fact that the original draft was written by a fourth grader. Without her, this book would not be where it is today, and I mean that.

To my front cover illustrator, Davynn Martinoff, and to my back-cover illustrator, Eden Gross, who do so many wonderful things. I am lucky to have them as not only my wonderful illustrators but also my friends. Their art is beautiful, and they deserve credit! I truly appreciate the time they spent to help me accomplish my goal! They truly show that a book can be fully written and illustrated by kids and embody the message that you can write, draw, act, or be creative at any age.

This book simply would not exist without my teachers. Throughout Kindergarten, first grade, and second grade, I was mostly unaware of my passion for writing but was still pretty good at it. I had some amazing, encouraging teachers back then. They lent me books, encouraged and supported me, and helped me use and grow my imagination. Without my third-grade teacher, I would not be writing at all. She helped me through my first 'book', 'The Adventures of Super Victor', a little picture book that I wrote as a project throughout most of my third-grade year. Without that teacher, and without Super Victor, I never would have discovered my huge passion for writing. I am still so grateful for her encouragement, kindness, and her suggestion of starting the project in the first place. It was a lot of fun, and a little bit stressful, everything that writing a 'book' for the first time should be. Plus, I got to brag to all of my friends that I wrote, illustrated, and 'published' a book. That's when I really became obsessed with writing. Over that summer, I started on another story. When I arrived in fourth grade, I showed that to my teacher, who loved it. She was so fun, supportive, and encouraging. During a fiction-writing project that the whole class was assigned, 'Carl's Side', just called Carl back then, was born. Most of the class wrote just enough to receive credit and then forgot about their narratives the second we moved on from the project. I kept working throughout my fifth and sixth grade years. My teachers those years were amazing as well and encouraged me to keep going.

This year, I am entering seventh grade. I am forever grateful to all of my family, friends, and mentors. It has been a long and fun journey to get this book to where it is now. I know this book is far from perfect, but I could not be more proud of myself and my writing, and I am lucky to know that all of these amazing, beautiful people feel the same. Thank you to everyone in my life. I would not be who I am today without all of you!

About the Author

Lila Drowos is an 11-year-old girl from Florida who is entering seventh grade this year. She absolutely *loves* books. She's been writing ever since she knew how. Her favorite genres are fantasy, science-fiction, poetry, and dystopian fiction, and she's almost always writing. When she's not writing, she's probably singing, dancing, acting, playing the violin, studying, or hanging out with her friends. She also loves baking, art, and reading. Carl's Side is her first novel. She has been working on it four two years (since fourth grade!) and she is so excited to share her work with the world. You can email her at lpdwrites@gmail.com or check out her website www.lpdwrites.com.

Discussion Questions for Book Clubs

Below are some suggested discussion starters based off my book to spark conversations between book clubs or groups of friends who enjoy reading together. Feel free to send me your answers or any other questions/feedback using the 'Contact Me' page on my website: www.lpdwrites.com. I love hearing your thoughts!

1.   Who do you think was the true villain in 'Carl's Side'? Is there more than one? Was Drake a good or bad character?

2.   Who is the hero of the story? Is there more than one?

3.   What are the themes of the story? Why are they important to Carl.

4.   How did Carl's relationship with Jean affect his views on family? How did these change once he met Clover and Jolly?

5.   Carl connects with Jolly and Clover because they don't 'fit in' in their own communities. What do

you think about the importance of community and how it drives the choices the characters make?

6. Write or consider an alternate ending of the story. How would it end? Who would be the main character?

7. Discuss the importance of Ivy's relationship with Carl and its impact on his journey. How do their views about being orphans differ? If you were to write a story from Ivy's perspective, what details would you include?

8. If you were in Carl's position, what would you have done differently? What aspects of his journey would have scared you? Which would have excited you?

9. **BONUS QUESTION:** If you were to live in the magical world, would you rather be a troll, a fairy, an elf, a magical being (wizard/witch), or a vampire? Why? What would your role be?

Made in the USA
Columbia, SC
17 July 2022